The Thread

Lara Magill

JaCol Publishing Inc.

ISBN: 978-1-946675-16-3
For information regarding permission, write to:

JaCol Publishing Inc.
195 Murica Aisle
Irvine, CA 92614
818-510-2898
Editor-in-Chief: Randall Andrews
Technical Editor: C.E. Hilburn
Illustrator: Eva Taylor
www.jacolpublishing.com

ACKNOWLEDGEMENT

To my family and friends, my wonderful loved ones who have inspired, encouraged, and supported me to chase my dreams. Thank you for all your work, all your time, and all your love, and know I love you back. To Randall, my patient and funny mentor, and to Eva, my clever and intuitive cover designer, thank you both for bringing this all together.

TOC

CHAPTER ONE

Henry wondered for the thousandth time why him. His physical performance and grades, a couple peaks among averages, didn't deserve recommendation to the military's elite unit, the White Wings. The honor to serve couldn't settle his unease because he knew what grunts like him were supposed to do; they fought and they died.

Macabre anxiety hung over him as country called him from home a second time. Something in the air, the weight on his back, imparted permanence. Before, he'd marched toward the Yard, a military academy on Handakau, swollen with patriotism and his mother's pride. Six bruising years tempered that hubris. At the end of the first, he turned fourteen years old. Fourteen. He adapted mentally, but his body never caught up. Always too small, too weak. Henry got that. He also got six years of advanced field training. Five years of remedial PT. Four years of individualized physical programming. Years of hard work manifested in legs like fire, and little else. He grew, hardened but trim, as one of the Yard's least impressive soldiers.

So, dread nestled in his belly when he was promoted early sixteen days ago. Nobody left early—no one. His doubts tripled when Shai Jukita advanced with him. Jukita embodied prodigy. He maintained top grades without effort. Good looking, with gold-streaked black hair complementing dusty skin, and a soldier's bulk. His angular permutations hinted he could even be one of Handakau's rare giants.

The giants, more like shapeshifters since their growth came from a bestial transformation, only came from Handakau. All the Kau had the genetics for the transformation, but only half the population could achieve it. Henry had learned the hierarchies associated with giant culture, but as a Morosi, he forgot most of it.

Henry could reason why Jukita could have been promoted early, sent to the Tower, humanity's stronghold. Standing next to him, Henry couldn't fathom what he had to offer.

Henry hefted his pack, home's anchor ceding to his doubts the further he walked toward his new life. He loved his mother, but six years away stripped him of the childhood she remembered. He floundered to lift the solitude society dealt a widow. For the last two weeks, Henry stumbled through the gaps in conversation, and hugged her when his words failed him. The inability to relate didn't bother him; she was family. They wore the same braids and laughed at the same jokes. They shared the same tattoo, the Kinyu, on the backs of their necks. Most Day Walkers, like himself and his mother, had black ink on coffee skin. Henry's night-black skin required white.

When Henry said goodbye, his mother didn't cry. She held him, gave him a kiss, and sent him off with strength. He stopped at the end of the path, turned around. They waved. She turned her back on him and went inside. He turned his back on home and walked on, just like six years ago.

Her strength lasted him to the space port on Pol. He hated flying, so much that his anxiety outstripped his growing disquiet. Henry got into line and counted faces, minutes; his nerves curdled in his intestines.

"Welcome, Cadet Harbor," a hostess read his ticket.

"Thank you."

Henry followed the other passengers onto the open catwalk suspended a meter above calm water. The Weavers emerged like trees from the water at the end of floating bridges. Henry had seen them before, but they still took him in.

The Weavers stood at thirty meters, twenty of them tentacles, grey with dark blotches, flat triangular heads with no mouths, and shiny orbs for eyes. Their pale underbellies oozed a slimy, sticky mess. Small suckers, covering the eight whip-like tentacles, allowed the creatures to grab and hold onto anything in the galaxy. They lived in the Web though, only diving into reality for humanity. Without them, no one would have ever recolonized Old Home, humanity's first planet.

More than that. Without them, humanity wouldn't exist. Centuries past, Old Home failed. The planet had been torn apart, and humanity abandoned their home in search of new ones. Those were always Henry's favorite stories. The ones about his namesake. The ones about Henry the Dark, who fought back evil with his own darker power. How Henry saved humanity by sending them off group by group to other viable planets in the solar system. Henry achieved it with the Weavers. The Weavers could enter the Web, a separate dimension of light and wind overlaying the real world, allowing the Weavers intergalactic travel. Henry the Dark's stories ended when humanity scattered, his legend living through oral tradition until the colonies developed written word, digital records. Humanity lost the stories of the Weavers, but Henry dreamed they helped because Old Home had been theirs too.

Humanity survived for over a millennium, enough time for each colony to reflect natural selection. Henry revered the Kau's giant adaptation, sensational and strong compared to the mundane variation in skin pigment the Morosi evolved. Interplanetary travel maintained the underlying genetics across all the colonies for fourteen hundred years until the Kau and the Morosi Cooperative Engineering Committee built humanity's first space port. Another century passed before a co-op mission reported stable life conditions on Old Home.

A jab in his side brought Henry back. A nerve-ridden Day Walker apologized. Everyone filed into an oblong tube and strapped luggage to the walls. Henry readjusted the latches on his pack. He breathed shallower, especially once he entered cubicle four. He counted each pant.

"Please secure your belts," a host called out. "The mechanic is descending."

Henry shivered. He knew the Weavers were smart—brilliant. The legends would be impossible if the Weavers were as dense as herd sheep, but not having a pilot bothered him.

The hosts sealed off the entrance. Henry strapped into industrial strength cinches before the hosts slid a protective door over every cubicle, empty or full.

Henry peered out a small porthole, two slimy tentacles sweeping up. The nose of the tube tipped upward. As the tube came full vertical, Henry craned his neck to watch two sets of tentacles unfurl from the Weaver's belly.

The small suckers on every tentacle pulsed. White light circled each one and the tail thrashed below the tube, pushing them into the air. The other tentacles writhed around each other, building a tangled ball of glowing strings between them. The higher they went, the more the ball grew until it tripled in size. A jolt and the tube spun. The Weaver's tentacles stretched the mess of strings as wide as they could go. The strings pulsed, a life-like energy humming through the air.

All the tentacles snapped around the tube. Henry's cubicle darkened, and a thunderous clap signaled the Weaver ripped through the Morosi atmosphere and into the Web.

The float light came on a few breaths into the flight. Henry removed his cinches and slid the privacy guard over his capsule.

Henry's mind drifted with him. His heart thumped. The Tower, a figureless giant, overcast the journey. A few times, flashes of his mother's eyes tearing up, her hand fisting against her chest, her voice brimming with pride, rose next to his worries, soothed the menace of the unknown.

Henry couldn't shake his cyclical questions. Hours passed and he still mulled over his instinctual concern.

A shudder wracked the tube, a sickening lurch in his gut. The Weaver broke into Old Home's sub-space.

Henry grimaced. He breathed. In, out. In, out.

The tube pointed down.

Down. Down. Down. Faster and faster. Fear swallowed his vision like a flooding pond. Sealed into a tight space, falling at fatal speeds toward hard ground—no control.

A breathless moment later, his stomach hitched. Their speed lessened. The window lightened. Colors blurred past the glowing ball around the tube, but the horizon started to make sense. Tentacles held the ball beneath them, the strings stretched wide; a luminous net between them and deep water.

Henry clamped fingers over his racing pulse. The sight of shore pressed his anxiety, the dread of carving out a new life he didn't deserve hot in his throat.

CHAPTER TWO

The Weaver landed in blue water a kilometer from shore. A motor boat sped out to meet them. The ride back disoriented Henry. The spray stung his eyes, the smell clogging his nose—saltwater. He'd only read about it. He marveled over the expanse of ocean, the size dwarfing his anxieties about the future.

Boots on the sand broke the water's spell. Henry followed crowds trudging up an orange slope. Over the rise, hundreds of paved paths wound inward. He people-watched as he joined the swarm: soldiers, doctors, lab coats, suits, and bags all plodding on.

When he arrived inside, Henry followed signs to his ticket line. A mix of everyone: Morosi, both Day and Night Walkers, Atal, their skin all the same pine green, Kau, in every shade of brown, and the bright red hair of Horns. More Horns than anyone else. No matter the color, the accent, the origin, all were dressed like him.

The stranger ahead of him blurted, "Can't believe I got North Sound." An Atal. A few weathered scars on her hands. Half an eyebrow missing and a chunk out of her chin.

"Me either. First in my family to go." The Horn in front of him.

"Congratulations." The Atal eyed him. "Quite an honor to be placed there so young."

"I was top in my academy, but didn't like officer training as much as I thought I would. Think special ops is more my style."

The Atal laughed. "You'll have plenty of company. More than half the candidates are officer drop outs too. What was it for you?"

The Horn grinned, flushing.

"Relax boy, I'm no rat."

"I wasn't interested in eating the correspondent's asshole."

She slapped him on the shoulder. "You and me both, kid."

"Heard they have Rahnus on base."

The Atal shrugged. "My sister was at North Sound for five years and said she never saw one, but she wasn't high up."

"Shame. Always wanted to see one."

"You and me both, kid."

"Next!"

The scarred Atal smiled at the Horn before she left.

Henry's stomach tingled. North Sound, the largest special ops base on Old Home, housed the military's research center. It was the only residence on Old Home too, the planet's scarring only able to sustain a small population. Earning North Sound, especially out of academy, made most kids' dream come true, even would have for Henry.

No one knew the Tower's name. No one knew the people who served there or remembered their families.

Every child knew North Sound because it trained the only soldiers who faced the Rahnus. When Old Home failed, the Ages said the Rahnus devoured the remains of the planet. Still hungry, they took to the Web, plaguing the colonies in their infancy. The Horns suffered the worst losses, but an alliance with the Atal saved them. History aligned around the Rahnus' attacks, humanity's survival.

"Next!"

The Horn slouched off.

Still, twenty-four years passed since the last sighting. There was no surrender, no truce—just empty space. Two decades of peace couldn't stifle humanity's memory, so Henry had dreamed of North Sound and pledged his stick-gun to humanity's finest.

The rumor of Rahnus at North Sound gave Henry hope that the Tower would have one too. What he wouldn't give to face one, to taste humanity's oldest glory, no matter the odds. It was everything the Yard ever promised him.

"Next!"

Henry approached a grumpy Kau. She checked his papers and pointed to him to an attendant. Henry followed the guide deeper into the space port, stopping by an unmarked door.

"You'll wait here for your next flight."

Henry let himself in. The room had a few lonely benches, a pack, and Shai Jukita lounging against the wall.

"Henry!" Shai's face lit up. "Glad you're here man, I've been waiting hours. Are we departing soon then?"

"I don't know."

Shai grimaced. "Well I wish they'd hurry. I'm getting hungry."

Henry didn't respond. The Atal's words stuck in his mind. He ignored Shai glancing at him every now and then. Shai didn't push small talk, just looking. "Why do you think we're going to the Tower?" Henry gave in.

Shai's tawny eyes settled on him.

"Beats me." Confidence and caution mixed in his voice.

"Nervous?" Henry asked.

"Definitely. Death, life, and Web, man." Shai smiled. He held his nerves well.

Death, life, and the Web: the three dimensions of duty. Henry had fallen asleep under those words ever since he'd been accepted to the Yard. The obscure phrases imprinted on his nationalism. Death finds us all, but life still deserves guarding, and the Web kept them all alive.

Less than an hour later, the same attendant escorted them outside. The sky had gone from blue to purple.

"Fucking missed dinner," Shai grumbled.

Henry chuckled.

They flew a Mini this time, a smaller cousin of the Weavers. They appeared the same, except scaled down to a sixth of the size and bright green. Henry buried his nerves during the fifteen-minute open-air flight. He couldn't breathe until they touched down on the southern tip of the eastern continent.

Henry and Shai stood on top of a cliff. Henry gaped at the landscape around him. The thunder of the Thalweg below, a rush of water two hundred kilometers across between the continents, awed him. The grassy plains, hills and valleys, and far-off mountains replaced the hot sands, tropical plants, and light pollution of the western shore.

A pop shredded through sound, startling Henry from the sunset. An enormous man spewed from a glowing hole at the edge of the cliff. A Horn, wearing a black, skin-tight suit. Three white feathers hung from his shoulder—a strange uniform. Shai shouldered his pack and approached. Henry followed.

They descended a ledge hewn into the cliff-face for over an hour. When they got close to the water, the ledge turned into a man-sized hole in the rock. Inside, smooth walls sloped up around Henry. Silver glistened far above, the light too faint for comfort. The flat stone gave to the sky after only minutes. They emerged onto orange sand and kept walking.

Henry breathed for calm. Walking and waiting and flying and waiting and walking and on and on. He wearied despite his nerves.

The rock next to him grew darker. He turned for verification. It wasn't the night or the water. The rock truly darkened. Farther down, the rock looked black. Farther still, the rock gleamed as if polished.

The Horn stopped and pressed a hand against the glossy surface.

"Second Lieutenant Caspiano escorting Cadets Jukita and Harbor."

Silver light sizzled under Caspiano's palm, and he pulled back. The air cracked, popping and sizzling like lightning. The light emitted a low, gravelly voice.

"Welcome home Second Lieutenant. Cadet Jukita, Cadet Harbor, welcome to the Tower."

CHAPTER THREE

Ro woke with a sour taste in her mouth, the sweat on her face clinging to the pillowcase. Her muscles strained. White knuckles disturbed Akira's sheets.

Breathe. Breathe.

She closed her eyes, drawing focus, and freed her will from drowsiness.

Flow. Movement.

Her will responded, the mental muscle flexing against the dream gripping her mind.

Move.

The blood pulling through her veins lessened like she'd been demagnetized. She sighed at the relief her conscious will could lend her marking. Ro's blood had been exchanged for the Web's light—her marked blood. In her veins flowed molecules of light, biologically compatible enough to sustain her body but constantly driven by the Web's hunger.

Hunger I can master.

With a huff, Ro snapped her will in warning against a tendril of the Web leaking from her marking. The Web's tugging through her marking's molecules receded to nil.

Ro sighed into her stiff spots, the pain flaring through her nervous system retreating behind her will's leash. Despite her marking's daily intrusion from sleep, the dream lingered. It overwhelmed her, and she forgot the day's burdens ahead. A new dream this time, not her age-old nightmare.

A figure, swathed in fog, fled to her grove. She loathed intruders. She chased the shadowy man through the trees, her feet springing over familiar ground.

My ground.

They came to the pool. Instead of her beloved moon-lit clearing, the space was cramped, dark, and forbidding. The green underfoot turned to ash. In real life, she would have acted, but paralysis ruled her dreams. The man grabbed her, wrapping her tight against his chest. Furious silver eyes met hers and her vision whited out.

Her heart pounded, and fear thudded through her veins. When her pulse steadied, Akira's light touch drew her back. His snoring, one arm around her shoulders, sheets unruffled— familiar, warm… *home.* She relished the comfort against those silver eyes.

Light sparked on her side of the bed. She detangled from Akira and stood. As her skin contacted the floor, the Web's pull sank through her flesh, her marking an inherent invitation. Her blood jerked in response toward her feet, zapped against her will's restraint. She ignored the prickle inside. She'd mastered much worse reactions to be able to live in the Tower.

She breathed deep, beginning her morning ritual. Simple manipulation. She pulled her marking away from the Web's yearning, moving her blood through her vessels in regimented normalcy. She flexed her will. Her marking jumped, concentrating blood in specific pockets. Feet. Hands. Core. Shins and forearms. Head and spine. Last, her will directed her marking on the onyx under her feet. Blue-touched silver swelled in the black beneath her, the Tower accepting her touch like a lover.

She dressed and leaned over Akira. He cupped the back of her head and pulled her in deep. He filled her up, abolishing the dread from her darker thoughts. She kissed Akira back.

"I'll see you later."

She hummed in assent, pressing a final kiss on the shell of his ear. She relished the comfort Akira gave her, but it'd have to last a while. She wasn't ready to see Ham yet.

She met Kekoa, her uninjured teammate, on the training fields. They conditioned in silence for hours. Ro pushed herself hard. Kekoa didn't try to keep up. They trained in a mismatched rhythm, the off-beats marking the absence of their teammate.

The time outside the Tower at least helped with the relentless nagging of her marking. She wished the sun didn't sap her time up, when the Tower only ever felt like an eternity.

The hours are melting away.

The morning swept past and she faced the infirmary. Kekoa stood behind her. His presence, albeit dimmed, reassured all the same.

She took his hand and glided through. Neither of them walked forward. He too didn't understand how to respond to this…

This first time one of us has been in here.

His breathing deepened, and his voice projected clinical precision: his medic voice. It hurt Ro even more to hear that from him for one of their own.

"Is it time then?"

Ro couldn't answer, but she pulled him forward.

Ham's skin had sealed, and the concussion hadn't done any serious damage. Her subconscious writhed knowing she put him there.

I failed him.

Ro found herself on the verge of tears hours later, under her shower, with riveted skin. Her lips hadn't stopped trembling.

She toweled off and slid into bed. Normally, she craved routine. Not today. The moment her head hit the pillow, she shut her eyes and shut down her mind.

Just focus on breathing. Nothing else. In. Out. In. Out. In…

The man sprinted into the distance. He moved fast through the trees, but this was her grove. She knew she would catch him this time, knew she had him. She followed him to the pool, where he stood clouded by mist.

"Why here? Why always here?" she unleashed her pain at his invasion.

The man turned. He did not speak. He did not breathe. He took a step toward her, and another, and another. She watched mute, her chest heaving from the vicious chase.

He hesitated for a moment and vanished. The mists evaporated. No indents in the moss witnessed his passing. A small sense—a warning—flitted through her spine. A hand grabbed her shoulder and wrenched her around.

She woke, startled and gasping. She shook herself and staggered to the bathroom. Wild, untamed fear lurked in her reflection, her shoulders bent. She did not recognize the defeated girl in the mirror.

This isn't me!

From some depth she never could find, Rolyn breached. The woman that commanded attention everywhere she went, the Lieutenant that outshone every other White Wing in all disciplines, the marked Wing that submitted to no one, not even Roxar; she surfaced and recovered her features.

She restored control. The desperate girl, that had arrived at the Tower unable to contain her marking, was unseated.

Again, and always.

Ro straightened her shoulders, pressed thick lips into a thin line. She tried to recall the dream. It evaded her. She knew it changed, again. She didn't understand what went on, what it meant, why it changed.

Who is that guy?

Mask covering her lurking questions, she faced the Web.

Ro had fed the Tower a few drops of her blood, once she could tolerate living there, and ever since she was linked to this Webbed wall. Here—here alone—the color of the Web changed to match her emotions. Mercurial orange swirled, a lighter shade that gave way to wisps of yellow. She frowned, focusing. The color faded to cream.

Such a trusty wall.

She dived into the softer color and shot toward the mess. She barely had time to sit down with Akira, before she felt the tug on her marking's peripheral senses.

Roxar had asked her to drop in.

CHAPTER FOUR

Great.

She got one bite before the flash skidded to her feet. She scooped the flaming embers up. Akira's smile faded.

"You're needed." Roxar's voice died, and Ro closed her hand over ashes. She grimaced at her boyfriend.

"C'ya later," Akira sighed.

She winked at him and stood. She caught his eye roving low. "My room or yours?"

He pointed at his chest with his fork, mouth stuffed.

"Kay, I'll flash you if it looks like Taizai is involved." She waved and left.

Annoyance set in. After everything today…

And this late at night? Such an ass.

She doubted she'd withstand it if he decided to push her.

She knew he'd ask about Norvin, had been preparing for this the minute she realized what she did. Her innards clenched as she remembered Ham's animated face going slack, looking down at red.

She ran around a bend, and a vein gleamed before her. Flinging her hand in, she grabbed the first thread she could find.

I want Roxar.

She pushed into the sucking vacuum, noise cracking around her.

One…

Two…

Three…

Four.

She popped into reality, snapped toward the desk, but not fast enough.

Roxar's unnerving silver palm glowed, eight meters away, centered over her left eye. His marking's proximity raised her blood into spikes in her veins. Ro calmed her marking's usual warning, and approached.

"Such an unnecessarily rude entrance."

Calm and cool.

Roxar dropped his luminescent arm and sat. "Sit, Rolyn."

"Ugh. Don't call me that." She goaded him with the same back and forth that started their mutual dislike.

"As always, I insist. Sit."

It wasn't a request. She sat on the proffered bench. She scowled at her mentor but avoided eye contact.

"Why am I here, Roxar? If this is about Norvin then I prom—"

"Well, not directly, but I would like to hear your version of those events."

Asshole.

She glared, her brow flattening, locking her eyes with his.

He bored into her, silent and stalking. Stubborn or not, she could read that danger sign. Where brawn was her specialty, intricacy was his, and right now, her marking hardly pulled toward his. If he had already concentrated his marking to a singularity that small...

Such high stakes? Why?

She allowed her marking some slack, and used her will to channel it into defensive wards around her mind. They'd break if he forced them, but she couldn't afford anything stronger without alerting him. Since she wasn't as soft with her hand, she stalled.

"You know what happened."

"Rolyn. Let's both agree I know what happened and I know I've taught you better than that. How could your control slip so easily?"

Well, shit.

His marking still registered as small and defenseless, which she knew was the most ingenuous facade.

"There was a seam."

"Really? Is that all?"

"It was the biggest I've ever seen. It…"

"Well, then. Now for Lieutenant Hammond, your accident has made him a desirable test subject for Taizai. I'm reassigning him to the lab for a year-long rotation."

"What?" Fury fractured her self control, and rage took center stage.

In her moment of weakness, Roxar flicked his marked palm. Thread clamored from the walls all around her, writhing into a cage of light for the two of them. Her marking spasmed at the oppression, her body agonizing in consequence.

Roxar's menace seeped under her skin, her marking quailing, but her fury swelled to replace it. Malevolence grew in her gut. He knew the pain she could feel, and he deliberately used it against her.

Bastard.

"Turn one of the best snipers into a lab rat? For what! Are you insane?"

"No." The cage's thread walls collapsed to wrap around her. Ro's marking seared in her veins as if it were Roxar's actual silver fingers tightening around her skin.

Have to move, get out!

She couldn't. The weight of his ability was too heavy, too constricting. She didn't think he'd go through with it—a real Possession. Brute strength wasn't his style, just his pride.

"I'm pulling you off rotation, too. You have a new assignment. New recruits start tomorrow. They arrive this evening, in an hour or so in fact…"

"This is weaver shit—"

"Rolyn!" His cage assaulted her consciousness. Her will shriveled and broke. Her marking wailed, nearly ripping through her skin. Her body tried in every way to escape the onslaught, knowing how close he was to Possessing her again.

No!

She clamped down on her will, beating her marking into control by giving up on freeing her body from the pain. She forced her lungs to pump air in and out.

Roxar eyed her, the threads constricting her with immeasurable strength.

"What are my orders sir?" she managed defiance.

"Cadets Shai Jukita and Henry Harbor."

"Cadets? You've got to be joking…" she kept her tone civil. The cage bludgeoned all her senses, but she kept her marking under an iron grip.

"I do not joke," his voice reflected a darkness that never failed to shut her up. Any rationality in Roxar winked out, and he projected his infinite expanse of power into the small space still left between them, goading her marking with a battering ram. His arm glowed with purest white, a sight familiar only to her.

Double shit.

When Roxar outmaneuvered her, she always resorted to her physical superiority, though it worked less than a third of the time. She slammed her body forward into the cage, crashing against the thread encircling Roxar. She stretched her hand forward and locked her grip around Roxar's glowing wrist.

"Don't you dare," she whispered.

Roxar froze. He didn't let the cage up, but he didn't force the threads down on her.

She balanced on the balls of her feet, waiting. Roxar didn't let up one detail; he was an immaculate instructor. Roxar was one of the few who challenged her, but the converse wasn't true.

Yet… not yet.

So, she waited.

Roxar snapped once. The silver threads drooped, then wafted back through onyx to return to the Web.

That unprecedented release induced paralysis driven by shock. She simply stared, her hand falling limp.

What are you playing at?

He came nearer and laid the tips of silver fingers on her cheek. Her marking wrenched. She met the eyes of the sadist who stood too close.

"You do not know what you threaten. You've injured one of my own."

Ro couldn't contend that.

"You will meet the cadets at oh-six-hundred on the supplementary fields. New schedules will be assigned by tonight; dismissed."

No trace of danger in sight, his marking thrumming normally against hers.

"What's the catch?" she snapped.

"There is no catch, Rolyn."

C'mon give me the real answer shithead.

"Lieutenant Omika will do their intake tonight. I'm sparing you that much so you can adjust your… attitude. Their documents are available whenever you're ready. Dismissed Lieutenant."

<h1 style="text-align:center">CHAPTER FIVE</h1>

Crap. Shit. Fuck!

Logic prodded her to escape while she could. She revolved on the spot and dived into the light.

The moment her fingertips felt the heat of the Web, her anger melted to grief.

Winner, Roxar... unbelievable Ro.

She was breathless.

One.

How could he replace Ham?

Two.

He knew it wasn't entirely her fault.

Three... And new cadets? Shit. Just let me float.

The Web welcomed her mourning. Ro hung, suspended in light, in the belly of the Tower as the foundations of her home crumbled.

Why did Roxar break them up? Santos had earned its prestige among the White Wings. Ham was on track to be one of the top snipers in the last ten years. Kekoa was already such a skillful medic that captains and higher would take him on specialized missions.

And me...

Trained by Roxar himself, youngest promoted to Lieutenant, and the only Marked Wing on active duty.

Ham, Kekoa, and I are the best ones here.

Everything they had been through—everything they had fought through—it was over now.

Worse, she never saw it coming. All those extra hours working her ass off with Roxar and she could sooner predict weather than his actions.

She was spent. Her bones ached, her head hurt. She wished she could purge the last few days from memory.

She dived deeper into the heart of the Tower. Her marking stilled, buried in the light it craved. She clung to the temporary high, because it was all she would afford herself. It was all she would admit she needed when she felt like running away.

She resurfaced half an hour later trying not to think of her mentor. She left in search of company on foot. Walking prolonged the Web's bestowed calm.

Knock, knock.

"Yeah?" Akira's voice muffled voice made her smile.

She pushed through and his bare chest greeted her. She pressed him against the wall, needing his heat.

"Is it your turn to give me a peep show?" she asked. His body dissolved into liquid against her, except for one part, but he groaned.

"I would give you anything you want, you know that." He guided her hand down and pressed it against his hardening length. "But I can't yet, Taizai says I need to meet some new cadets in the portal bay." His face crumpled when she frowned.

She folded into his hug. She nestled her face against his neck so he wouldn't see the pang of loneliness.

"How long do you think?"

"An hour, hour and a half tops. I'll come right back, promise."

"Can't wait for later then."

He followed her out and spanked her as she headed toward the nearest vein. She returned to her bed, wallowing in her colored light since Akira couldn't hold her. She didn't want to think about how the two cadets he registered were the new Santos replacements. She didn't want to confess that Roxar was pulling her and Kekoa off rotation to train two rookies.

She sulked. Kekoa would be busy with the cadets too, and Pia, her best friend, was on mission. She thought about talking to Opal, but doubted the ethereal woman would sympathize. It was hard to lose your team; it was harder to lose your life.

The wall shone a venomous shade of blue. Her marking tugged through her at random, spiking with the actions of the people in the Tower.

She remembered how she used to start when she felt the tug in her blood. With time, she'd honed that magnetism into her sixth and deadly sense, but that only worked here, living where the Web permeated black walls. Out on mission, she had to be more creative with her marking. She learned that the hard way, thanks to Roxar.

Unbidden, her thoughts turned to him. In the beginning, when she had managed to keep herself under control enough to reside in the Tower, she spent sixteen extra hours a week doing intensives with Roxar, beyond her marked practice.

I hated it.

She hated the man's guts and his ridiculous secrecy. She hated that they disagreed on almost everything. She hated how he used her marking against her.

She hated that she resented him. Roxar—only Roxar—taught her control, taught her the luxury of freedom. She never could have amounted to anything without his grueling instruction. With every hour she spent practicing each technique, fixing every hole, drilling over and over, he was folding the steel of her soul, forging her into a sharper blade.

A sudden tear through her chest left her shuddering on the floor, her wall blackening.

Pain. Stabbing, searing, boiling pain ratcheted through her veins.

She hadn't felt this since her first months after being marked… the mind-stopping torture, the confusion as her faculties blacked out, the chaos wracking her body.

Minutes dragged by as Ro clenched her teeth, praying to the brightest stars that this would pass. It didn't. A millennia or thirty seconds could have swept her by and she wouldn't know, hunched up, fists bruising into the cold floor.

The pain never diminished, but the part of her that wouldn't quit rose to meet it. She gritted her teeth harder and struggled up.

She stood, gasping for breath. She flexed her will just to see. Her marking oozed from a cut along her finger, and her blood seeped into the Tower.

Her marking located that fierce agony stemmed from someone she had never met before. Through the Web, the person was bright, a luminosity that rivaled even Roxar's and her light. Curiosity swam through the cloud of misery, and she dived toward the stranger.

When she emerged outside the mess, a flash bumped into her feet. One name penetrated the pain. Harbor.

CHAPTER SIX

The light popped to black, and an explosion of sound ricocheted through Henry's chest.

Sand shifted and rolled as the cliff's maw opened, welcoming them into cavernous darkness. Caspiano strode forward. Henry's breath hitched. Shai also hesitated.

"Keep up."

Henry and Shai hustled, straight-backed. Something hovering near Caspiano's feet illuminated him, a small, spherical flame. Its glow permeated a meter of the gloom. Henry kept within the light.

The light exposed a wall, rounding up away from their feet. Caspiano put both hands against the black surface. He spread his hands apart—one north, the other south. A silver line trailed his touch. Caspiano slid his palms into the wall. Black engulfed his fingers.

Again, Henry's breath stopped in his throat.

Caspiano hauled his hands apart, dragging black with them. He constructed a compact room in the wall and entered.

"Well, come on."

Henry shuffled in, his tension growing to fill the gaps between cramped bodies. The hair on the back of his neck stood.

Caspiano sealed them in, then smeared his hand on the seamless wall.

"Commander Roxar."

The glowing hand print pulsed twice and the floor moved. Henry listened but heard no detectable mechanics. He only felt a soft thud when the lift stopped. Again, Caspiano's fingers pushed through the wall. The black melted back.

Henry paused, inhaling deep, before following Shai out into oppressive darkness.

"Do we go that way?" Shai pointed forward.

Caspiano shrugged and shut them out. The faint light vanished.

Henry rubbed his eyes; Shai cleared his throat.

"The fuck is this?"

"I don't know."

"Why didn't he take us to the Commander?"

Henry sighed. "I don't know."

Shai stayed silent a moment. "Think they're testing us?"

"I don't know, Shai."

"Not much of a talker are ya?"

"Guess not. Let's go."

"Right behind you."

Henry stretched his hand out and penetrated the unknown. He hit a wall. A glow appeared under this touch and dissipated when he pulled away.

"Check it out."

Henry pressed his palm flush. Brightness traced his hand, pushing black back with silver.

Henry balled his fingers and pressed his fist against the wall. He grazed the surface. Light streaked with his skin's path. He flexed his arm, punching his fist fast. A ball of light rocketed forward from his skin. It disappeared behind a sudden curve in the tunnel. To his satisfaction, a glowing trail smoldered.

"How'd you do that?"

"No idea, just tried it."

They fell into a synchronized rhythm, years of training guiding their boots. They walked until they found the smoking remains of their guide. Its embers slid to the bottom of the tunnel.

"Try it," Henry said.

"Well…" Shai approached the wall and crouched. He spiraled back, throwing his arm under hand. A streak of silver looped the tunnel. It lacked the brightness of Henry's, but the glossy black reflected the light. The eerie luminescence turned the huge tunnel, fifteen meters across, into a gloomy cage, the light pulsing against sterile walls.

"Hey, you like to bet?" Shai turned.

Henry grinned. "On what?"

"Uh—actually, I don't know yet, but first to the end?"

"A race then."

Shai smiled, aware Henry was faster. "Speed," he pointed to the walls, "and light."

"You're on."

They ran, slid, and tumbled across the smooth black. Henry gained a lead, but Shai spent more time throwing silver. His lights caught up to Henry, and Shai's laughter drew nearer. Henry skid to the floor, launched three quick shots, and rolled to his feet, keeping his lead.

When Henry flew around the last bend, the brightness blinded him. He retreated behind the corner, Shai slamming into his back.

"Sorry. I get competitive," Shai held his hands up shielding his eyes.

Henry shrugged behind his own hands. "Me too."

The lights jostled, making a full circle around the tunnel. When his eyes adjusted, Henry touched the luminous line. Mist crept from the silver, like smoke filling the space of the tunnel.

Taking a deep breath, Henry plunged through. A freeze on his skin made his blood simmer. He came out gasping.

Shai emerged beside him, holding his sides. "What was that?"

"No idea. Really weird."

Henry and Shai walked into a long room, the domed ceiling just as high. Three swirls of silver swam the length of the ceiling, brilliant eels in a dark ocean.

Two soldiers in the same skin-tight uniforms stood near a desk. The shorter, a Horn, stood at seven and a half feet. The other, Kau and angular, like Shai.

A desk flowed from the floor, arcing around another huge man; another Morsosi, another Day Walker. The creases at the corners of his eyes looked misplaced. Even sitting, the man radiated like a wildfire. Dark hair fell behind him into elaborate braids. He wore the same uniform, on his shoulder three encircled feathers making a bisected X.

Another seven foot Kau stood behind the Commander.

The seated man stared bright green at them.

"Join us Cadets."

Henry and Shai lined up with the other two soldiers, saluting.

"At ease. I am Commander Ilo Roxar. Your reporting officer, Lieutenant Omika. Your commanding officer, Captain Berto Gamabre." The Commander gestured to the two beside them. "You'll meet Lieutenant Sech tomorrow, your second reporting officer. Your orders, Cadets, are to demonstrate your skills for acceptance into my division. The White Wings are an integral system in locating and tracking Rahnus, and only the best will stay on. Your reporting officers will conduct series of tests and provide remedial training as needed prior to attempting the Wing's exam. Train hard, Cadets."

"Yes sir," Henry and Shai intoned with pride.

"Good. Lieutenant Omika will take care of your initial workups and then to your quarters."

"Yes sir," the Kau's response expressed crisp obedience.

"Astounding potential," the Kau behind the Commander murmured.

The Commander pressed his lips together but glanced at him. The Kau continued, eyeing Shai, then Henry, "Recent discoveries necessitate that we divert a certain number of skilled persons, the top graduates and specialists, toward more refined missions. You are lucky to have such genetic compatibility with the Web. To have the chance to be considered at all for this division."

"But we aren't graduates, sir," Shai blurted.

"While we require independent thought for our line of work, we also expect a healthy regard for tradition and discipline. More prudent cadets wait until invited to speak, no matter how highly commended they are, Cadet Jukita."

Shai lifted his chin. "I apologize for my breach of conduct, sir."

"Principal Foster praised your skills, Cadet—"

"And I expect the same outstanding results and behaviors you demonstrated at the Yard," the Commander interrupted. Henry couldn't maintain his eye contact. "You are here because you could be good enough. Looking at the pair of you, one spoiled by talent-inflicted privilege and the other just as inhibited but by of all things a lack of muscle, I guarantee if you achieve a position within my White Wings, it won't make a difference if you graduated or not."

"Yes sir."

Shai didn't shake, visibly. Henry, though, was used to honest criticism.

"Enough," the Commander waved his hand. It was silver, like the light above. "Send the reports to the lab but let me know when they're complete. Dismissed."

CHAPTER SEVEN

Out in the tunnel, Omika groaned and rolled out his shoulders, but smiled at them.

"You gave me desk duty for a month." He brushed a finger tip on the wall. "Portal bay."

The smear of light pulsed twice then flared down the hall. Omika followed the glowing trail.

"Well, come on." He glanced behind and stopped. "Honestly, life here ain't so bad. You even get used to all the black," he threw his arm wide.

"I miss the sun already, sir," Shai protested.

"You'll get plenty of it. From now on, report to the supplementary fields at oh-six-hundred. If you're going to be a White Wing," he tilted his head in Henry's direction, "you especially, then learn now when the stakes aren't so high… And call me Kekoa. You can relax a little," he chuckled.

"Yes sir," Henry and Shai said.

"Fucking kids," Kekoa kept laughing. "No, in a good way! You two are the first cadets ever to screen straight into the Wings from the academy level. How high did you score?"

"It's not in our files?" Henry confirmed.

"No. Scores can vary up through your thirties, and our measures are more precise than the screenings," Kekoa explained.

"Three forty-six over seven," Shai offered.

Kekoa whistled. "Really, really high. No wonder you got in so quickly."

"Really high," Henry agreed.

Shai scrunched his face, but didn't comment. He knew that Henry scored higher.

"Well, to be fair, you need a good score and a good performance. The White Wings… well, I imagine you have a lot of questions. You didn't even get intro since you skipped a few years."

"What intro?" Shai asked.

Henry's breathing stilled, his ears perked. "All we were told is the name."

"Figured as much. All right, here's a crash course. Let's see… the White Wings wouldn't exist without the Commander's military funded research, but that's all backstory, and a lab rat would tell it better than I would. The only important thing you need to understand is the timeline. As soon as the Commander figured out how people could dive, the Rahnus stopped raiding our planets. As soon as the first White Wing team scouted, the attacks ended altogether."

Henry absorbed the significance without Shai blurting, "So they stopped because of you? Why aren't the White Wings public knowledge?"

"Because we learned it from the Rahnus themselves and turns out diving is part of the process of becoming one."

Henry gaped.

"Yeah, that's about right. The thing is, as far as the Commander knows, that only happens after centuries of use, and even then there are other factors. So, no human should live long enough to turn into one."

"But any connection would not play well in the public eye," Shai said.

Kekoa nodded.

"Doesn't sit well with me, honestly," Shai grumbled.

Kekoa eyed Henry. He shrugged. He couldn't wrap his head around such power and such cost. He wondered how the Commander had done it, and darker questions lurked.

"So what's this diving then?" Shai asked.

"In a moment," Kekoa held up a hand. "Diving also introduced humanity as a player in an intergalactic territorial war in a system called Mergana. That now takes up half of White Wing operations, but the teams specialized enough to handle those missions are few and far between. While the Rahnus haven't attacked recently..."

"Death, Life, and Web," Henry and Shai chorused.

Kekoa grinned, "Death, Life, and Web, kids."

"So diving?" Shai prompted.

Kekoa beamed, "You're going to find out soon enough anyway. Why spoil it?"

Shai snorted, "At this rate, we'll miss breakfast too."

Kekoa's generous chuckle left warmth between them and the dark walls. Henry couldn't help gravitating toward his ease.

"We'll get food too, promise. Might as well ask whatever else you wanted to know now," Kekoa encouraged.

"Where to begin?" Shai said.

"Who is a lab rat?" Henry started.

"They are techs working under Taizai, that Kau behind the Commander earlier. Taizai runs R&D for the Commander and recruits at a higher rate than the Commander can. You can study onyxian physics enough to be good at it, but you can't help how you're born."

"Onyxian physics?"

"You only learn about it once you've proven yourself in government weapons development labs. Top secret clearance and stuff. This..." Kekoa extended an arm, brushed the shining black. Silver reflected his passing touch, "... is onyx, the only element we know of that can embody the Web. Visibly similar to the common mineral, but structurally very different. Beyond different."

Shai scoffed.

"Really," Kekoa pointed to the smear bouncing in front of him. "That light, that's the Web. As physical as it could ever be, housed in onyx. Outside of onyx, just photons and waves like any other ray of light."

"How…" but Henry couldn't finish his question.

"Good thing you're meeting my buddy, Akira. He works for Taizai, an onyxian engineer and physicist. He knows loads more about it than me. Anything else?"

"Tell me more about Taizai," Shai said.

"Taizai is actually second commander, but I've never met anyone more disassociated from the military. He has the rank, but he doesn't use it."

"How does that work?" Shai frowned.

"It is weird, but you'll get used to it. Anything else?"

No question could distract Henry from diving. Whatever it involved, it deemed top-secret military status and hefted enough power to dispel the Rahnus and host intergalactic peacekeeping. He didn't deserve it.

Henry clamped his mouth against too many unknowns. Shai grumbled about getting to food sooner, and they followed Kekoa in silence. When Kekoa slid to the floor, Henry copied him. He fell down a terrifying vertical chute. He gulped at the air rushing past him as he free fell for fifteen seconds.

"What. The. Fuck?" Shai demanded at the bottom of the slide.

Kekoa's laughter boomed in the tunnel. "Your face! Man…" he sighed. "The slides are the fastest way through the Tower. It's better the first time if you don't know what's coming."

"That's not funny."

Kekoa beamed. "You're right. It's hilarious."

CHAPTER EIGHT

Kekoa led them at a jog, but Henry itched to go faster. Adrenaline still hijacked his heart rate, his body eager to expel the slide's thrill. When they came to another bright circle, Henry surged through the mist. A grey haze filled the cavern on the other side. Shining beneath the smog, puddles of light spanned the floor, some large, some small, meters apart. Henry walked to one and crouched. The light roiled, as if liquid, entrancing Henry.

"You've seen it before." Kekoa came over and dipped fingers in the silver. He shivered, closing his eyes. "The screenings… didn't you ever see what they used your blood for?"

Memories flooded his mind from fifteen years ago. An old face, a delicate syringe. The glowing substance shimmered beneath a glossy black stopper…

"What is it?"

"The Web."

Henry reached out with one finger. He jerked back at the range of extremes on his skin, scalding ice, jagged fur, pointed curves. So small a touch for such grand feelings… Henry's finger reached again as Kekoa kept talking. The next touch wasn't as intense.

"Addictive, huh? You develop a tolerance pretty quick, though. A separate dimension made of light, wind, home of the Weavers… but they aren't the only ones who use it. That's what makes the Wings so powerful."

"Wait… White Wings…"

Kekoa beamed. "You'll see soon enough. Before you two, none of the cadets started in the portal bay unless Taizai recruited them. Even those though…" his eyes followed a tendril of mist escaping from the pool. "Just wait for your first dive," he winked. "Oy, Akira!"

Another Kau approached. He had the same build as Taizai, awkward angles through the hips. Brown hair fell to elongated shoulders. A slender nose dominated his face. He wore a loose fitting all-black uniform. A lilting purr rolled through his voice; he must have learned the common tongue late.

"Hey, I'm Akira Iraiza, assistant lab technician. Welcome to the Tower."

"Don't flatter yourself, Rat," Kekoa said.

Akira rolled slanted eyes at him and handed Kekoa a hand-held mirror. "Can I go to bed after this one?"

"Nope. Updated stats are high priority for these two, Commander's orders."

Shrugging, Akira knelt to place a long fingered hand on the ground. The silver on the floor highlighted his leonine features, reminding Henry his bloodline was once wild.

Shai's voice was muted with reverence. "You're Old Kin."

Akira paused, his hand outstretched. "I am. Please don't bow."

Shai grinned, "How'd you end up here?"

"I chose to go to the academy when I was first screened."

"That's incredible. I didn't think anyone with Old Kin lineage was allowed to leave Handakau."

Akira chuckled. "I'm only half. My mother is Lady Mirai of the Clan Mazu, and my dad is not. I can't preserve our cultural heritage with half the genes."

"Mazu? No shit."

"Yeah, but I wasn't a fraction as good as my half-siblings. They'd give even our own giant Wings a rumble."

"Still, Old Kin lineage and a warrior clan at that... why aren't you a Wing?"

"My giant is good, but my brain is better."

Kekoa snorted. "Good means he spars with our senior giants and keeps them on their toes. So, imagine that, but a million times nerdier."

Shai brightened. "Will you spar with us too?" he motioned between him and Henry, then paused. "Well, me."

"Sure, whenever you're free."

Akira pressed his palm to the floor. Two shots of light skittered across the ground from his fingers. Kekoa lifted his eyebrows.

"One for Ro," Akira admitted. Kekoa rolled his eyes.

"I heard you two had a falling out last night." Kekoa earned an impish smile from Akira.

"We didn't fight, but we did make up for long time."

Kekoa chuckled. "Trust me, the other side is a pretty different."

"Yes, well, for the record I was right."

"Sure, man. When she's not here."

"Some friend you are. So, Shai, Henry, where are you assigned?"

"Uh…"

"They're coming into Gambare's detachment under me and Ro. Didn't she tell you?

Akira shook his head. Kekoa shrugged, but Henry caught the scrunch of his nose.

"Rough job. Of course, being with Taizai, I'll be seeing you a bit."

Kekoa grumbled. "Not for the first chunk. That's for training at least."

"Ah… well there's that at least, hm? Did the commander say why their elementary training wasn't finished?"

Kekoa didn't stifle his negativity. His silence engendered more questions than anything else had that night. Henry quashed his surging dread, kept it hidden in his gut.

Akira studied Henry and Shai for a moment. "Well the commander wouldn't have put them with you this early if he didn't foresee its benefits."

Kekoa's grim quiet persisted. Even Akira wasn't willing to lift it.

A burst of light skid to Akira's boots. Akira scooped it from the floor. He held a small flame. It spasmed to emit a familiar guttural voice.

"The landing pad is clear. You have half an hour before Team Amrah arrives."

The fire popped, and ash fell into the haze below.

Kekoa let out a long breath. "Finally. Okay. You're about to take your first dive."

Henry 's stomach squirmed, like it would drop out his ass. Shai's face pinched, his hands balling into fists.

Kekoa muttered, "Well don't look too happy."

"Will it hurt?" Shai couldn't hide his morbid curiosity.

"I assure you it's nothing like, like, what you think it will be. It's difficult to describe. I mean, the noise is awful, but it's nothing to worry about. Just remember: never open your eyes. The light inside the Web is too extreme. It will burn out your retinas, and our medical expertise still hasn't found any way of reversing the damage."

Henry's breath caught.

"Nervous?" Kekoa asked.

"Yes," Shai admitted.

"All right then," Akira chuckled. "Henry first?"

CHAPTER NINE

Henry quelled the riot in his innards and stepped into the silver. It bubbled around his boots. Frostbite stung his feet. Cold climbed his limbs, seeping through every pore, soaking up his body heat. Henry grit his teeth to push air through his lungs.

"Don't worry Cadet, it's normal. Chest tightening?"

Henry nodded.

"Feels like your blood stopped moving?"

Again, Henry jerked his chin.

"Then you're good."

Shai sighed. "That looks bad."

Akira joined Henry.

"Grab my arm and don't let go. Keep still and—Don't—Open—Your—Eyes. No matter what, until you feel ground again."

Henry's double grip secured around Akira's wrist.

"Good." He closed his eyes, and Henry copied him. "Dive in three… two… one…"

The atmosphere split around them, the noise ripping through Henry's conscious thought. The world outside his sealed lids turned dark for a space too small for time.

Light infused every particle of Henry's body and snapped him into a heatwave. The immense pressure pulled like fingers squeezing him through the Web's rays.

Light seared through his eyelids in vague colors. Silver. Black. Blue. A wind, hot and fast, burned against his face. Henry pictured himself falling from the rim of outer sub-space, an unknown cosmic fate at his descent.

It horrified him, but there was peacefulness. Somewhere, between the fear for his life and the burning in his mind, he found a restful calm. Henry relaxed for the first time since he left the Yard. The longer he stayed inside that bright chaos, the better he felt.

In a single breath, the air cooled to the opposite extreme. Thunder rang his ears. The dive halted, warping back into reality. The landing sent him sprawling. Small stones imprinted on Henry's palms and thighs. Lying on the ground, bruised where he thudded to earth... he preferred the heat? Light? Chaos? Henry couldn't find the right word.

He pushed himself up, looking around. Even in the night's gloom, he could tell they were back where he and Shai landed hours before. Henry started, realizing the Tower was underground, hewn into the cliff below him with the Web's light.

Shai and Kekoa tore into existence. Shai landed with a grunt. Henry hoped he didn't look so awkward.

"Not what you expected right?" Akira asked.

"Not at all." Henry smiled, but Akira grew pale.

"What is it?"

"What did you score on your last screening Henry?"

"Four hundred seventy eight over three."

"No kidding," Akira whistled and gave Henry a small mirror. "Look."

Despite all the familiarities, the person in the glass was a stranger. Molten silver eyes dominated Henry's features.

Henry saw remarkably well—improved vision. Not a change in the colors, or his focus, but the clarity. The minutia, like the pinch above Akira's angled eyes, shed subtlety.

"What's going on up here?" Henry asked, pointing to his face. He struggled to ignore the inundation of data his eyes picked out.

"You've been marked as we all have been," Akira answered, pulling up his shirt. Three silver bands paralleled his bottom three ribs on the right. "Kekoa's left foot is marked. It happens to us all, even those who don't make White Wing."

"Yeah, but it's not the same. I see, uh, more."

"Well, that's… that's just…" Akira motioned to Kekoa. The Lieutenant came over, Shai following.

"What's up?"

"Guess," Akira answered, taking the mirror from Henry.

"Shit Cadet…" Kekoa gasped. Shai took a step back.

"This is going to change everything," Kekoa grumbled.

Henry searched their darting eyes and tense jaws, looking for answers. He found anxiety in Kekoa's frown. Akira's eyes relayed guarded curiosity. At least Shai's shock matched his own.

Henry turned to Shai. "What about you?"

"On my back, left shoulder."

"Over the heart? Touching," Akira didn't turn toward the other giant.

"Okay… okay," Kekoa tore his eyes from Henry and shook himself. "Henry, yes—your marking is different from ours, but you have to prove that you can use any ability that comes with it. Until then, it doesn't matter too much. Akira, I'll be right back, gonna take'em to the mess."

"Hurry. The commander will probably alter orders." Akira gestured at Henry.

Kekoa nodded. "Fucking paperwork."

"I'll tell Ro," Akira waved.

A tear in space swallowed Akira whole, silver outlining him for an instant.

"Can't we dive back?" Shai pointed to the drop off.

"Nope. Rules," Kekoa shrugged.

"I can't wait until we get to do that," Shai whispered.

Henry nodded. Shai still looked at Henry wide-eyed. Kekoa wasn't any better.

Henry chose to bring up the rear. It helped. He didn't have to make eye contact with the other two. The Thalweg's turbulence lured his attention far out over the cliff. He caught the white tips and black troughs with precision. A faint bump off the coast several degrees north made the water calmer—a tiny island.

An hour passed in silence, the hike taking less time since neither Henry or Shai carried their packs. When they got to the beach, the stars captivated Henry. Henry stared like he'd never seen them before. The moons pierced the sky with brilliant light. Stars glittered against the deep, deep blue, winking secrets. Two planets, hues of green and blue on their star-spangled canvas, hung above the horizon.

Still craning his neck, Henry walked into Shai.

"Come on, Henry," Shai complained.

"Sorry, I was…" he trailed off. He didn't know words good enough for the opus above. "The stars are really nice."

"Sure." Shai didn't look up.

Kekoa turned. "Can you see them differently?" His eyes read pure curiosity, no apprehension. Any progress let Henry breathe easier.

"Yeah. I see them better, clearer."

Shai grinned. "But you can't clearly see me."

Kekoa laughed. Henry smiled back. When they continued on, Kekoa's shoulders didn't ride up his neck. Shai didn't glance back anymore.

CHAPTER TEN

Kekoa took them back through the gates and deeper until he came to an atrium, pillars of silver lining each corner. Kekoa walked to the nearest pillar.

"This is a vein, part of the Web. They run through the Tower. Once you are cleared to dive, you will have full access, but for now, if you ever need it, you can use it for basic transportation."

Kekoa pulled a pocket knife from his boot. He threw it into the light, creating shimmering ripples. The knife floated, weightless but stationary in the viscous silver.

"Quarters, Omika," Kekoa ordered. The vein pulsed twice. The knife sped off, lost to light. Even Henry' eyes couldn't find it.

"Got it? Basic transport only."

Henry nodded.

"Great, can we eat now?" Shai asked.

Kekoa chuckled, setting his palm to the wall. A new light bounced off to the left.

Henry realized his empty stomach at Shai's words. The excitement of the evening kept him busy enough he ignored the pangs of hunger until now.

It didn't take long to get to the mess. When they entered through the mist, the smell of grilled meat consumed him. He salivated for the same grub he was used to at the Yard; it was hot and filling. He went up for seconds. Neither Kekoa nor Shai matched his appetite.

"So where are our quarters?" Shai asked.

"Where all the other White Wing quarters are: random. You two will be rooming together until after initiation."

"Cool," Shai shrugged.

Henry didn't mind sharing. He'd shared his quarters with his team at the Yard. Sharing with one would be luxury.

"Well, you two should get to bed as soon as you can. Just use a comet when you're done and send it toward your quarters."

"A what?" Shai asked.

"A comet. Press your hand. Light comes on. Tell it where you're going, just like using a vein," Kekoa instructed. "There should be basics in your room. Press your hand on the wall and think of a drawer. All your clothes and linens will be there. If they don't fit, wear your old ones."

Both nodded. Kekoa left.

"Well I'm wiped," Shai said. "Mind if I go ahead?"

Henry gestured him on, mouth full. Shai left with a yawn.

Henry took his time, sifting through the night with each bite. Onyx. The commander. His marking. He circled his doubts, wondering how any of the White Wings learned to trust anything related to the Rahnus. He didn't know where to begin.

A glow outside the mist distracted him. A soldier entered, her austere presence filling the room. Henry's keen eyes watched. He slid his pelvis under the table.

She was Syll, the only one he'd ever seen. Unlike the rest of humanity, the Syll preferred isolation, only trading necessities and barring all outsiders. The Syll had blue skin that darkened as they aged. Hers was clearest blue, like an early morning sky. It glowed, as if light danced beneath her skin.

She was far taller than him. Her dark hair was pulled back from an exquisite face. High cheek bones, wide blue eyes, full lips. Her eyes alone splintered his thoughts. Two tiny moles above her left eyebrow, and one high on her right cheek. Her movement, soundless and sure-footed. Predatory, even. Lean, but toned through her whole body. Conditioned muscles stretched her loose-fitting uniform. Curves Henry eagerly pictured taunted him through fabric.

She twisted her hips to sit opposite him, making him stare. Her most prominent curve sent a hot shiver through his spine. She faced him, her long braid sliding over her shoulder. The thick hair fell below her breasts. He wanted to stroke it.

Part of him was speechless. The bigger part of him was wedged under the table.

"You are Cadet Harbor."

Her tone halted his fantasies. Resentment. Condescension. Pity. He regathered forgotten logic.

"Yes."

She leaned forward, her eyes skimming him over. "You don't look like a soldier. You barely look seventeen. I can't believe Roxar brought you here. You are you at least twenty, aren't you?"

"Nineteen."

She smiled, leaning back. Stress drained from her face, but something else took its place—darker, more sinister than disdain. He couldn't read her like he could the others; it frustrated him.

"And you didn't even finish your training before you got here."

"That didn't bother the commander," he emphasized the rank and met her gaze.

She jerked. "Most candidates arrive fully prepared to take on initiation. But you," she paused allowing an icy tone to edge her voice, "You are here unprepared, untested, and unfinished. The time it will take to train you up to the point where you just might pass—which will be a stretch for you I can already tell—takes away valuable time from White Wings who have already proven their worth."

The huge room around them vanished. Henry could only see the sneer on her face.

"The commander thinks I'm worth it."

She laughed. It made her cheeks flush, making her skin even more touchable. Henry hated it.

She lifted off the bench and turned her back on him, more appealing than ever when she walked away. The room shrank when she left.

Henry sat at the table, food forgotten. His body fought with his brain. He'd never met anyone so attractive, but she was an asshole. Everything about her teased his senses. He wanted to watch her, touch her, know her, but her ego squashed those thoughts. Despite that tantalizing body, only her condescending sneer stuck with him.

His thoughts drifted to Petal, the only other girl that made his body react back home. How she'd always be his friend, but he couldn't feel for her. He couldn't picture her, instead reliving cold blue eyes laughing at him.

He promised himself that he would never let her get the better of him.

He would never give her reason to sneer.

When she was ready to fight about it, he would never lose to her.

He would win.

CHAPTER ELEVEN

Henry lay in bed, stewing in the image of the Syll's contempt. Restlessness guided his fingertip around a circle on the wall.

The circle he traced pulsed. Once. Twice. Then it sunk into the dark.

Henry didn't breathe, controlling panic. After a few moments, the circle floated into view, a window looking on her. Henry blinked.

She was naked, pressed against Akira, their legs wrapped around each other, their faces slack in sleep.

He snapped his eyes shut. Heat flushed up his neck and down, lower and lower.

He turned back, in spite of himself.

Something wrenched the window from his control—sideways. A pair of wrinkled milk eyes peered at him through the window. They stared, unblinking, unseeing.

Henry stopped breathing despite his thudding pulse. He didn't make a sound.

A ghostly message surfaced on the wall in front of him.

Tsk, tsk.

The silver words quivered in front of him. Henry stared, awaiting discipline. After a breath, the words dissipated into black.

Are you illiterate?

Henry rolled his eyes.

No.

His response sank into onyx.

You could be interesting.

Confusion replaced Henry's regret.

Who are you? He scribbled.

I am the Gatekeeper. Been enjoying the view?

How do you know?

You shouldn't have looked again, you know.

You're right.

Silence passed.

I'm sorry. Henry tried.

The apology goes to her.

Shame stilled his hand.

Really nothing?

I am sorry.

Again, wrong person for that apology. I shouldn't have to repeat myself. You won't do well here if you need to be told twice.

Henry paused. *I know. Thank you.*

I'm giving you the benefit of the doubt. Who are you?

My name is Henry.

Henry. Your marking is bright.

Henry hesitated.

Roxar may have brought you here, but I could teach you too.

His focus sharpened, wary of another unknown. The Gatekeeper was the second person to refer to the commander so casually. Kekoa hadn't, and neither had Akira.

What could you teach me?

The window widened. In it, an unfamiliar figure floated. Mist hazed the exact outline of her body, but she looked stooped, contorted. Those milky eyes looked at but didn't see him; blind eyes.

I didn't think you would be so picky.

Henry could hear the annoyed flicker in her words.

Why teach me then?

The milky eyes narrowed.

Do you belittle yourself so easily?

Henry pushed back his own annoyance.

I am not little.

My son was a smart-ass too. The writing softened. *Your first lesson, Harbor, is to answer this question. What is Death?*

Henry snorted. *It's when you die.*

Such shallow perceptions are meaningless. When you are ready, write your answer. When you are correct, I will return.

The window disappeared and the writing faded.

Wait! Henry scribbled furiously, but there was no response.

Henry drew another circle, tried to spy on the blind woman. Swirls of silver shrouded his view.

How could he sleep? What did she mean? Who was she?

The questions lingered in the dark as he slipped, unwilling, into sleep. The Gatekeeper's question interrupted his dreams and left him sore in the morning. It rattled in his head as stretched in bed. His lack of drive annoyed Shai.

"We gotta hurry. We have to be there in half an hour." Shai already wore the skin-tight all black uniform.

Henry rolled out of bed. He needed a hot shower to mellow yesterday's lingering intensity and the new stakes the Gatekeeper presented. The water thudded on his head, neck, and back, a rhythmic feeling pushed it all back. His mind didn't stay empty long, focusing on the indeterminable training ahead.

His new uniform didn't cling like Shai's did. On Henry, the black fabric was a layer of loose skin. It emphasized his thin frame, especially standing next to Shai. Three white feathers hung on his right shoulder, set in a line, none touching.

They exited their quarters and jogged to the mess.

"Couldn't sleep so well." Shai jabbed his fork at his food. "Kept waking up for no reason at all."

"Me either," Henry said. "I met a girl after your guys left."

Shai stopped chewing. His eyes glinted.

"Who was she?"

"No idea." Henry admitted. "She wasn't very nice."

"Oh," Shai sighed. "There are always bad eggs Henry. Best to stay as far away from them as possible." He patted his stomach and winked.

They finished eating and returned to the black corridor.

Henry turned to the black wall. "We need to meet Lieutenant Omika." The comet whizzed away.

"Ready?" Henry stalled.

"Don't look at me like that with those, man," Shai pointed to Henry's face. "Makes my spine tickle."

Henry laughed and they took off. Ten minutes later they stood before a misted circle, but this time it only spanned the right side of the tunnel. Rather than a doorway, this mist lasted, a wet clinging fog that grabbed at Henry through the black suit.

Henry broke out under the sun, the light coating the ocean below in diamonds. They were half way up the cliff on a narrow ledge on the East side. Manicured grass stretched for a couple kilometers up the coast. No one else used the fields, strange for any military compound's training area.

"We're early."

"Could have slept more." Shai flopped on the grass.

"Good morning," a sharp voice echoed. Sky colored skin. Dark hair and wide, blue eyes. Muscular with curves. Henry met her hostile eyes.

He groaned.

CHAPTER TWELVE

"Morning ma'am," Shai scrambled to stand.

"Stop right there," she snapped. She took two steps toward him, close enough he had to look up to her face. "I realize you've only been on base a few hours, but still. White Wing is a rank, not a title. Here, all of us have earned our Wings the same way. The proper way to address any Wing is by their rank, and in conversation 'sir.' Only sir," she paused. Her eyes narrowed. "Should you make my time worthwhile, perhaps you'll earn it too."

"Yes…" they answered.

"Sir," she finished.

"Yes sir," Henry and Shai repeated.

"Good. Lieutenant Omika and I make up Team Santos. Cadet Harbor, I'm Lieutenant Sech. You're with me. Cadet Jukita, you will report to Lieutenant Omika. He will arrive momentarily. Until then, two basic rules. One, always light a comet when traversing the Tower. Two, no diving. That last one gets lifted once you make Wing. Apart from these rules, everything is the same as it was wherever you came from, which was…?"

"The Yard, on Handakau, sir." Shai had recovered, and still seemed eager to engage her. Henry imagined Shai would enjoy that challenge.

"Fine. Questions?"

"Excuse me Lieutenant," Shai ventured, "but why are the comets always needed?"

"The Web makes onyx malleable or solid as needed. None of those tunnels are permanent. The Tower makes new paths each time you travel through it."

"The veins stay in place don't they?" Henry blurted with gut instinct.

"I'll remind you to address me as sir, Cadet." Her posture shifted so she stood at her full height. Sech peered at him, meeting his eyes. That crisp authority was contradicted by an intense… something. Something darker. Again, she eluded his sight, and it annoyed him.

"The veins are like the Tower's foundation, but don't think of them as physical. They are access points to the Web, and that's it," she answered, staring Henry down.

"Do you mean that none of those rooms… none of that is actually real?" Shai's eyes lit, curiosity pitching his voice higher.

"Sir," Sech snapped at him.

"Sir," Shai smiled at her.

Her brow flattened. "Yes Cadet. That is basically what I mean."

"Then where does it all go, sir?" Henry asked, incredulous.

"It remains in the space provided for by the Web."

"But how sir?" Henry prompted.

"I'm surprised by your curiosity Harbor. Typically only Taizai's candidates pay so much attention to the finer details of onyxian nucleophysics. When you fail to make the White Wings, perhaps Taizai can squeeze you in somehow."

Henry bit back his tongue. Her indifference didn't surprise him, but Shai couldn't shake the disapproval off his face.

Henry warmed toward his new bunkmate.

"Oy, Ro!" Kekoa emerged from mist.

"Ah, finally," she sighed.

"Started the party without me?" Kekoa sauntered up.

"As usual," she responded without turning.

"Lighten up, it's their first day," Kekoa punched her in the shoulder. She flashed him a quick grin. Her stony facade returned when she eyed Henry.

"I'm sure Lieutenant Sech has scared you right stiff, she can be an ass that way…" Kekoa said.

Sech smiled, but it didn't touch the something in her eyes.

"But you listen to everything she says, and you do your absolute best to remember it," he directed his comments to them. "She is first off, my co-leader for Santos and your direct superior but beyond that… she is the Commander's personal protégé. You have a lot to live up to Harbor."

"Quite right," Sech added. Henry forced his stomach to settle.

"Well," Kekoa said, "shall we get started? This first week we are doing preliminary work-ups on your current physical fitness, combat skills, recon strategy, and Web compatibility. No assessment will be made now except for an evaluation to figure out how best to prepare you for Initiation. The actual exam will run very similarly to this first week, just faster paced and way more stressful."

"You will know whether or not you passed or failed on the final day of the exam," Sech concluded.

Henry's stomach started kickboxing with his esophagus despite his best effort.

The two Lieutenants waited a few seconds. Henry didn't have questions now, just nerves. Shai stayed quiet too.

"Alright warm up for cardio, you have five minutes," Kekoa motioned to Shai.

Sech turned to Henry and locked eyes.

"Ready?" she asked.

Three hours and forty-five minutes later, Henry's muscles didn't ache. They screamed. Sweat poured from his brow, neck, and back. The staccato bursting through his jugular left him wheezing when he wasn't retching.

Henry's body sharpened at the sound of Sech's boots approaching. He willed himself to get up. He ground the heels of his hands into the grass and shoved up to one knee. Still, too little, too late.

"Stand up," Sech commanded.

"I... I don't- I... can't sir," Henry gasped. His vision swam. His body shook from the effort it took to stay semi-vertical.

"Stand up or prove me right."

"Lieutenant, I can't... please, I need... some water."

"Ro!" A new shadow joined them. "Stars... this was just an assessment. Seriously... C'mon," Kekoa lifted one of Henry's deadened arms and jerked him to unready feet. The lurch made Henry's stomach flip.

"Can you stand?" Kekoa asked.

"I need water," Henry didn't want to invite more criticism.

Sech's expression looked like someone held shit under her nose. She made no move to help Kekoa carry her despondent charge.

"Ro, stop beating him up and rest him," Kekoa admonished her.

"My Cadet walks on his own two feet," she replied, turning her back. A misted circle appeared, and she vanished into the silver.

Kekoa grunted.

"Thanks," Henry muttered.

"Don't mention it. Did she let you drink at all?" he asked.

Henry nodded.

"Well there's that at least," Kekoa's relief sounded bitter.

He helped Henry shamble to the Tower. Kekoa alternated between checking Henry's feet were still moving and yelling at Shai.

"She has high standards, and the last few days have been hard for us both," Kekoa started. "Don't take it personally."

It wasn't much comfort, but Henry appreciated help that didn't think less of him for needing it.

"You good now?" Kekoa asked once they reached the wall. Henry sagged against the rock.

"Yeah, thanks."

Kekoa nodded, frowning, and jogged back to Shai.

Henry let himself fall through the mist. Dragging his feet behind him, he crawled through. He only stood on the other side by bracing against the wall. Gritting his teeth, Henry struggled after Sech.

CHAPTER THIRTEEN

He didn't have to go far. He found no mist, but a sheer cut in the wall. Silver flowed down the back of the large alcove, illuminating a table and stiff shoulders. Sech sat, a cruel thinness in her lips. A pitcher and cups waited in front of her. She poured both cups and pushed them toward him.

Henry took the seat opposite her, gulping down the cool water. His head spun. He rested on his forearms, trying to focus his vision.

"You did not do well." She poured him two more cups.

"I know, sir," Henry answered between mouthfuls of water.

"How did you do at the Yard?"

"Not well either. I took remedial training."

"I'm not surprised. I recommend you continue remedial training."

"Recommend or order, Lieutenant?" Henry picked his head up. She stared at him. He didn't conceal his exhaustion.

Both her eyes widened, her spine stiffening. Her breath caught for a moment. "Order, Cadet." Her voice softened, but her accusing eyes made up for it.

"Yes sir," Henry answered. "Sir?"

"Yes Cadet?" Sech continued in the same tone.

"What'd I do? To you," he added.

"I—"

Her eyes narrowed. "Absolutely nothing. My personal feelings have nothing to do with why I pushed you harder than Kekoa did Jukita. You tout Roxar's support as one of your defenses, right? Well, Roxar believes new recruits should dog a mentor's footsteps rather than mass training. He thinks it may be of use to candidates who would fail otherwise. So, you want to keep up with me? You'll have to do better than that burnout today. By a long shot."

Henry heard it, the arrogance. "You don't believe I can make it."

Her eyes grew round with pity for a soft moment.

"Harbor, regardless of my efforts, Initiation is designed to break people like you."

"If I don't have a chance, why am I here?" Henry demanded. She shrugged, pouring him another two cups. She opened her mouth, but shut it again.

Henry didn't move toward the water, holding her gaze.

She blinked and carefully looked toward the Web's glow.

"Roxar's thoughts are a mystery to all, including myself. His decision alone brought you here, not your score," she said. That something edged her eyes again, that indecipherable feeling, but it vanished as quickly as it came. A monotone continuance, "I am going to keep breaking you down until you finally get back up stronger than me, or until you stay broken."

"And when I am stronger than you?" Henry challenged.

She relaxed her shoulders. Her eyes flicked toward him—a flash of fear.

He was too riled by her words to think what frightened her.

"If by a miracle you do pass, you'll be promoted to Wingman and join Santos." Sech's words belied her eyes. Henry's insides ice over.

"Any other questions?" she asked.

The one question he hadn't dared think tumbled from his mouth.

"What happens if I don't make it?"

"You go home."

"That's all?" Henry asked stunned.

She didn't answer, turning to the radiant wall. "What was your score, Cadet?" she diverted.

"You don't know? Sir."

"Scores rarely matter here as only scores over three hundred are eligible, and even then they change following the first dive. Because of that, no incoming scores are reported until after acceptance to the White Wings."

"I don't know if it changed after yesterday."

"Be that as it may, what was it?"

"Four hundred seventy-eight over three, sir."

Sech jolted, swiveling to him, her mouth gaping. Her eyes grew laughable, large, an open book for Henry. Jealousy mingled with frustration. Pain-driven fury, and... recognition?

That something darker flooded her eyes, masking all she felt.

"Why does that bother you Lieutenant?"

She sighed—the steely kind.

"You are the first cadet who has ever scored better than I did." She would not meet his eyes.

"Why does it matter?" Henry gave into an inquisitive edge.

The Lieutenant's expression shifted to irritation. "For the second time Cadet, scores don't count anymore... it's just a number."

Henry saw that darkness leak from her gaze, knew she lied.

"When you are ready Cadet, we will begin part two of today's assessment." She smiled. The sadistic authority that drove him outside was back.

"What?" he exclaimed. Heat and anger rolled off him. He knew his body would fail another assessment.

"Relax, Cadet. The second phase is not physical, but something else entirely. Can you guess?"

"My marking," he answered.

"Correct." She pulled a small knife from her boot leg. She sliced along a thin line on the side of her second finger. Though shallow, the cut dripped. She pinched her finger, increasing the flow. Blood gurgled forth, making a small, silver pool. Too silver for it to be the light emanating from the back wall.

"Are you… blood marked, sir?" Henry asked amazed. Wonder superseded disgust as the silver blood fell from her callused finger tip.

"How observant," sarcasm dripped. "You should have known by looking at my skin. I am far too pale for a Syll."

"I have never seen a Syll before yourself, sir."

She looked down her nose at him. "Obviously. I'm the only one off-planet. But, not even a picture?"

Henry shook his head.

She huffed.

"Why aren't there any other Syll off-planet?" he asked.

"Why do you care?" she bit back. Her voice grew harsh, an iciness colder than her dislike of him.

"Nothing, sir. Uh, what is the second assessment?" he changed subjects.

Sech sighed. She put pressure on her bleeding finger. "I am blood marked and you are…?"

"Eyes, sir."

"Yes, unlike most others, we both are marked organically. That really means that part of us, in its cellular entirety, is marked by the Web. All of my blood is marked. Roxar's right arm is marked. And Opal's marked, but she's even more of a special case. We used to be the only three organically marked, and now you came along. Any idea what that means, Cadet?"

"Unique abilities?"

"Right. Our abilities are inherently powerful."

As the words left her mouth, she flicked her hand. The pool of blood flattened, thinning itself to its minimum. She raised the cut finger, and the disc of blood took to the air. She drew a circle in the air. The silver disc started to rotate. Henry couldn't stop staring.

"Is that really…"

"Yes, that's my blood."

CHAPTER FOURTEEN

Sech leaned forward across the table.

"'Why does it look metallic?"

"I'm happy to explain, but I'd rather use the next hour figuring your marking out."

"Fine," Henry accepted. "Can I do that Lieutenant?"

"No and yes." She moved her hand. The blood fell, splattering the table and their uniforms. "Because of my marking, my blood cells are both real and part of the Web. My ability manifests based on what my cells can do. Take my red blood cells, for instance. They absorb and transport oxygen. Well, my strongest ability is called Blending, absorbing anything into my blood to store and transport as I want. That said, conceptually, all marked Wings can achieve the same things, just in their own ways based on the nature of their marking."

The implications staggered Henry's thoughts. He couldn't even process the beginning of her explanation.

"Real and part of the Web? Isn't the Web real?" he protested.

"I remember telling you to address me as sir, Cadet," she said.

Henry didn't care what she thought. "Yes sir. Can you give me an exact answer? Sir?"

That dark something grew deep in her eyes.

Henry knew he crossed her lines.

She answered anyway in a soft, controlled tone. "To understand ability, first you must recognize what your marking really is. Your marking exists both in reality, here," she pointed to the spatter of blood, "and in the Web," she gestured to the silver flowing down the wall. "Of course, the Web is real. Calling this reality is just a simpler way of understanding it than getting into a breakdown of the dimensions. What this means for you now is your marking exists biologically, as your eyes, and transcendentally, as an access point to the Web."

"So it's a vein?" Henry clarified.

"Yes, but on a cellular level, and because you are alive, your marking is way more potent than any vein in the Tower."

Henry nodded. "Ok."

Sech raised a single brow. Heat Henry ignored tingled down his spine.

"That's it?" she prompted.

"Sir."

"Good. As far as Taizai can figure, ability falls under three types: Blending, what I do, Possession, what Roxar does, and Reflecting. Technically, I can all do all three, but as I said, because each marking is unique, some abilities come easier and some come harder. I can do this," she flicked a finger and made the blood jump on the table, "through Blending my blood and air to suspend and mold every molecule how I want."

"Sir, does that mean your ability is also limited by how much chemistry you know?"

She hummed in assent. "Knowledge is the second greatest inhibitor for any White Wing, but for a marked Wing especially. I have to keep studying in addition to training... Roxar's just had so much more time for it."

She stared at the silver droplets splattered around them, her gaze unclouded. She dropped her walls.

Henry saw frustration and wonder. Anger and gratitude.

He had no idea what to make of her.

With a tiny bend of a finger, one large drop on the table rose up. It floated to her finger tip, hovering above her skin.

"What can I do?" Henry asked.

She dropped her finger. She let the drop of blood settle in the middle of the table and drew her fingers into a fist. Henry watched, entranced. Blood came off his shirt, leaving it spotless, and collected with the larger drop. It swelled as blood from all around them gathered on the table. With a soft scooping motion, Sech guided the blood back through the thin cut. It was the strangest thing Henry had ever seen. When she finished siphoning the blood back into her body, she pressed her fingertip and thumb together. She presented a healing finger to Henry.

"Well, if you've recovered enough, we can find out. Ready?"

"Yes, sir."

She turned her back to him. Her shoulders dropped, a minute decrease in her tension. She lifted her cut finger to her lips and sucked hard, her cheeks hollowing. She spat into the silver.

Specks of her blood fanned across the liquid wall. Blue emanated from the drops like swirls of dye intertwining with the Web. Sech inhaled, then let it out slow. The blue streaks shifted, sinking or rising with purpose. Where they met, the blue turned dark and the silver around it brightened. Then, the color vanished. The Web swallowed Sech's blood.

"Watch."

Sech closed her eyes, her arms stretching away from her body, palms facing the glow. Her head tilted back and the lines on her forehead smoothed. Her lips quirked up on one side, content to be lost.

A hazy shape, deep in the silver, snagged Henry's eyes from Sech. The shape moved toward them, almost walking. Henry squinted. A silver-speckled blue body walked toward the Lieutenant. The figure, lithe but muscular. Distinctly feminine. Two sets of palms faced each other, both still as statues. Sech, eyes still shut, raised her left hand, flexed two fingers. The figure in the wall mimicked her.

Sech never opened her eyes, never turned toward him. "It's called casting a Shadow. It's the basics for more advanced techniques like setting a Drone or making a Ringer," she said, playing with herself. "For Roxar and I, it was the first thing we mastered. It's the easiest because you don't have to use your will actively."

"Will, sir?"

"Think of your will as the mental muscle that controls your marking, and consequently your ability. It taps into the Web through your marking, and affects as much of the Web as you can manage to hold. The stronger your will, the more of the Web you can manipulate, the greater your ability."

"I can do that? A Shadow?" Henry hesitated.

"Probably."

Silence hung between them for several minutes. Not the bad kind, the only in the moment kind. He enjoyed watching. Whatever held her, she reminded Henry of his first dive. The ecstasy. The perfect chaos.

"They did change, Harbor. Your scores," she broke, eyes still shut.

An alarm bell clanged in his head.

"Usually the change isn't so drastic after just the first dive, but, like the rest our organically marked few, yours jumped. A lot... you're a perfect score. Five hundred over zero."

CHAPTER FIFTEEN

Shock stiffened Henry's spine. "How is that possible, sir?"

"I don't know. Roxar doesn't know. Taizai doesn't know. Roxar scored a four ninety-one over four, and he had the highest score until you showed up. Don't think he's too pleased about losing that record. Regardless, it doesn't matter if you can't actually use your ability. Taizai speculates you could harness more of the Web's power than us all combined because of your nonexistent dependence on proximity… zero, none whatsoever…" she trailed off. The Shadow's brilliance dimmed.

The peace on her face died without his help. Henry held in a sigh. He didn't want to fight with her or shoulder more slashing criticism.

"We should find out whether or not you will be the strongest of us all, don't you think?"

"Yes, sir," Henry kept his voice even.

"It doesn't take much effort. Come here, Cadet."

Henry obeyed. His legs quivered like his bones turned to jelly. His heart ached.

"Have you noticed any differences since you took the first dive?" Her Shadow started to sink into silver.

"Like what?"

"Sir," she reminded. She breathed deep, once. Then, "Anything that relates your eyes to the Web. Roxar doesn't let anybody know anything about his powers, but Opal feels her spine tickling whenever she interacts with the Web. I usually feel a prickle on the inside of my skin. I'll bet for you it's something visual."

"My vision is better?"

Sech frowned.

"Uh, I can see better than I used to. Sharper. Clearer. I can see better far away."

"All the time, or only when you interact with the Web?"

"All the time, sir."

"That's not it then. This change has to be when you interact with or are near the Web, though perhaps since your dependence on proximity is so low it is different for you. When you took the dive, when you create a comet, did you notice anything specifically during these times?"

"No sir." Henry staved off discouragement.

"Well." Her frown deepened. Doubt looked strange on her features. "Do you use physical touch to make a comet?"

"Yes sir, but doesn't everybody?"

"No, not all of us need to. Opal just asks to be sent wherever she wants. I use touch for convenience, but a blood spatter does the trick. My marking allows me some proximity diving, but I still have to be pretty close to a vein. Maybe three meters. Try touching the Web and doing whatever you do to cast a comet."

"Just see if I can do it? No… no procedure?"

Henry fumbled. The military epitomized structure. Rules and more rigid rules. The right way. Henry's first years at the academy enforced military routine: how to keep your bunk, how to do a push up, how to clean his plates, how long to brush his teeth. Everything had the same unyielding methodology. The last thing he expected was no protocol to learn his marking.

Annoyance froze his response. More than that. The Yard overwhelmed him, but he at least had teachers. Henry kept his indignation to himself. He walked to the Webbed wall, near Sech.

"Try," she commanded.

He stood there, staring into the silver depths, observing the swirls, fractures, and beams of light. He pressed his hand against the silver. Shapeless, formless, but a great amount of mass. He closed his eyes and let the Web fill him. Joyous heat spread through his veins like a drug. He tried using his hands to outline the shape of a head and torso, as if his eyes could pull the figure into his molding hands.

Nothing.

"Again."

He tried. Nothing. He failed again. And then again. He'd change his strategy, his angle, his mental image—no adaptation yielded any result. Each time, Sech commanded him to try again.

Shame colored his neck and cheeks, leaving a cold lump of determination in his stomach. He tried shouting and throwing comets into the Web along the onyx walls. Try after try, the Web would not respond. All he felt was something… missing. Something deeper.

He plunged his whole arm into the Web. Sech snapped out of her commands to grab Henry's shoulder. She threw him back like his deadweight limbs were lighter than air.

"Don't you ever, and I fucking mean ever Cadet, submerge yourself in the Web. You don't know how to dive and fucking up by going deeper than you can handle does not end pretty. If you ever so much as turn toward a vein I will flatten your ass like the burnout you're proving to be." Wild darkness stole her blue eyes. "We will train each day until you get it. Until then, report to me every morning like today. I will send remedial training regimens to you. Do them on your own time. Do not fail that simple task at least, Harbor."

"I wasn't going all the way in!"

She slashed her cut open. If his eyesight hadn't improved, he would have missed the practiced motion. Blood welling, she dived into the Web, backward. She hovered. The glow of the Web clung to her sensuous curves, her skin luminous. With a twist of her wrists, Sech swept her arms together. Black slid to cover the Webbed wall, cutting her off from Henry.

Henry sighed. He faced the now-onyx solid wall, giving the black a dark look. His body ached in places he didn't think possible. Soreness threatened to tie him up in knots. Longing for a shower, Henry instead casted a comet towards the mess. His shower could wait compared to the moaning in his stomach.

CHAPTER SIXTEEN

Every step stretched his tendons, ligaments, and muscles. Every step moved him further away from failure. Every step healed the parts Sech savaged—his body, his pride. The further he walked, the more resentment he felt, more productive than the frustration she left with him.

He sulked all the way to the mess. There, Shai, Kekoa, and Akira laughed over empty plates.

"Oy!" Shai called to Henry. Henry joined them. Shai held ice to his shoulder. Kekoa's left eye was blackening.

"What happened?"

"Close combat. Ice is just a precaution, no real injury, apparently."

"Those bruises will suck," Henry grinned.

"This one especially." Shai pointed to a black mark on his forearm. "Man, can you believe how much bigger the shooting range is? Stars, I mean, c'mon, it's—" he mimed his head exploding.

"I didn't see the shooting range," Henry admitted.

"What? How about the arena?"

"Nope."

"The tank?"

"No."

"Well where did you go? We assumed you were getting the tour or something."

"She took you to one of the Webbed rooms," Akira interrupted.

Henry nodded.

"A what?" Shai looked interested.

"The Webbed rooms are for training in Web manipulation. Only marked Wings can do it," Kekoa answered.

"What can you do then?" Shai turned back to Henry.

"Uh, nothing. I couldn't do the basics."

Kekoa shrugged his shoulders. Akira looked away.

"So what? It's your first day," Shai reassured him.

"Yeah."

"Some things take time to grow," Akira said.

"Kekoa," Henry turned. "She wouldn't tell me. What happens if I don't make it?"

Kekoa and Akira met eyes, an exchange of silent caution.

"She didn't say anything?"

"Just that I'd go home."

"Well, that can't be all it is, right?" Shai jumped in. "No way they'd let you go back home just like that. Not after coming here."

"You're right," Akira said.

"So what does happen?"

"I can't give you specifics. Everyone who didn't make it has been sent home for a couple months then re-stationed, usually to special forces."

"No way. We would have heard about the White Wings if the failed ones go home. A rumor or something, at least," Shai scoffed.

"I can't go into specifics," Kekoa said.

"So there is more?" Henry confirmed.

Keko sighed.

"It's for your own good," Akira frowned.

"Why?" Henry probed.

Neither answered. Shai shook his head and mouthed "later" at Henry. Henry nodded.

"Fine. Any tips on using my marking then?"

"Not from me," Akira said. "I think Taizai might be able to help, though. Let's take Henry to the shooting range, then I'll take him to the lab."

"Fine by me, but I'm going to meet up with Ro to start that intake doc. See you tomorrow." Kekoa dipped his head and bumped fists with Shai when he left.

"Better hurry that dinner Henry," Shai urged.

"Go on," Henry said. "I'll catch up in half an hour."

Happy with that, the other two also left. Alone, Henry wolfed down chunks of meat, watching the pace of the mess. A loud group entered. A few celebratory hollers greeted them. The group waved to their friends before getting in the food lines. They stood close together, laughing and bumping against one another.

The team got their food and walked around searching for enough seats. Henry shoved food in his mouth, trying to clear his plate. The team wound its way toward him. One of them, a Horn with lavender eyes, smiled at him.

"Mind if we sit?" she asked.

Cheeks bulging, Henry nodded. He kept his head down.

"Thanks!" she chirped. She and her team sat down around him. "I'm Lieutenant Gelipia Lagarre, but please, call me Pia. This is Lieutenant Will Mont, First Lieutenant Masera Ya Xue, and Wing Leader Charles Smith," she told him. She held out her hand. Henry took it, gulping his food down.

"Cadet Henry Harbor," he replied, not meeting her eyes.

"Truly? Let's see them then." Without care, she took his chin and turned his face toward her. She gasped. "Your eyes really are magnificent. You know, I didn't believe Ro when she told me about them."

"Sorry, who?"

"Ro? Rolyn Sech?"

"Oh. I didn't recognize her first name."

"Weird... but you're new aren't you. We would have met earlier but we were out on mission. Congrats on the early graduation."

"Thanks. Where were you?"

"Just finished scouting and setting up mining operations on Norvin. The Commander and Taizai only found out about the onyx on Norvin a couple months ago so all the White Wings have been scouring the planet for the where that signature was coming from. A few days ago, Santos found it near a local village, but for whatever reason—probably Ro's temper—things got out of hand. Santos barely got out of there and ruined all the relationships we had been bridging with the Norv. Today though, Bardos, Infection, and Sekhmet, that's us," she swept her hand across the table, "were able to patch up the relationship with a hefty bribe." She smirked.

"Oh, cool. Good work," he flushed. A quality right down to how she smelled set him at ease. He looked away from her pretty face. Her smile made Henry's insides squirm.

"Don't be embarrassed," She put a hand on Henry's. Her calluses scraped his skin. "You see, as White Wings our primary missions are recon for later infantry units, but the whole purpose is to locate onyx. About three percent of the planets emitting signatures actually have enough onyx to mine. So, when the Commander identifies a signature, he sends out his White Wings, yours truly," she winked, "to go out and figure out where it's coming from. Then, if we find it, and we can access it, Taizai's teams go back to mine it. While the rats are working, all the Wings have some down time until the Commander finds the next signature. It's always up in the air. Sometimes we have no break at all, and once we had almost a month off rotation. Right now, he hasn't found a new signature yet, so we will at least have a day or two off."

"I didn't realize we got vacations."

"It's not vacation," she slapped high on his shoulder. The touch zinged through Henry's skin and jittered through his stomach. "The Commander likes us on hand in case of emergencies. I have no idea what he expects would happen at the Tower of all places, but hey, being able to sleep in my own bed for a week is pretty sweet."

Henry absorbed her words but couldn't take his eyes off her face. Henry liked the way she licked off her lips. The rest of her teammates eyed him behind spoons and forks. He cleared his throat.

"Sorry, I have to go. People are waiting for me at the shooting range."

"Oh… well have fun!" Pia smiled big and bright. "I'll see you around Henry."

"Yeah. Good to meet you," Henry murmured to the whole team.

He pushed away from the table and left. He chanced a look. The other woman smirked, and the two men teased her. Pia's head tilted back, her white teeth flashing.

CHAPTER SEVENTEEN

After such a depressing first day with Sech, the gun recoiling in Henry's hand gave an outlet. The steady rhythm hung over him the same way he sunk into his stride when he ran. The bullets whizzed through the target.

Akira interrupted. "Henry, now's a good time."

"Aw c'mon, he just got here," Shai groaned, lining up his reticle to the target. He fired.

Henry tracked the speeding bullet into the second ring of the target. One of Shai's worst shots. Shai, silent, fired again. Perfect shot.

"If you think now's best," Henry shrugged.

Henry handed the hardware off to Shai and followed Akira back into the Tower. Akira's comet bumped along to his smooth gait. Henry kept mute, pondering how Taizai could help him when Sech couldn't.

They came to mist. Akira looked at him askance.

"I'm ready," Henry nodded.

The lab sprawled like the portal bay, but paper littered every surface: on tables, counters, lab space, chairs, and sinks. Diagrams, charts, and notes in every color and size covered the walls.

"To be fair, we try to keep it clean. It just doesn't stay that way."

"Don't you lose stuff?"

"Sometimes."

Akira led Henry deep into the lab, stopping in front of a room with a table and smoke. The smoke rose in a column, but didn't smell like fire. The opaque, dull grey looked out of place in the luminescence of the Tower.

Taizai stood at the table, limp arms hanging, palms facing the smoke.

Akira whispered, "Master Taizai, I brought a visitor for you."

"Have you brought Harbor?" Taizai asked. "I wondered when we would meet again."

"Yes. Good night, sir," Akira slipped away. Taizai kept his back to Henry.

"I expected a visit from you, Harbor, but I am surprised you chose such an hour. What can I do for you?"

"Akira suggested now, sir."

"Personally, I choose to believe you have the foresight to make your own decisions. You came here. Why?"

Henry stilled, looking inward. He couldn't use his marking, but he'd struggled through every year at the Yard. He never expected anything different. He couldn't discuss Sech, not with a superior. He felt vindictive, but he'd shed childhood with his first salute.

"I can't use my ability."

"You mean to say that you can't use your marking. Ability is only a manifestation of the Web's response to your will. A fancy title for a simple reaction. Though useful, certainly. Do you question you are organically marked?"

Henry frowned. "Every one is marked. Is mine really like Sech's? Or the Commander's?"

"Yes. We don't understand much about organic markings, Harbor," Taizai offered. "There are no answers in research, data, books. Not from Commander Roxar. Not from Opal or Lieutenant Sech. Not from your preliminary tests. All we know is organic markings are highly individual."

"Sech said something similar," Henry muttered.

"Lieutenant Sech's marking," Taizai emphasized her rank, "is a painful one."

Henry peered at him, reminded of that something darker he couldn't identify. "Painful how, sir?"

"Physically, but the Lieutenant is the only one who really knows how her marking works. The Commander and Opal do not relate to Lieutenant Sech's marking any more than she does to theirs."

"Permission to speak freely, sir?"

"Granted."

"If everyone's marking is different, how can Sech figure out mine? Seems pointless."

"Lieutenant, Cadet. Maybe it is. Opal studied under the Commander and so did Sech. All three seem to be competent. Ask them about what they learned, and maybe you can help yourself."

"Why can't I study with the Commander, sir?"

"His White Wings, his decisions."

"Who did the Commander study with, sir?"

"He didn't," Taizai admitted. He met Henry's eyes for a fleeting second.

"Sir, can you explain the basics to me? Theory? Anything?"

"The basics... Death births us all. Life divides us all. Thread binds us all."

"I know about the dimensions, sir," Henry said.

Taizai chuckled. "Basics or no?"

Henry shut up.

"The basics are just that. Basic. Three dimensions, three abilities. Take you, Lieutenant Sech, Opal, and the Commander. Technically, you are beings of the third dimension, since you all embody the Web through your organic markings. I like to think I'm right about that," Taizai nodded to himself. "That's only one half of the equation though. Human control of the Web is only possible because of the relationship between the second and third dimensions: Life and the Web. You see, they oppose one another, yet Life and the Web coexist so intimately woven that they are in constant conflict for control of their own shared space."

Henry had no inkling what Taizai meant. The dimensions... weren't about his duty? The motivation behind every blaring wake up call, every drop of sweat, every hour in the field? Sudden anger pierced through Henry's confusion, but he forced his face neutral. "Back up. Sech mentioned three abilities too, but I still don't get it," he avoided his ire.

"A good, if complicated, question. How about the short version, hm?"

Henry nodded.

"Each ability manifests in different ways because of the nature of the marking itself and the human whose will controls it. As far as we know, we being the Commander and myself, despite individual nuances belonging to markings or will, there are only three actual mediums that connect the marked to the Web. So, three abilities. The first I came in contact with was Possession, the Commander's ability. The second was Blending, Lieutenant Sech's ability. The third, Reflection. I have never personally come across it. The Commander swears it exists."

Henry remained quiet. His vision still pulsed red, but he thought through the haze. None of this information gave him answers, just more questions. "Sir, how will this help me?"

"You're the one who asked for the basics, Cadet. Can you not think of any application of what I have told you?"

Henry escaped into the smoke's fluttering. Taizai confounded him. The basics upended the foundation of the last six years of his life—the last few centuries of human glory—and his foreseeable future. He could vaguely relate to the marking and will discussion, though the finer points were lost on him. "All I can come up with is studying the other marked Wings doesn't make sense. Too much depends on me."

"Yes. To a degree. Depending on your will and your marking, some aspects of Web manipulation will be easier and some harder." He paused. "Everyone here made themselves here, Harbor. Marked Wings in particular have to stand on their own two feet. Earning those Wings is a greater freedom and a greater burden than any of the others can or will carry. Only true ambition will get you there.”

The words paralleled Sech’s contemptuous insult, but this time, there was no derision thrown in Henry’s face, only facts.

“Where do I start, sir?” Henry contained his frustration.

Taizai turned with a challenge. “Those Wings can’t be earned through another’s work. Good night, Henry.”

“Yes, sir. Good night, sir.” Henry saluted and strode out.

CHAPTER EIGHTEEN

Just inside the mist, Akira emerged from a side room filled with broken stools.

Henry relaxed his face, aware his anger pushed each footstep.

"Go well?"

"Not really."

"Bet it was better than you think."

Henry didn't bother. He was tired, bone tired. And seething. He wanted nothing more than the privacy of his quarters. Henry followed Akira out of the lab.

"I need to stop by the mess. Have a good night, Henry."

Henry nodded. He set off hoping Shai was up, someone sane he could talk to. Henry entered empty quarters.

Sighing, Henry paced the room, too restless to fall asleep.

Three dimensions. He fumed over Taizai's complete dismissal of everything Henry knew. Those words made him pledge his life to the military. Sure, he could accept the Web was a real dimension. But Life? Death?

Death births us all.

Life divides us all.

Thread binds us all.

Those words... how did he miss this? Henry knelt, writing messily.

Death is the first dimension.

Slow, yet accurate.

Why didn't I see this? He asked. A lull of darkness fueled confusion.

My guess, you brushed it off as military propaganda. Many do. Most never have to understand what it truly means.

You mean most aren't marked.

Yes, and no. Taizai is not marked the way you are, but he understands.

Henry had nothing to write.

Well, I'll admit I thought you would have asked someone else long before now. But you got there in the end. Ready for your second lesson?

Wait, I don't understand. What does it mean?

That is your next lesson. Find out what it means.

Henry stilled, sifting through which question he needed first.

Harbor, stick with Sech. Her handwriting faded fast.

Why?

He waited.

Why!

"Why what?" Shai peered over Henry's shoulder. Henry jolted upright. He slammed the back of his head into Shai's chin. Shai yowled. Henry appraised him with panicked eyes, rubbing his head. Shai massaged his jaw, glaring.

"Uh," Henry blanked.

"Why. What?" Shai ground out.

Henry took a breath. He told Shai everything he learned from the blind woman and Sech, and Taizai.

"Stars. That's definitely the longest you've talked since I've met you."

Henry recognized what Shai hid under his humor. He too couldn't face the implied conspiracy between the White Wings and the military Taizai exposed.

"Well, any ideas?"

"I didn't think you could even talk for that long. A breathing thing, or something."

"Any ideas?"

Shai sighed, then grinned. "I know why I'd stick with Sech."

"I don't think she meant it that way," Henry snorted. Shai rolled his eyes, but got serious.

"Come on. It's easy. Ask Ro this time, flat out."

"But there was no condition last time."

"Maybe only she knows?"

"I doubt that's it."

"Why?"

"She said Taizai truly understands."

"So the Commander would know too."

Henry nodded.

"So?" Shai prompted.

"It's not a condition. It's a warning."

Shai's tone shifted to curious. "A warning for what?"

"Can't say."

"It could mean not to go around her back."

"Maybe."

Shai shook his head. "Then again, probably not. Talking with me is kind of like going behind her back, isn't it?"

"I guess."

"Well, assume talking with me is allowed. Talking with other non-marked Wings is ok too."

"But Taizai-"

"Ok, non-marked and non-lab," Shai put his hands up. "Ask Ro tomorrow during PT in front of Kekoa."

"That's brilliant."

"Thanks."

"But I won't."

Shai looked at him like he was crazy. "Why not?"

"Well—" Henry exhaled long and slow.

"I assumed you were awkward around her because she's crazy hot."

Henry glared.

"I'm not judging. She's, like, a twelve. Just so-"

"I know, dude," Henry cut in. "She just—" Henry sighed, frustration choking his throat. "We don't get along."

"Sucks."

"Yeah," Henry nodded to the floor.

"So what will you do?"

"I'll figure something out. Maybe Pia."

"Let me know when you decide," Shai flopped on his bed. "Until then, what do you think Kekoa and Akira were hiding at dinner?"

Henry sunk into his pillow, relieved to turn toward questions he had better answers for.

"You believe Akira? That it's for our own good?"

"I don't. We've been trained our whole lives to get here. They should tell us what will happen to us if we fail."

Henry grunted agreement.

"But, I don't think we will fail. So, moot point," Shai said.

Henry couldn't share his confidence. He was no star soldier like Shai. He had no control over his marking like Sech. He had no reason to be here beyond numbers on paper.

Doubt consumed him, eating at the crumbling foundation the Yard instilled in him.

"Dude. It's ok. We got this."

Henry nodded to the ceiling.

"No, I really mean it. Henry, c'mon man."

Henry turned to face him. Shai's sincerity was transparent as glass in his eyes.

"We can do this."

"I can't lie to myself about what I am."

"I know we never really knew each other at the Yard. I know," he held up a hand. "But I remember the first time my team beat yours. You didn't win the next scenario because your team magically got better. I remember what you did."

Henry shook his head. That day he thought he was going home, had already packed his bag just in case. When he stepped on that field though, his fear of being kicked out dissipated in his desperation not to fail his home, his country.

"You're not... you know. Strong," Shai air quoted, "but you're worth it. I know we can do this."

Henry picked his head up, looking at Shai in a different light. He never thought Shai had noticed anyone else at the Yard, consumed by praise and attention. Henry regretted he'd underestimated the giant.

"Death, Life, and Web." Shai held out his fist.

"Death, Life, and Web," Henry knocked his knuckles against Shai's.

Despite the intended comfort, the hollow words drowned Henry's ears, a meaningless pattern that once meant home.

CHAPTER NINETEEN

Ro liked watching when the needle slid in. She couldn't watch the silver sliding up. The humming through her marking provided enough sensory information as she allowed her cells to leave.

"So, your first day with the cadet. What's your impression?"

"Is this a formal or informal report?"

Taizai smiled, "Just my curiosity."

"That potential is something."

Taizai agreed, removing the needle. His slime-coated finger smudged against the injection site. The healing substance sent an icy tingling into Ro's skin. She relished the physical sensation, uninfluenced by the Web's pull.

"His potential, indeed," Taizai nodded. "Do you have a free block sometime soon?"

Ro shook her head.

"A shame. I am on the verge of achieving stem cell regeneration, and my latest experiments were successful with blood cell types."

"Shut up."

"My weaving codes still require refinement, but right now? I could theoretically add thirty percent to your spec."

Ro beamed, marveling at the possibility. Her suit's unique spec relied on Taizai's coding genius, genius resulting in onyx fibers with four times the plasticity of any other suit. Adding thirty percent to her spec effectively meant she could draw on thirty percent more of the Web's power to boost her ability. It also meant she waited extra for alterations and repairs because other coders didn't have the acuity.

"If I could regenerate any blood cells at all, I could be unbeatable."

"But never infallible."

Ro threw her hands up, "I know, I know."

"Do you? Unlike the Commander, I won't allow your lies. A seam? Really?"

Ro averted her eyes, sucking on her tongue.

"Admit it."

"There was a political situation we did not include in our reports. Kekoa failed to navigate it, and I got cocky in the cleanup."

"And your arrogance bought you?"

"A debt owed and a burnout Cadet."

"You're lucky you didn't hurt him worse."

"Come on, give me a little credit. As soon as my marking came in contact I did everything I could to lessen the damage. And what damage is there really?"

"He had—"

"Nothing requiring a year's rotation in the lab."

Taizai softened, "That I can't deny."

"Did you have any part in that?"

"I didn't decide to split you up, or bring in the cadets, but I did offer Lieutenant Hammond space in the lab once the Commander made up his mind."

Ro understood the unspoken; Taizai kept Ham close to home for her.

"Thank you."

"He is my best friend, but you are my favorite."

"Someday he will get jealous."

Taizai's teeth flashed, "In your dreams."

"Nightmares, more like."

"Do you see the Commander in your nightmares?"

Ro waved him off, "Even in my worst dreams, I'm somewhere better than this."

Taizai paused, frowning. "I can never remember any of my dreams, good or bad."

Ro stalled. Despite her easy confidence in Taizai, even knowing his intimacy with Roxar, she stumbled when he traded affability for transparency. He only looked a decade older than herself, but she believed he faked his appearance. Any coder with his skill could. No matter how much she enjoyed his company, she always recognized alien depth when he displayed empathy, a reminiscence in passing, like talking of dreams. The words never sounded real coming from manipulated lips.

He pointed to the samples. "I'll inform you of any changes. One last question, if I may."

"Of course, sir."

"I have yet to finish the initial reports, but if you had to, how would you compare yourself between the Commander and Cadet Harbor?"

"What, are you insane?" She admitted she let her temper slip. Since the Web first made Henry's marking, Ro's marking had gone haywire in response. It took her years to overcome her response to Roxar's marking; Henry's marking drove her to pain she'd never known. The pressure her will exerted to keep her marking in a semblance of balance drained her endurance only hours into the morning with Henry.

At least I lasted this long before snapping at someone.

"At my age, probably," Taizai nodded.

Ro quelled a shiver down her spine, instead sliding from the exam table. "Why, sir? There is no hard data beyond his score. It's only his first day; Roxar's had years."

Taizai shrugged, "I am curious in our new Cadet."

"More so than in me?"

"Never," Taizai inclined his head.

"Well, candidly, I've never liked Roxar, and so far, I don't like Harbor."

"Surely your experience lends a little more substance than dislike."

"I really don't like Roxar, and I'm pretty sure I really won't like Harbor too."

"If you insist," Taizai turned to collect the samples. "Good night, Rolyn. Try to get some sleep."

"Then don't make me crunch data every night."

Taizai chuckled and waved.

Ro remained on the exam table, legs swinging with her thoughts. Unease she only experienced with Roxar set in, turning her stomach.

Roxar deserves it, but Taizai…

She could reason why to draw a line between herself and Roxar; putting Harbor on the same side with Roxar raised suspicions Taizai didn't mean but Ro couldn't avoid.

Roxar's earliest training brutalized her, in rigor and in loyalty. After running from home, then running from her planet, she thought she could find home in country if not in family. Ro ran to the apex of the military only to suspect the same exclusion and betrayal she faced at home. No matter that Roxar's methods turned results, she couldn't rationalize how her training could ever benefit people, only him.

I will never be his tool again, but Harbor…

Resolution stilled her swinging feet. Adrenaline pumping, she left for the training mats despite her body's exhaustion. She had hours left before she faced Harbor's torturous marking again. Exercise brought focus, pushing past her need for sleep. She sighed, returning to her quarters to shower off sweat and paranoia.

She spent her last free hour eating and meditating in her grove, a small island Roxar gave her where she could be free of the Tower's web.

She hadn't needed it in over a year.

She approached her meditating pool and lay beside the trickling waterfall. She watched the stars dim as the sun woke, and reminded herself of sanity.

Taizai has always been on Roxar's side, no matter how he treats me.

Harbor is not colluding with Roxar against me.

I am stronger than I was then.

CHAPTER TWENTY

Any peace Ro gained in her grove dissipated as soon as she met Harbor. Her marking thrashed against her will at the proximity to him. Harbor failed through the day, again, burying what little patience she'd reserved. She snapped when his hand moved toward silver again in front of the webbed wall.

She hauled him back, "What did I tell you, Harbor?"

"Lieutenant, it's different today. I think if I could—."

"You really think that's all it is? Today? Five hundred over zero! Zero! You don't depend on proximity for your marking to activate."

"I do, sir. It's like something is… blocking me, or… I'm not sure."

"You think I'm wrong, Cadet?"

"My marking doesn't work. Touching does."

Just like Roxar.

Ro's revelation distracted her from hours-built exasperation. She searched his eyes, bearing her blood shooting into her skull, but she found no trace of Roxar there.

"The Web is much stronger than even the best of us. Rookies can't dive because the Web will suck you in without training your will first."

Harbor didn't answer. His gaze pierced, but Ro held it. Sincere, stubborn, and pleading, Ro couldn't find fault in his wordless optimism.

He found his spine faster than I did mine.

She managed, "I'll put your request through to Roxar," before fleeing into the Tower's depth.

She sulked in the Tower's belly, but even this pressure couldn't stop her marking's response to Harbor. Skewers jabbed against her blood vessels as her marking traced his movements through the Tower.

He really did grow a lot, even if it didn't show.

Overnight, Harbor had grown, a natural reaction as his body adjusted to the Web's invasion. She hadn't expected Harbor could have come so close to Jukita's level in a single night, no matter how much harder she pushed him. Harbor remained leaner, lankier, but his frame…

Such wasted potential indeed.

She sent a flash toward Roxar despite her misgivings. His reply found her fingers in moments.

"There is some risk, certainly, but if you take the right precautions you can ensure nothing happens to him. You can cover those basics, can't you Rolyn?"

She growled to herself. Her best judgment kept her from surging toward Roxar and taking her skin-thin temper out on him.

A gentle nudge from the Web pushed a different flash into her hand. Akira's voice whispered to her. As much as she hated data analysis, she welcomed Akira anytime he volunteered to help. She left her ruined respite to join him.

"I'm so lucky to have such an eager assistant," she grinned when she saw he'd already started the video analysis of Harbor's failed Web efforts.

"Why don't you thank me later," he paused the video and snaked his arms around her waist. "Missed you last night."

Ro ran fingers through his hair, "Worked late."

"Figured. So, Iraiza reporting for duty."

"Did I already say how lucky I am?"

"Yes sir."

Akira stayed with her the whole time, but left for dinner when the numbers were done. Ro stayed to finish Harbor's remedial program.

"His performance warrants it."

"Sure, but I think you've earned at least a small break. Come eat with me."

"I'll never finish tonight if I do," she kissed him quick. "I'll come to bed later."

"Later tonight, not tomorrow," he rubbed her arm before he left.

It took Ro an hour to map out the training circuit and benchmarks. She struggled to keep eyes open as she finished the instructions. Her subconscious screamed for sleep, but something kept chugging her brain back to waking, a niggling worry in the shadows of developed thoughts.

After food, she turned to her own bed instead of joining Akira, longing for undisturbed rest. Even in darkness, that concern repulsed sleep. She tossed and turned, until she gave up.

Ro rolled to her feet, checking the time. If she worked it out quickly enough, a few hours remained. Invigorated, Ro sat in front of her wall and meditated. She watched the color shift. She decided Harbor wouldn't act against her behind her back, not after his entreaty today. Roxar, though, stooped as low as necessary to preserve his profit.

If Harbor ever did use that potential... Roxar could...

Cold, clawing instinct choked her throat, froze all thought.

Run.

She didn't.

Run. He'll hurt me.

Her nails dug into her knee caps, but she didn't move.

Run. Run. Run.

Muted knocking shocked Ro back to breathing.

"Can I come in?" Pia's voice carried just enough.

Ro croaked, "Yeah."

"Stars' light, what's wrong? You look awful."

"Didn't sleep last night, can't now."

"That's some burnout shit," Pia curled up next to Ro on the floor.

"So why are you here?"

"I just sent Henry to bed."

"Oh? If you like him at all, please take him off my hands."

Pia laughed, "Come on, it can't be that bad."

Ro rolled her eyes at Pia.

"All right, all right, I don't get it, but, stars, Ro, he's going to be an incredible wing."

"Really."

"Really, really."

"Why?"

Pia sniggered, "Between you and me, he'll be immaculate. Come on."

Pia tugged Ro's arm up, and Ro followed without hesitation. She guided Ro into bed, cut the light, and initiated a white noise program Ro never used.

"Rain ok?"

"Yeah."

Pia always asked. She still always asked. Ro squeezed her pillow as her best friend's snores soothed her to sleep.

CHAPTER TWENTY-ONE

Henry's muscles ached in the morning, but not as bad as he expected. Light creased the domed ceiling, growing like a real sunrise. Shai turned from it under his blanket. The light grew brighter.

"I'll shower first, all right?" Henry offered.

Shai grunted.

Henry rolled out of bed, headed to the shared bathroom. Again, Henry's reflection was a stranger. The silver eyes hung eight centimeters higher than they should be. His neck, thicker. Shoulders, broader. He walked back out into the room.

"Get up."

Shai, cached in his sheets, turned over. "I've got a few more minutes."

"Come on, man," Henry insisted. Shai sat up rubbing his eyes.

"Damn Henry, is that you?"

"Yeah," Henry answered.

"You put on ten kilos! And you're taller too!" Shai ripped through his sheets. Henry stared at the giant's growth.

"What happened to us? I'm not complaining or anything but…" Shai inspected his hands.

"Yeah, I know," Henry concurred. His new height overwhelmed him. His knees shoved up when he sat on the toilet. He ducked under the shower curtain rod. His ankles and wrists stuck out of his basics. He couldn't fit in his boots.

"What do we do about this?" Shai hacked at the tongue of his boot with his knife.

Henry shrugged.

90

"Well this is pointless," Shai gave up.

They jogged to the mess in their socks. When they entered, ripples of laughter waved across the room. Shai showed his enlarged feet to every woman who smiled at him. Henry kept his eyes on silverware and food. Sech and Kekoa laughed in a corner. Sech's mirth bothered him. A red head and wide smile bobbed forward from the food line.

"Trouble this morning?" Pia beamed.

"Why am I bigger?" Henry pointed out his exposed wrists.

"Better question, what else was bigger this morning?" she winked.

"His bunkmate," Shai joined. "I'm Cadet Shai Jukita," he leaned on Henry's shoulder.

"Lieutenant Pia Lagarre," she offered with a quirky smile. "You also seem to have clothing issues."

"A temporary inconvenience."

"I can help you with that," she looked to Henry. She towed them out of the mess.

"Here we are, the closet!" she pulled up in front of another silver circle. Pia activated the mist, and they plunged through. Five people in loose black clothing ran up to them, waving tape measures like bad swordsmen.

They touched everywhere with abandon. Henry flinched when one pulled the tape up under his balls. Pia floated around the room, chatting. Henry and Shai refitted and received a barrage of instructions on how to use the closet service from their quarters. Everyone hugged Pia goodbye.

The uniform issue made them late for training.

"Legitimate excuses," Sech said when they arrived. She looked at Kekoa, and they both cracked huge smiles.

"I promise, you'll make up for the time lost," Sech turned to Henry. "Time for first weigh in."

Neither Sech nor Kekoa were as invasive as the closet technicians. Kekoa explained how they used the measurements to adjust their training regimens to maximize growth.

"Speaking of growth... why do I look doubly spectacular today Lieutenant?" Shai flexed.

"The Web alters and shapes your body. Molds you into the best soldier you can be," Sech's tone flat.

"Will we keep growing, then?" Henry confirmed.

"For a while. Expect physical change for the first month after your first dive. But the first day is always the most dramatic..." her voice trailed off.

"Shall we get started then?" Kekoa diverted.

If Henry thought Sech was brutal the day before, the second day proved her sadistic streak. She stood over him and yelled words like "faster," "more," "harder," "bigger." None of them filtered through the pounding in his ears.

The sun went from pleasant to blistering. At the end of the sixth hour, Henry heaved on all fours. She didn't yell this time, just watched.

When Henry stood, he had two minutes to walk out his protesting body. He received two bottles of water. One he drained. The other he poured over his head and neck. Then, she ran him to the Webbed room.

"You run well, Harbor."

Henry's stomach threatened to heave again. "Yes sir," he panted.

"Good. Go stand next to the wall."

Sech drilled him over and over. Nothing worked, but something was different. When before Henry had felt nothing under his fingers, now he battered against a barricade. He spent two hours at it, before frustration drove him to submerge his arm again. Sech seized the neck of his uniform and hauled him back as his fingers touched the light.

"What did I tell you Harbor?" Sech demanded.

"Lieutenant, it's different today. I think if I could—."

"You really think that's all it is? Today?" she growled. "Five hundred over zero! Zero! You literally don't depend on proximity to the Web for your marking to activate."

"I do, sir. It's like something is... blocking me, or... I'm not sure," Henry mumbled at her glare.

"You think I'm wrong Cadet?" Her tone went frigid.

Henry shoved his retort back down his throat. "My marking doesn't work," he said instead. "Touching does." He calmed himself.

She tilted her head. That something lurked in her eyes again, and Henry remembered Taizai mentioned her pain.

"Rookies can't dive because the Web is much stronger than even the best of us. You need time to train your will before you can touch it without losing control." Her tone shifted to introspection.

Henry didn't needle her despite his instinct. There was something preventing his marking today, something beyond his grasp.

"I'll put your request through to Roxar," her voice was cold, but not toward him. She dived—a blue gem in silver waters. Blue-speckled silver streamed forward, and Sech slammed onyx over the Webbed wall.

Henry didn't see Kekoa or Sech the rest of the day. Henry and Shai ate with Pia's team, Sekhmet. Pia explained their lieutenants had to analyze the day's results.

"That's the worst part of training new cadets," she said. "Tons and tons of lab work."

"Think Akira likes that part," Will joked.

Pia snorted into her water.

Henry stayed until a flash scooted to his boots. Sech's voice issued instructions, his remedial training. He groaned. His mood lightened when Pia offered to do it with him.

"Can't hurt," she took Henry's hand. Her comet led them to a room of mats, weights, equipment of all kinds. Pia worked through Henry's regimen with him, correcting when needed. He was at ease with her beside him. No stress. No animosity. Though his body yearned to be done, he didn't mind pushing through with her. When they finished, Henry swayed on his feet.

"At the rate you're growing, you won't need remedial for much longer," Pia encouraged him.

Henry nodded but didn't get his hopes up.

Pia hugged him before leaving. The feel of her body against his warmed him all the way to his bed and into sleep.

CHAPTER TWENTY-TWO

On Henry's third day, he feared Sech would kill him. She made him do everything he'd done yesterday twice as fast. He stopped before he was an hour in. He threw up. Twice. Once nothing more came up, Sech grabbed him by the back of his uniform, dragged him to standing.

"Why fight?" she asked.

"I have to!" Henry's throat burned like hot coals.

"Foolish answer. Everyone has to. The weak die. The strong fight." She shoved him forward.

He started to run again, relieved she didn't push him back to the ground.

Henry finished by mid-morning. He couldn't keep Sech's pace all the way through.

"New training today, Harbor." She marched in a new direction. He followed Sech back to the closet.

"We are starting suit training today," she told him.

A tech held his hand out.

"Your suit, sir. The Recovery packages were low, so we had to do a full replacement. Could we do your next drawing now?"

"Not now, I'll come back tonight," Sech answered. The tech nodded and gripped her hand. The black material of the tech's sleeve grew. It covered their joined palms.

The basics Sech wore darkened, absorbing the light in the room. The material shrunk, gaining a glossy sheen and merging into one piece of cloth. The three white feathers on her shoulder glowed brighter. The black uniform hugged her body instead of covering it. Her curves could make him delusional.

Another tech came forward, holding her hand out to Henry.

"A non-specialized package, sir," she said.

"Thanks." Henry laid his hand on hers. Black crept up his arm, and Henry felt heavier, bigger too. Fabric clung to his skin.

"What happened?" he asked Sech, trying to lift his heavy arm.

"This is a suit. Its fibers are woven onyx with threads of the Web woven in. The combat program the tech transferred to you is standard issue. No specs," she paused.

"No. I meant why do I feel so heavy?"

"The amount of onyx per fiber has to be dense enough to store a lot of the Web, so it's heavy on its own. The point of using a suit so heavy is the specs. Specs are programs you can use to boost your strengths, fill out a weakness, even out imbalances. For example, a Defender spec expands the onyx in the suit and hardens it to make shields. Makes them the perfect complement to combat and recon. Thing is, they add weight too. The more you train with your suit, really the more of the Web you can carry, the bigger your arsenal can be."

Henry flexed his fingers and rolled his shoulders. "How come I don't look bigger?"

"Same way the Tower can create and adjust rooms, passageways, and space."

Henry nodded. He tested out other parts of his body. Henry worked harder to do the simpler stuff—raising his arms, walking.

"What specs do you use, sir?" he asked Sech.

She ignored him, eyes downturned.

He didn't mind. He preferred her silence over her temper. Though, it tempted his curiosity. He wondered what weight she carried.

"We are going out now. The acclimatization process will take a couple of days."

Henry nodded.

"Bye! See you soon!" the tech waved.

For the rest of the day, Sech and Henry hiked all over the compound. She made him take the path from his first day up the cliff. When they reached the top Henry struggled to breathe, but he wouldn't complain. The Lieutenant nodded once—a hint of approval. A wave of heat filled Henry's stomach, burning his aches away.

She turned and continued into parts Henry hadn't yet seen. Hitting his second wave, Henry followed.

They wore the suits for two days. Each day, the physical training left Henry boneless. Never was the Yard so grueling. Never had he experienced this kind of tired. Sech kept increasing the work so Henry couldn't tell if he got better. As the hours dragged on, Henry stretched thinner and thinner. Late the second day, Sech took him back to a Webbed room. Hours passed. The useless repetition against the blocked off Web pushed Henry's control.

"I'm going nowhere!" he shouted once. He was mid-way through another failed attempt.

"Are you giving up?" Sech's chilled voice goaded him.

Henry wouldn't stoop to her condescension, his silence fueled by frustration, anger, and exhaustion.

"I once called you unprepared, untested, and unfinished. Do I add undeserving to the list?" Her ice fractured to fire. No hatred. No contempt. Pure fury.

No one riled him up so much in so little time. His hands fisted, but he wouldn't give up. Bolts of lightning burst from his feet. They crackled along the floors and walls, thundering his rage. Across the Webbed wall, the lightning fizzled out into silver.

Silence hung when the walls went black again. Henry turned to her. She hadn't moved, the question still stuck between them.

Henry refocused on the Webbed wall. He fought over and over to shove her words in her face.

He didn't.

"Sloppy!" she snapped the next day.

"Then teach me—"

"Teach you what? How to manipulate my marking?" Dislike dominated her eyes, but underneath it that pain was there, driving her.

"I…" he stopped. "Sorry, sir."

Six days passed. Exhaustion sapped him of all energy, even his curiosity to answer the Gatekeeper's new question. Still, he pushed through PT. He powered through suit training. Pia worked with him every night on remedial. He tried again and again at the Webbed wall. Every day, Henry drove himself to wipe the taunting glare off Sech's face. On the sixth day, Sech stopped him early after only an hour in front of the silver.

"Go. Eat. Sleep. We go out tomorrow."

"Out?" he asked.

"Out. Easy mission, but you should rest. Wear your suit tomorrow. The closet will set up your standard gear so no need to pack."

"Web storage?" Henry clarified.

Sech nodded.

Henry kept quiet. He'd learned to adjust to added weight.

"Relax," Sech said, mistaking his silence for nerves. "Last time you carried a real pack, you weren't seven feet tall. You'll be fine."

Henry jolted, meeting her eyes. He couldn't trust such sympathy from her.

An uncomfortable silence fell between them until she left without another word. He left the intimate tension behind, lighting a comet toward Pia, hoping for a different kind of intimacy.

Pia invited him to eat with her in her quarters. He decided to ask her about the Gatekeeper, but she had more immediate plans.

As he walked back to his quarters hours later, he couldn't help the bubbling in his stomach. Waking up for Sech's training was awful. The prospect of tomorrow excited him. His first off-world mission, and he'd be tailing Sekhmet. Pia would be there the whole time.

"Good night?" Shai asked when Henry returned.

"Really good," Henry mumbled.

"Atta boy!"

"Yeah," Henry beamed. "We're trailing Sekhmet for the mission."

"Seriously?"

"Yeah man."

"Lucky bastard." Shai's smile was genuine.

"Where do you think we're going?'

"You'd have a better guess than I would."

"They don't talk about missions when I'm around."

"Like a team only kind of thing?"

"I guess so. Think we'll go somewhere far off?"

"I don't see why not, right? It doesn't matter how far we are."

"I guess."

"Dude. Don't be nervous."

Henry shrugged, turning his eyes down. Far from nervous, the anticipation thrilled him.

"Henry, that's what we do. We fight. Not at home. Out there," Shai gestured at the ceiling above them.

"That's what I'm excited about," Henry said. "Leaving."

"Didn't peg you for an adventurer," Shai scoffed at him.

"Didn't peg you for a giant," Henry quipped back.

Shai grinned, then they both lay on their beds. Henry's palm brushed the wall, and light faded to night.

CHAPTER TWENTY-THREE

Henry couldn't sleep. His mind kept drifting back to Pia's distraction. In three hours, light crept toward his bed. Smoke shifted in his palm. Opal's voice was quiet.

"Meet Sekhmet, Lieutenant Omika, and Lieutenant Sech at the portal bay in twenty minutes."

Eighteen minutes later, Henry and Shai stood ready. Luminescent mist engulfed their boots. Stuffed packs crested the mist like islands. Everyone got there before them. Pia flashed a big smile when they arrived. Neither of their Lieutenants looked as enthusiastic.

"Morning rookies, ready for hazing?" Pia teased them. Sech scowled. Kekoa groaned.

"Don't make this harder for us, Lieutenant Lagarre." Kekoa emphasized her rank.

"Of course, Lieutenant, how could I be so careless, letting them in on it so early," Pia winked. "Cadet Harbor, Cadet Jukita, are you ready?"

Both nodded. Shai radiated confidence. Henry's stomach fluttered. Pia kept trying to catch his eye. It didn't help.

"Excellent," Charles stepped in front of them. "I'm lead. Mission objective, meet with Delegate Prima on Optra in two days' time. Escort the cargo home. Expected duration—three days."

"Yes sir," his team saluted.

"It's good to have you, Sech, Omika."

"Back at you," Sech yawned.

"Once planet side, Cadets will tail Lagarre and Mont. Cadets, any White Wing gives you direction, follow to the letter."

"Yes sir," Henry and Shai chorused.

Charles bent; a flash whizzed away, like a fish darting into the glow. Henry and Shai followed Pia and Will's instructions to absorb their gear. Henry didn't stagger when he hefted the weight. He caught the approval on Sech's face in his periphery.

A bright message flew to Charles' feet.

"The signal is locked on Optra. The veins are clear. Stay safe, Charles."Opal's jagged voice grew soft. Charles smiled.

"We will travel in pairs. Ya Xue, with me. Mont and Lagarre. Lieutenants, your cadets."

"Yes sir," voices rang.

Roaring signaled Sekhmet's departures.

"You want to go first?" Kekoa asked Sech.

"No, I want to try something with Henry."

All Henry's excitement ratcheted into tension.

"Okay."

Shai nodded at Henry as the silver grew bright around his boots. The reassuring smile disappeared into space and sound.

"Cadet, you're going to dive."

"Are you joking?" Henry choked out.

"No. I brought up your concerns with Roxar. I'm allowed to pursue a different approach with you." Her monotone alerted Henry's caution.

"But I'm not a White Wing." Henry wanted real training, not throwing himself into another unknown.

"Harbor." She almost sounded patient. "Remember, although my opinions matter a great deal in your training, Roxar makes the final call. He brought you here—early, untested—because he is confident that you and Jukita belong here."

Her attempt at comfort made him uneasy; left him silent.

"Now Cadet," she said in a stronger voice, "If you've quit your whining?"

"Yes sir," Henry stifled bitterness.

"Grab my arm," she instructed.

Henry took hold above her elbow. She passed her other hand across the back of his forearm, brushing his suit.

"I just passed you coordinates for the planet. Can you feel a pulling, almost a pinpointed vacuum?"

"I don't know about a vacuum." Something drew him, more like a handshake than tug, an invitation. The feeling prickled through his arm. "I got it."

She turned and looked at him. Henry was her height now.

Henry's breath caught in his throat. She was too close. Her blue eyes drew him down like gravity. Flecks of gold danced in turquoise seas and indigo depths—for a moment.

"Well?" she demanded.

"Sorry, sir," he blinked. He took a deep breath, and then— nothing.

"How do I do this?"

"It's the same as casting a comet, but using the direction from the coordinates. Focus your mind on that pull."

Henry turned to her again, but her face relaxed, her eyes closing. Trusting. That look unnerved him more than her attempted reassurance. A new weight burdened his shoulders, as heavy as her grip on his arm.

Henry stretched his free hand up, palm facing onyx in the direction of the pull. Silver breached in the black, and a jolt fizzled down his palm through his body. He breathed deep. Focused. Henry punched his palm up into a fist. He shut his eyes as his body was ensnared in sound.

He plunged like a dark star through the Web, wind whipping through his braids. Heat bathed his cheeks, shoulders, and torso. His every care melted away in that mad euphoria.

Until Sech's grip tightened on his arm. Wide, trusting blue eyes flashed through the chaos in his mind. He resisted the urge to open his own eyes, check she hadn't slipped despite his hold back on her.

A jolt made the muscles around his eyes spasm. The Web jittered through his marking. Intent pulsed through his consciousness, assuaging his fear for Sech.

His awareness sharpened, cleaving his senses. Henry processed a new separation between his physical feedback and the information sifting through his brain. An ethereal part of himself grew outside the confines of his skin—out and out and out.

Henry's expanse overlapped Sech's form, and her mind laid bare for him.

No rejection. Not one iota of dislike. Joy sang through her veins and mind, the same way the Web bubbled through himself. Carefree, they hurtled through the Web, bound together.

The dive ended too soon. When he landed, he visualized landing feet first. Solid ground sent tremors up his legs, but he stayed upright. The bubbling in his body drained.

He took in the scene. Sekhmet, Kekoa, and Shai sat on a grassy plain that stretched for kilometers all around. The knee-high grasses came in shades of yellow, bright green, and lavender. The sky, a cloudless blue. Such a clear atmosphere allowed him to see straight through sub-space. The stars winked at him past the single sun's shine.

"Holy shit, are you ok?" Shai asked.

"What?"

"Your eyes!" Pia gasped.

"What's wrong this time?"

"No man, they're- you're- glowing," Shai answered.

"What happened Ro?" Kekoa's face blanched

Sech glowed from within. Her veins stood out, shining so brightly her skin seemed transparent. Her eyes fluttered under her lids like she was in REM sleep. A smile Henry had never seen before exposed a softness in her he never expected.

"Ro?" Kekoa projected clinical calm.

She did not answer. Henry reexamined that enthralling softness, and his stomach dropped.

CHAPTER TWENTY-FOUR

Charles demanded, "Harbor what's wrong with her?"

"I don't know sir."

Everyone circled Sech. Masera and Will stood with their backs to the group, assuming watch positions.

"What did she have you do, Henry?" Kekoa asked.

"She told me to dive, sir."

"Really? I wonder why." He knelt.

"Omika, what's wrong with her?" Charles turned from Henry.

"I've never dealt with this situation before."

"Well what should we do?"

"We could wait, I suppose."

"I'd rather not."

"Then we have to wake her up."

"How?"

Kekoa pinched Sech's arm.

"Ow!" Henry blurted. Everyone, even Masera and Will, turned to him.

"Cadet?" Charles prompted.

"That—I—" It had hurt. Even though Kekoa pinched Sech, the spike of pain jabbed Henry's nerves.

Kekoa pinched her again.

"Will you stop that?" Henry snapped. A growing bruise ached at the same spot that Kekoa touched on Sech's arm.

"She's Possessed," Kekoa said.

"What?" The protest came from different people, Henry included.

"Possessed. I've never seen it before, but she told me about it once. Happened during training; scared the breath right out of her."

"What can we do?" Charles asked.

"We can't do anything. The Cadet can."

"I didn't do anything," Henry insisted.

"Yes you did, Cadet," Kekoa addressed him. He didn't sound angry. "You took her brain and body away from her. Our Lieutenant isn't up here right now," he tapped on her head. The fingers resounded in Henry's own ears.

"But how, sir? I don't know… the Web did everything for me."

"You mean you knew you had control over her?"

"Not like that," Henry backtracked.

"Well, you need to let go of her."

"How?" Desperation fueled the guilt in Henry's gut.

"I'm not a marked Wing. Give it any try you've got," Kekoa told him.

Henry took a deep breath. In. Out. He drew his focus in, creating an image of her in his head. Many memories surfaced. Blue eyes. An icy voice. A sharp reprimand. Dislike and awkward comfort all in one.

In each mental image, Henry housed Sech's body. Henry's outline overshadowed hers. He looked three times his true body size. He concentrated on that. Sech was there, strong, proud, and venomous, but all her fire flickered under his bulk.

Henry peeled the two images apart in his brain. Minutes dragged by as Henry worked. The bond between the two bodies resisted his efforts, growing stickier as he shaved more off. Sech's consciousness began battering against him in muted bursts. He was happy to feel her bite.

Henry opened his eyes when his mental image normalized. The two images didn't overlap anymore but were still connected. Satisfied, he yanked the rest of his consciousness in. He strained against a sharp, quick tug against his mind, like an elastic band snapping back on his brain. It hurt.

Sech's body went rigid. Her arms shook at her sides. She opened her eyes; they filled with tears.

"Ro?" Anguish softened Kekoa's voice.

"No, no, no, no, no…" Spasms convulsed her frame. Her eyes rolled into the back of her head. She collapsed to the ground, twitching and jerking.

"She's having a seizure. Get back."

Henry and Charles moved to join Pia and Shai. Kekoa stayed by Sech, worry clear on his face.

Pia whispered, though her eyes were glued to Sech. "Are you all right?"

"I'm fine." Guilt constricted his throat.

"You didn't know, right Henry?" Shai asked.

"No! I would never-"

"I know you wouldn't on purpose," Shai pacified him. "But you know what it means though, right?"

"What?" Henry snapped.

"It means you've used your marking. It means you'll make White Wing."

Henry stilled.

"Not like that he won't," Pia interrupted. "The Commander would never accept a marked Wing whose ability cripples the team."

"But that's not fair! Henry's got the best scores in history."

"How good is any score when your teammates keel over?"

Shai glared at her. She turned from Ro to glower back.

"I won't make White Wing." The words constricted Henry's throat. He hadn't been at the Tower long, but he had worked damn hard for this assignment.

"Oh no, you can still make White Wing," Pia still stared daggers at Shai.

"How?"

"You get to choose your specialty for Initiation, and there are plenty of others besides marked Wing."

"That's perfect Henry," Shai clapped him on the shoulder. Henry didn't respond.

At that moment, Kekoa sighed. Pia swiveled back toward them. Sech's body relaxed. Kekoa turned her on to her side and stood up. Charles approached him.

"Her seizure lasted just over thirty seconds. No serious trauma to the head or other physical injuries. She went back to glowing though."

"How soon until she's up and moving?" Charles asked.

"Honestly, I'm not sure. She's never had a history of seizures, and I have no idea what other possible damage might have occurred when Henry Possessed her."

Charles brooded. He pulled Pia aside. Shai inched closer to Henry, both trying to catch some of the conversation.

"Any insight?"

"No more than Kekoa. I've never seen this either."

"I don't like it."

"We are safe here. The Optan don't have any issues with us, and its harvest season anyway."

"Still. I don't like sitting out in the open. Not to mention all the ground we'd have to cover tomorrow."

"We don't have much choice."

Charles grumbled under his breath. They moved further off. It was impossible to eavesdrop anymore.

"Any idea what's wrong with her?" Shai asked.

"No."

"Doesn't look too good does it though? She ends up convulsing on the ground after your first dive."

"Don't remind me," Henry muttered.

"Good thing you don't have to test as a marked Wing."

The encouragement didn't work on Henry. Deeper, he did feel relief knowing he didn't need to rely on his marking to make it. He believed he would fail if it came to that. The new information slid off his mind. His stomach twisted. His throat, too dry.

Sech lay facing away from him. All he could manage was to watch her, watch her breathe on her own.

CHAPTER TWENTY-FIVE

"She's waking up!"

Everyone, except for Masera and Will, closed in. Sech stirred. She worked her jaws, but no sound came. Her eyes shuddered open. She flexed her fingers, wiggled her toes. She sat up, smooth to stand.

"You know, taking someone's will away is really bad manners, Harbor."

"Yes sir."

"Explain yourself."

"I got worried. The Web took over."

"Did it ever cross your big head to just use your other hand to secure the grip?" she rubbed her eyes.

"No sir," Henry admitted. "I'm sorry sir."

"You realize if we had landed in the middle of hostile territory that some of us could be dead?" Sech asked.

"I hate to interrupt, but I do need to take your vitals," Kekoa cut in.

Anger eased off her face. She turned from Henry, sighing and sagging.

"Of course." She grabbed her wrist and slid her hand up. The suit revealed skin. Kekoa pulled onyx across his palm, prodding her.

"Any ideas why you're still lit up like a star?" he asked.

"I do actually."

Kekoa paused his test. Charles leaned closer.

"My Cadet's like a walking vein. He embodies the Web as much as I do."

"Get to the point," Charles crouched beside her.

"My blood is attracted to Henry because of the huge amount of the Web he carries within him. Thanks to his Possession, my marking's overcharged."

"He's like a mobile power source for you, but Possessing you was more like plugging you in," Pia chimed in. Sech nodded.

"Can you use it?" Charles asked.

"I haven't tried to really use my marking yet," Sech hesitated, "but, yes. I can." She locked eyes with Henry. Big, round, open eyes.

Henry held his breath.

"Does that mean he eliminates your handicap off base?" Pia asked, eyes alight.

"It does," Ro answered, meeting Pia's heat. Their intimacy bothered Henry.

"So?" Charles addressed Pia.

"When she's off base, her ability is inhibited because her proximity to the Web decreases. With Henry around, it's like she's back in the Tower."

"Damn. Like you need another power up," Charles smiled. "Still, you're glowing for all the world to see. Can't you control that?"

"Not right this minute," Sech's eyes accused Henry.

"You had a seizure when Henry let you go," Kekoa said, taking her forearm again.

She sighed. "Roxar never slapped me around enough for anything like that to happen."

"How did I give you a seizure?" Henry interrupted.

"You can't just go around blundering with other people's consciousness."

"How soon until you can shut it off?" Charles cut Henry off.

"A couple hours," Sech said. "I can probably run though."

"No, you're not fooling me," Kekoa rejected. "Sit down."

She sank to the ground, scowling at Kekoa.

"We set up camp for tonight, make up the time tomorrow after I'm sure she's fine," Kekoa told Charles.

Charles sighed, but he started issuing orders. Henry and Shai followed Pia and Will. Kekoa continued to talk with Sech.

While they set up camp, Henry's shoulders weighed a ton a piece. He strained to overhear Kekoa's questions, Sech's answers.

Sech sounded desperate. His Possession took something from her, something more that he couldn't give back. Henry sweated.

After dinner, Charles issued watch pairs. He excluded Kekoa and Sech, leaving Henry with Pia and Shai with Will. Charles and Masera would go first, letting the others sleep.

Henry curled himself inside his sleeping bag. He looked over the low fire to the lone tent. Kekoa busied himself around Sech's prostrate outline. Kekoa's low tone soon lulled him asleep.

Foggy dreams made his eye lids heavy when Pia's cold fingers woke him. They walked a few paces outside the fire light and picked up circles around their campsite. Henry's mind drifted. Pia slipped her hand into his, tethering him.

He Possessed Sech. Progress should make him feel better. Possession sounded like an advanced skill. Sech convinced him nothing like that was within his range. Usurping her mind disgusted him. He never meant to invade her. He was wary what his marking really meant if this ability manifested without his help. Then again, he didn't consciously do it. The Web weaponized his worry.

A thud in the tent. Henry and Pia tensed, both listening to within rather than without.

"How are you feeling?" Kekoa's voice radiated concern.

"Awful," Sech whimpered.

"You fell on my medic trunk."

"What?" Sech grumbled. A faint click. A soft, red light glowed.

"Your vitals are within normal range, but your heart rate is elevated." Kekoa said.

"It's the dreams."

"Possibly. Do you want to talk about them?"

"No." Pia squeezed Henry's hand at Sech's answer.

"That's fine." Kekoa used that calm tone only physicians had.

Quiet reigned for several minutes. Pia relaxed and watched the plains again.

"I do bad things in my dreams," Sech started. "Atrocious things."

"Like?" Kekoa prompted. Pia flicked back to the tent, stilling.

"Like genocide."

Kekoa said nothing.

Sech's breath fluttered. "I slaughter hundreds, probably thousands, for almost no reason. Men, women, children, animals, plants… all of it… anything living."

"You're a soldier Ro." His shadow leaned into hers. "Death catches up to us in its own way."

"It's not like that. You've seen me kill. You know how I deal with that. This is different. I walk through worlds I've never seen before, and I walk alone. Not because I am alone, but because I am alone, alone. I'm the different one. I'm Roxar." Her voice cracked, remorse, spite, and fear all wrapped into one confession.

Pia stopped breathing. Her grip on Henry's hand tightened like a cinch.

"You're the only one besides Taizai who really knows him," Kekoa began, "but you know you're the only one who has those doubts."

"I know. It doesn't change the fact though that that's me in my dreams."

"I can listen, and I can give advice, but I can't fix what's eating at you Ro," he said. "That's your job."

"Some doctor you are."

"I can give you something to knock you out for three hours."

"Please."

After several moments of movement, the small tent went dark.

Henry dragged Pia further away where their voices wouldn't carry but they could still see.

"What was that about?" Henry asked.

"I'm not sure." She wouldn't meet his eyes.

They spent the rest of the watch in silence, eyes on the horizons. Pia held his hand the whole time.

CHAPTER TWENTY-SIX

In the morning, Sech assured Charles of her fitness.

"See? No glow," Sech swept her body with her hand.

"Good," Charles smiled. "You said yesterday you wanted Henry to track?"

"He's perfect for it," she nodded.

"I've seen him set pace. He's a natural. Little fast, though," Kekoa added.

"Your Cadet, your call," Charles motioned Henry forward. He passed two fingers over Henry's forearm. Henry's suit shifted over his hand, gaining a vibration in his palm rather than weight.

"I transferred a nav spec to your suit. Focus on it until you can tell which direction the coordinates are," Charles ordered.

Henry steadied his breathing. The pulse sharpened to a sting, dragging his palm northwest.

"Got it," Henry pointed.

"Good. Move out."

Henry had to limit himself. The boring terrain gave his boots traction and the wind blew with him. He could have run nonstop, but Charles kept calling them in every two hours. Around midday, the grassy plains gave way to hills. Every few kilometers, a patch of soil waited for seed.

"Where are all the people?" he asked Pia during the next mandatory break.

"What do you mean?"

"Fields, but no farmers."

"Right. Those aren't fields like the kind on Handakau. Optra has no real agriculture above ground. The Optan live underground and farm the fungi below. When a farm has been fully harvested, the top side loses the grains that feed off the fungi.”

“Oh.”

“Yeah. I’m doing the delegate trial in a couple months. Have to know all the agricultures, languages, economies, social structures, and governments with a trade rating of five or higher.”

“Had no idea.”

“Might as well put this mouth to use if I can’t shut up, as Will fondly says,” she smiled. “You’d be a terrible delegate.”

Henry chuckled. “I wouldn’t be bad.”

“Bad enough,” she laughed back.

“Hey, I talk with you.”

“True,” she leaned back, sighed. “You barely talk with Ro.”

“Who?”

“Lieutenant Sech,” she saluted Henry.

He snatched her hand. “Should I?”

“Of course.” The humor drained from her eyes. Even serious, Pia managed adorable. “Besides the fact that you Possessed her twelve hours ago, she’s your lieutenant, and for a reason. They broke up Santos just so you and Shai could work with Kekoa and Ro. It’s a big deal.”

Henry looked down at her palm in his hands. The ridges and calluses of her palms scraped; the backs of her hands, smooth like butter. He ran his fingers over that paradox.

“When you’re a Wing—no matter your specialty— you’ll join Santos. She’s going to be your partner soon, as well as your lieutenant.”

Henry grunted. Being around Sech every day would be a nightmare come true.

“You should get to know her. You’re so serious around her all the time.”

“I don’t think you understand her very well,” Henry grumbled.

“I think I know my best friend a little better than you.”

"What?" Henry stuttered.

"I thought you knew. I just assumed…" Pia smiled, pulling his hand toward her. "Ro and I graduated from Origins Base on Big Red. Same year. We were teammates."

"You're joking."

"No I'm not. Henry, you're going to be in a world of trouble if you can't relax around her. Someday she'll save your ass. Someday you'll save hers. In those moments, there better not be any issues between you two."

"Only if I make Wing."

"Of course you'll make Wing," Pia rolled her eyes. "Listen, I noticed you never call her by her first name. It's an easy place to start, and teammates are bigger than rank."

"Call her Ro?" It sounded ridiculous from his lips.

"You and Shai call Kekoa by his first name," she squeezed his hand before dropping it. "Just use your 'sirs' and your 'Lieutenants' when they belong."

Charles called everyone to get ready.

"Trust me," she said, smiling like the sun.

"If you say so."

Henry ran his mind against the drumming of his feet. Everything about Sech was too formal and distant, even if she had softened toward him. Though, that relationship worked. He grew monstrously, and then he Possessed.

Henry ran and rested and ran and rested in silence until the sky turned orange. Not even Shai disturbed him while they set up camp. Henry's pace left everyone too tired for camaraderie. Charles gave the watch assignments. Henry and Sech would take the last watch. Pia caught his eye as she walked out with Will to the perimeter. She winked again.

When Sech came to wake him, he thought it was Pia. He grabbed at her hand. Sech jolted, leaping back from him, clutching her hand at her chest. Henry blinked at the moment of vulnerability.

"I'm sorry, thought you were…" he trailed off, sleep making her expression more fascinating.

"Pia," she finished, her voice soft.

Henry nodded.

"Well, get up."

She turned and held her hand tight.

Henry rubbed his face. Sech had made him bitter, angry, determined. After he Possessed her, she made him guilty. He had little room for empathy for someone called Ro. Still.

They started walking. They didn't speak until Henry figured out how to say what he thought Pia meant.

"I don't understand what I did to you, but I'm sorry it hurt."

"Thanks." Her hands hung relaxed.

"You're welcome, Ro." It slipped out easier than he expected.

She stopped in her tracks for a beat before catching up. In the dark, Henry made out her surprise. Only in the corner of his eye.

"It's good that you can Possess," she said after a moment. "If you can do it outside the Web, especially. It would practically secure your placement in the White Wings."

"I didn't really do it," he admitted.

"What do you mean Cadet?" She angled toward him, ignoring their surroundings.

"I didn't Possess you."

She rolled her eyes.

"Ok I did, but I didn't."

"Care to explain that a little better?"

"I tried to focus. All I could feel was the Web and… well, you know. I thought about whether or not you were still with me. The Web took it from there."

"Is that really what happened?" The slight part in her lips turned her challenge into concern.

"Yes."

She sighed, shoulders breaking. "Well, fuck. Might as well sit down. I have a lot of questions."

CHAPTER TWENTY-SEVEN

Ro crossed her legs and sat, cupping her chin.

"Shouldn't we at least walk around the campsite?"

"Nope, no need. With you here, I can literally feel the entire planet."

"With what?"

"I'll give you a hint, it's not my feet," she joked. "You can't know because your marking isn't manifesting ability, but it might. Has, actually, if what you say is true."

"You're being confusing," Henry sighed.

She leaned back on her forearms. "So, number one. How did you think about me?"

"What?" Henry blanked.

"When the Possession happened. Did you ask yourself a question? Or like…"

"I—uh… pictured you, I guess."

Ro stiffened. "Pictured what?"

"Your eyes."

She let out her breath. Henry sank to the ground next to her.

"My turn."

"Excuse me?"

"Number one," Henry pressed. "How does your marking let you 'feel' the entire planet?" he air-quoted.

"My marking moves with the Web like a magnet. So, my marking draws me toward other Life, just like the Web, and my reach is far. Farther with you."

"Like radar?"

"That's an oversimplification, but sure."

"Can you track without a nav spec?"

"Yes. Number two."

"But—"

"My turn," she fell back against the grass. "Any change in your vision since the Possession?"

"No."

Her face scrunched.

"Number two. Why does my marking expand your reach?"

"That's a very long answer," she sat up, facing him. "I get five questions after this."

"Fine," Henry held out his hand.

Her hand gripped his too tight, too quick. "You know the Web binds us all?" she paused, because Henry went rigid. He couldn't control his reaction at those words. The third dimension. He had to stick with Ro.

Henry took a deep breath and picked his face up.

"Taizai said something about death that made me rethink the three dimensions. Is this part of it?"

Ro huffed. "Has he gotten to you already?"

"Who?"

"Roxar."

"The Commander? No?" Henry peered at her. "Wait, got to me how?"

Ro stalled. The tense moments reminded Henry of the nightmare he overheard, the Gatekeeper's warning—dread swamped his ambition.

She eventually deflected, "We got off topic. Markings attract the Web at a higher rate than a normal Life. The stronger your marking, the more Web you attract. Statistically, my marking is stronger than Roxar's, but my dependence on proximity to the Web is a big limitation he doesn't have. You even less so than him. With you around, proximity isn't an issue, so my 'radar,' as you put it, has a much bigger radius than usual."

Henry nodded, but she continued before he could ask.

"Alright. One of five."

"Wait," Henry interrupted. "You have to explain it. What did Taizai really mean? What did you mean by a normal life? And why is Roxar part of this?"

Ro's shoulders caved. "The Web is part of what Taizai explained to you, or at least I think he was trying to."

"I didn't understand it," Henry reeled.

"It's not what they taught you at the academy."

"I figured that out."

"Henry, one thing you have to understand is the world can't be the same for you with those," she nodded toward his eyes. "Those dimensions exist, are real foundations, for the people around us. Soldiers die and people live only because the Web allowed us to flee Old Home in the first place. We need that story to survive," her eyes dropped like anchors. "For you, me, and Roxar, it's more. We live in the third dimension. The Web binds us all, and Roxar and I at least can actually traverse it. When I say Life, I literally mean any living thing. Every living being, no matter what, is a pinpoint of the second dimension existing in the third, the Web. And the Web... it's a real, living web, Henry, made from the bonds between people and creatures and plants and everything in between. Every thread connects one Life to another, and another, and another. I can feel every living thing on this planet because the Web allows me touch Life. Any other Wing only gets to use this incredible organic network as a basic transportation system."

Henry stumbled to stand.

"What are you talking about?"

"The nearest life-form that could do us harm is four kilometers west. A pit vulture. I bet your eyes can make it out on the horizon. Go on. Confirm it."

Henry turned toward the faint separation between reality and wonder. A darker shape cut into the sky, an avian arrow through Henry's disbelief.

"The Web means I can touch it. I know where it is. My ability, something I've worked years to hone, isn't strong enough to Possess it at this range, even with you here. Roxar could. Kekoa never could. That's the difference. That's why they get to live thinking death, life, and the Web are rally cries and we have to actually bear those responsibilities. Have you ever killed anyone?"

Henry stared at her.

"No. You're alive, sure, but have you ever really lived?"

"My mother," Henry blurted.

"So, you understand just how important it is that someone like Roxar could touch, control, or take her life through the Web?"

"He wouldn't."

"The Web gives him that power, regardless of if he would or wouldn't." She turned to her lap. "There always has to balance. Life occupies singularity. Life, as a force in the universe split among these dimensions, is not conscious in and of itself. The bodies that house Life are. The Web is unity, but it becomes power through our Life. Look at how you Possessed me," she paused.

Henry held his breath.

"If you can't learn to control your marking, there won't be balance between your Life and the Web attracted to you. This time, you only Possessed me. I threw up enough of a shield that you only took my will, not my life itself."

"I didn't—"

"I know."

Henry swore, "I won't let it happen again."

She nodded. "Good. Can I have my questions now?"

Henry knew she deliberately wasn't answering his other questions. He decided he would still stick with her. He smiled and started walking.

"Was there anything weird about the dive? The Web?"

"Beyond how distracted I get, no."

"With time, you'll grow numb to it, just like the mist in the Tower. Did you have any other trouble?"

"No."

"Any pain?"

"No."

She sighed. "Really, nothing? I may be out of questions. You're really frustrating you know that?"

"Right back at you."

She chuckled and caught up to him. Henry fell into pace next to her. He reeled with the information she had given, but couldn't focus on her implications about his marking.

He couldn't fathom what the dimensions really were. He feared what knowing Death and Life really meant. The Gatekeeper's question lurked on his tongue the whole night but so did her advice. And Pia's.

Ro never glanced at him. She didn't bump into him or brush shoulders when they turned. Still, she chatted about small things and kept closer than ever before.

When the sun came up red, Henry fell back into to "sirs" and "Lieutenants."

"It's ok with Sekhmet," she murmured. "Ro's fine."

CHAPTER TWENTY-EIGHT

After a couple hours' run, they met the Optan at the bottom of a steep hill. They slid out of crude holes in the mountainside. Sweet-smelling goo encrusted their wrinkly hides. They had trunks for noses and short legs. Out of their caverns, the Optans' trunks trailed on the ground half a meter behind them. They brought baskets of mushrooms. Pia approached, thanking them while Masera and Will collected them. Ro took two mushrooms and handed one to Henry and Shai.

"Only one," Ro warned them.

"Why?"

"That's an Eyesore."

"A what?"

"An Eyesore. Three ounces of Nirvana per cap."

Nirvana, the strongest hallucinogen approved for military use, was a highly controlled substance on all bases. When combined with an onyx-compatible peptide, it made a potent and addictive narcotic. The subsequent connection to the Web induced euphoria-fed hallucinations so intense the brain and body disconnected. Henry had overheard some Wings discuss chemical desensitization but thought they'd been joking.

"You don't have to get me high to take advantage of me," Shai smiled at Ro. She rolled her eyes, and Pia sniggered.

"We all take a course every month to build up our immunity in case of capture. Nothing like the first time. Go on!"

Henry stared at the ruffled brown edges and stumpy cap. He closed his eyes and popped it in, chewing as little as possible.

Weird, shiny lines grew from his peripherals to cover everything. They refracted light into his pupils when he moved his head. They shifted with his sight, clinging to people, shaping plants, crisscrossing the sky with a brilliance that just… it was over, less than fifteen seconds.

"It takes four caps to get a serious trip," Pia snorted.

Sound blared through the atmosphere. A delegate team dived to the meet them. The delegate and the Optan confirmed the deal. The cargo transferred smoothly. They left in pairs, Ro taking Henry home. Lab rats waited to take the cargo off them. Ro disappeared with Kekoa for a while but came back before Henry and Shai left the mess.

"Henry, training is about to get worse."

"A lot worse," Kekoa emphasized. "You two are doing… well. The next phase is brutal. Sleep as much as you can, k?"

Henry gulped. His stomach was full and his first mission was over. All he wanted was sleep.

"Got it," Shai nodded. "What are you going to do?"

"Nap then remedial," Henry shrugged.

"First part sounds good," Shai shrugged.

They ambled back to their quarters.

"If I were a bum, I'd trip on Nirvana every day."

Henry laughed.

"What'd you see in yours?" Shai asked.

"Lots of bright lines that covered everything. You?"

"Man," Shai shook his head. His eyes closed, his cheeks tinted. "I saw Ro naked. Fucking. Awesome."

Henry couldn't fall asleep though. He brooded over Ro's warning the rest of the day, even after pushing through his remedial twice. He needed time to work out the information dump she gave him the night before. The anxiety she induced distracted him from making any progress. He turned to bed frustrated and confused.

It started three hours after he fell asleep. The light shined at maximum. Opal's voice projected from the floor, making Henry leap from bed.

"Meet Lieutenant Sech and Lieutenant Omika in the portal bay in ten minutes."

Henry and Shai rolled out of bed and jerked on their suits.

"Is this that bad part they warned us about?" Shai grumbled as they ran toward the portal bay.

"Has to be, right?"

"I hate it already."

Henry's comet sped up. "Hurry, or we'll be late." Henry accelerated to Shai's cursing.

Henry didn't sleep for days. The worst was the four-day streak. He got thirty-minute rest cycles twice. Maybe three times. He couldn't remember. All he did remember were commands, faces, and planets. Private Cassidy from team Xerxes. A small planet with plains of black sand and six tiny suns. First Lieutenant Frank of team Gorain. Green terrain oozing sludge and poison. Wing Leader Pedrau of team Kuat. Snow, ice, glaciers, and crevasses. As soon as one mission ended, a new team arrived with new orders. Mission after mission. Team after team. On and on.

"Seventeen days," Shai moaned. His eyes glazed over but they were open.

"S'long."

Shai grunted.

A spot on the horizon made both straighten despite fatigue. Henry jogged back to camp and reported. Ro and Kekoa returned with him to where Shai stood. They observed while team Rath received the envoy. Thirty minutes later, Ro held her hand out to Henry.

"Come on. We're going home."

Henry stared at her weary smile. He gripped her arm with both hands. Her palm moved up to the sky and sound yanked them into the Web.

The surging in his mind nursed his waning endurance. He clung to Ro harder. They popped into the portal bay a breath later.

"You can let go now." She smiled still despite the exhaustion in her posture.

Henry's hands swung back to his sides in a daze. Kekoa and Shai tore into space next to them.

"The hard part's over," Kekoa stretched his arms above his head. "We go back to PT and specialization training tomorrow. Go. Sleep. Eat."

Henry and Shai couldn't fathom food, just stumbling toward bed. Henry collapsed into his sheets without changing.

CHAPTER TWENTY-NINE

Freedom. It feels like freedom.

Harbor's Possession startled her with gentleness. Her marking ceased pulling every which way. Instead, her blood fawned over him. She knew she was gone, no ounce of control, no way to prevent her marking from driving her into death with the Web's endless urging to Blend past the point of living.

It didn't matter. Harbor held her just right, so her marking submitted to him. Her blood flowed without input from the Web to jar its course.

So...

Her wonder faltered. Roxar had held her this perfectly, had then taught her the fine line intention played in the Web with pain. Henry didn't wrest her marking from her, but the way his will held her—*so snug*—it was beyond similar.

It may actually be Roxar.

Then Harbor severed her. Her marking slammed home harder than the worst punch. Her will clawed against it. She collapsed and went dark.

She didn't remember much from when she woke, only the needles gouging through her body toward Henry. She couldn't remember the last time her marking pulled in a singular direction. The pain... her marking's addiction to him had eclipsed every lesson Roxar had imparted with pain.

She gritted through the rest of the mission. Being near Harbor was like standing on the brim of a volcano, but fear drove her nearer. If Roxar had used him to take her, she had to know.

She didn't blame herself for pushing away someone who made her hurt. But his Possession more than his apology broke her down. He'd cared for her. He'd gentled her. After everything she'd done to keep him at arm's length, he'd held her.

Roxar had held her, and used her.

… Henry is better than that.

The rest of the mission was fogged over by her reaction to Henry—the extremity—and the fight facing her at home. At least when she got home the Web could distract her marking's obsession. The Tower divided her pain, increasing it tenfold for every cell drawn from Harbor. She was shaking by the time she confronted a different torture.

One.

Two.

Three.

Four.

"Rolyn," Roxar greeted.

She glared.

"Scowling does not suit you. Sit."

She approached the bench he made. Her will whipped her marking to focus on Roxar instead of pining after Henry. She recognized Roxar's ability looming, but his intention remained murky.

"To what do I owe the pleasure so soon after you've returned?"

"Explain to me how Henry Possessed me."

"He Possessed you? Really?"

"Don't pretend. It felt just like you. I know you did it through him. Why?"

"Rolyn. I took you once, only once, and it was a very long time ago."

"Don't fuck with me. I felt it. It was his marking, but it was your touch. I know it."

Her marking flinched as he flexed his will, signaling his annoyance. His arm glowed, the Web clouding the domed ceiling above them. Roxar's cloud cracked and they were sealed in fog.

"Touched a nerve, have I?"

"No, a lesson in discretion. As much as you despise it, I value your life. I'd regret it if more devoted subordinates observed one of your outbursts... though that's precisely who you come to discuss, isn't it? Rolyn, think. I know you can figure this out."

"So, you deny you had any part in it?"

"Obviously."

"You're lying."

"You're bluffing. Think about it, instead."

Ro sat straighter. "His marking... like yours, what he can see, he can take."

"Perhaps. I'll have to run that one by Sochi."

"If your rat had a better theory, you'd have corrected me."

Roxar smiled.

"I still don't believe you. Even if his marking is just like yours, it doesn't make sense. He did it, but can't do it consciously?"

"Your marking required time to adjust before you could accomplish anything consciously, too."

She froze.

"I expected more from you than this."

"I didn't..."

"Of all the people who could sympathize, I thought you could have."

"I..."

"Close your mouth. Think, Rolyn."

Her head tilted down, her eyes welling. Roxar let her have her silence.

"When I came back, where did I even start?"

"You never had a true start, like he does. You ran away to the grove to establish yourself before attempting anything. By the time you came to me, your foundational skills were complete, so you achieved most training with ease."

Her voice dropped lower. "Then tell me how you began."

"Possession."

She didn't breathe. Her gaze snapped to the silver glow, her eyes blown dark with fear. "Someday I'm going to figure out what you're hiding."

"All children think that about their parents sometime."

"Don't try to twist this back on me, you ass."

"I think, Rolyn, no matter how effective my shroud, you should remember who you are speaking to."

"My apologies, sir."

"I hope you figure out how to best train your Cadet, Rolyn. Don't let him usurp your will again."

His fog released, pooling to the floor and vanishing.

"Yes, sir."

CHAPTER THIRTY

The Tower's depth held no comfort, the light's warmth numb against her skin. Her marking carved away at her will's hold, desperate to return to fawning over Henry. Ro couldn't stop her fears churning deeper and deeper.

Run.

No.

Run.

No!

Run.

Ro trembled.

Weak fingers prodded her shoulder. Ro reached out and took Opal's hand. The Gatekeeper's fragility, despite the power she wielded in the real world, called Ro's strength forward.

It's so much worse than I thought.

Opal's warmth seeped through their contact, her gravelly voice filling Ro's mind. *And still you stay.*

I can't… I don't…. I can't beat them both.

You still stay.

If I go to the grove more, Roxar will notice. I'm already on thin ice after Norvin.

Roxar made it for you. Use it when you need it.

Ro shuddered. *I can't live my life shut away there, and I can't be here. What if I can't do this?*

You fear you can't, but you are here, not out there, a pause, *because this is where you belong. This is your home.*

Ro squeezed eyes tight, remembering Pia's easy confidence, her wispy snores.

Help me, Opal.

I couldn't repel him if I tired.

Stop Henry, please.

I can't control your marking.

Can you shield him from me? Anything?

Nothing you haven't done already with your own will.

Ro's silence projected her shattered hope.

You shouldn't push Henry away.

Why not?

Roxar takes the people he wants; earn yours instead.

I never want to be like Roxar. I won't use people like that.

Don't underestimate what Henry could be, for both of you.

Henry is breaking my will.

You haven't succumbed yet.

Ro couldn't admit her limit.

You are stronger than this, Ro.

Ro couldn't repeat her mantra.

Your next lesson presented itself.

I can handle it, Ro lied.

Taizai has split from him. He no longer visits at night or reports on his progress.

Why?

That's what I'd like to know as well.

For how long?

A few days now.

I'll look into it.

Ro fled from the Tower's depths, hurtling toward the lab. Opal's intrusion left her disconsolate. If Taizai had given Roxar up, then the chances Roxar turned to Henry increased.

By a lot.

Ro rubbed weariness from her face when she emerged in one of the lab's storage rooms, furthest away from lingering rats. She snuck toward Taizai, finding him alone, observing a pillar of smoke stretching from floor to ceiling.

"Ro. I didn't schedule us tonight did I? I wanted to give you some time to yourself."

"No, nothing like that. Opal's been pestering me to check in on you."

"Oh? What for?"

"I was hoping you'd tell me."

"Something with her lessons I'd imagine. What has she directed you toward this time?"

"No content this time. Just you. Learn anything recently?"

"Nothing out of the ordinary."

Ro hummed, watching Taizai from the corners of her eyes. "Any luck?" she nodded to the smoke.

"Again, no. I'm determined, though."

"I'm surprised it's taken so long between the two of you."

"Was there anything else, Ro?"

"Am I intruding?"

"Of course not," Taizai's charm quelled any doubt.

"Thanks," Ro slid to the ground, lounging. "It's been a while since she's given me an assignment."

"Indeed. Why do you think now, when Harbor has you working overtime already?"

"Must be something on your end, not mine."

Taizai clucked disapproval. "It must be something we are both missing, then."

"You should run it by Roxar."

"It is your lesson, Ro, not mine."

"I'm too tired for this. No games. What's up with you and Roxar?"

Taizai's think brows lowered, his tone growing soft. "I don't meddle in your affairs with him, and you don't meddle in mine."

Ro shrugged, "Not my fault Opal knows more than you want her too."

"Opal isn't the one asking me questions."

"All right, then here's my very own question. Are you done with him?"

"Excuse me?"

"Are you still helping him?"

Anxiety bloomed as Taizai inspected her body language. She dreaded either answer.

Taizai frowned, "Ro, remember your station."

"If you aren't helping him, would you help me instead?"

Taizai lit with unique curiosity, the mind powering Roxar's dominion appraising her. "With what?"

Ro gambled, "You know my marking almost as well as I do. Make me as strong as Roxar."

Taizai chuckled, "A waste of time. That's not your kind of strength."

"Then make me however strong I can be. I can't do it anymore on my own."

Taizai set his tablet down, the onyx swallowing his notes. He circled the pillar of smoke and came too close.

"You made yourself a Wing. Now make yourself a better one."

"I need someone—"

"No, you've never needed others."

Ro flinched, her memories surging through her weary shields. She couldn't afford another breakdown.

Not here.

"You've never been stronger because of your team or your loyalty. You've only ever grown because you had to, otherwise..." he snapped his fingers. "You learned to survive before you learned the name Rahnus. Be that person again."

Ro's head pounded, the spark of fear and exhaustion and pain gas lighting loneliness she couldn't stop. "I guess Opal will be disappointed, then."

"I guess so," Taizai nodded.

Ro didn't bother saying goodbye. She dived to her quarters and fell into her mattress.

She was too scared to think. She was too tired to cry. She was too tormented to keep her darkest memories down.

****

She huddled at the base of roots, mouth gaping at the sight of another person.

"Who are you?"

Ro's voice cracked around the sounds after years of disuse. The younger boy frowned.

She managed, "Ro."

"Rolyn? Is that you?"

She nodded.

"How have you—"

She pounded her chest, "Rember?"

"What?"

"Rember me?"

The boy's cheeks blanched, his voice, a whisper. "We remember you."

"Ma? Da? Rember?"

"We all do."

Ro beamed, "Go ho?"

"What?"

"Go," she pointed up into the canopy, "ho?"

The boy's eyes widened as he took a step back.

She ran from him before his fear of her burrowed under her skin.

137

Unsuccessful with Taizai, Ro didn't bother returning to Opal. Instead, she dedicated herself to see past the fire Henry ignited.

To earn him.

Observing him through the psych tests strained even her basic control. She snapped once, but Kekoa put her back together. When they made it home, when she put the Tower between herself and everyone else, she thought she might be able to do it.

A new dream woke her with warmth.

"Ro… C'mon, lie down with me."

She scrubbed the dream's promise with denial, leaning over to kiss Akira.

"I have to be up soon anyway, go back to sleep."

He kissed her fingers before he rolled over. She forced through the day, leashing her marking, managing her pain levels, refusing to punish Henry.

But it happened again and again, day after day. The fourth night, she craved Henry's Possession more than sleep. Her racing mind never settled, refusing to lock away memories of freedom.

He still held on to parts of her marking that her will couldn't interrupt. That self-betrayal hurt more than any pain Henry could ever inflict. She wasn't strong enough not to feel bitter.

She surrendered to the Web. She relished the light and wind pushing all the lives tugging at her back. She dived deep into the belly of the Tower. Her marking veered.

The pain stabbed with familiar precision, even muted by the Web's depth.

But it's not his fault.

But I can't teach him and fight myself at the same time.

She hated being responsible for him, success or failure, and she couldn't even help herself.

But it's not his fault.

She suffocated her consciousness. She ignored her marking's masochistic desire. She emerged from the Web, resigned to a cold shower. She hoped icy water would quench the boiling in her veins. The soap scoured her disappointments, but nothing settled her blood lancing through her feet.

Ro didn't know how she made it to the training fields on time.

"I hate running after breakfast," Kekoa complained.

"I hate running too."

Before, Ham would have called them both pussies and outran them both, no matter if they tried or not.

"Henry doesn't seem to mind."

"Hm."

"Still not sleeping, huh?"

She glared.

"Side-eye all you want, but I know you better."

She huffed. "I can't tell if he's worth it or not."

Kekoa leaned against her. "You don't try unless you think it's worth it, so... yeah, he is."

The twang in her blood slid through her protest like a knife. Her marking strained behind, her nerves wailing.

"Excellent, and on time as usual," Kekoa said.

Ro faced the two cadets. Henry's eyes flicked down when she turned, and her blood jumped to the balls of her feet.

"Today we introduce skills testing," Kekoa started. "Emergency medical care, ranged combat, close combat, artillery, and on and on. Is that clear?"

"Yes sir!"

"Excellent. We are going to head up to the shooting range at twelve hundred hours."

"We'll go close combat."

Kekoa nodded and walked off with Shai. Henry stared at her like he was going to throw up. He hadn't looked so nervous since his first days in the Tower.

She quelled rage at his wallowing.

You have no fucking idea.

Shame flooded her cheeks. The pain he dealt her, unaware as he was to it, made a primal part of her hungry to hit back. For the second time since she met him, bile welled in her throat on Henry's behalf.

Henry stood there, head hung, shoulders drooping lower, and her blood thrashing to meet his averted gaze.

She steeled herself, blocking the pain out, blocking her marking out.

It's not his fault.

I am better than this.

She faced Henry's downturned head.

"PT first. You don't have to worry yet."

Henry took off. He flew through the morning, dragging her marking across the fields despite her will.

She ground her teeth.

She halted him early.

"It's time. Follow."

The pressure through her back, butt, and calves bit like hot pokers through her skin.

She had to conceded that Henry's brand was stronger than her marking's revolt during her first days in the Tower. Stronger than anything her marking had encountered before.

I am still stronger than this.

The sparring arena was almost full. She picked space on the far side of the spread of mats. Pia waved from the back. The blood wrenching though her side and away told her Henry waved back.

"How you feeling?"

"I'm ok."

"Good. Warm up however you did at the Yard. Let me observe."

She stalled. She waited as long as she could. "Enough. Your basic forms are decent. Let's see what you got."

She didn't flinch when her marking speared through her skin where Henry sighted. She read the blood-pull, moved like water around his strike.

Ro settled into battle-rigid precision; using her marking for combat, giving her pain purpose, helped her cope. She grimaced through Henry's offense, but her feet never faltered.

He never made contact, but she knew why.

"Why are you holding back?"

"I—"

"You think I wouldn't notice you're faster than this?"

"I'm not as clean if I go faster."

"All the more reason to practice. Come at me for real."

Henry nodded. He launched; her marking lashed. Undaunted, she grappled with Henry. She never struck until Henry made an obvious error.

She punched his kidney without power—a warning. "You're managing, but I won't accept shitty work."

"Yes sir."

Henry grinned. Her marking threatened to rip through her face.

I will be stronger than this.

CHAPTER THIRTY-TWO

She didn't stop until he grew tired enough to get sloppy.

"All right, enough. You're done."

Henry collapsed, bruises swelling across his knuckles and arms. Ro hid her pain.

"Your stamina has grown. I'm honestly impressed."

"Really?" Henry shot from the ground, his hope kindling a bonfire behind her eyes.

"That was pretty good," Pia snuck forward, flung an arm around Henry's shoulders.

"How long was your last rookie? Twenty some minutes?" Will called from the floor. He still panted.

Pia sniggered. "You weren't bad yourself."

Ro forced the corners of her mouth up, made it real. "Anytime, princess."

Henry looked between them. His eyes narrowed on Ro. "Were you holding back?"

"Today was just an assessment."

"Why? You thrashed me in PT."

Pia interrupted, "Because if she really let loose you'd be in the infirmary for a week."

"And Pia knows from experience," Will said.

"What? No never mind," Henry turned to Ro.

Ro's will held, but her control ceded ground to her marking by the second. She knew this feeling. His intensity was shredding her cell by cell. She broke his eye contact, landing on Pia.

Of course.

"What'd you tell him?"

Pia blanched. "Me? Nothing."

"Did you tell him?"

"Tell me what?"

"Of course I did!" Pia broke. "Ro, his marking... he had to know."

"It's not an option. Not with his scores."

"But Ro—"

"I can't use my marking," Henry caught her arm. "And I'm not going home. Not now."

The contact spiked through her shoulder. She tugged away.

"Your marking could be the biggest weapon in the Tower. The other areas of training are important, but to spend your efforts on them is careless when what you have is so overwhelming." Henry started to boil over, so she held up a hand. "Let me finish. Now, your efforts seem useless, but just as you have grown physically, your marking still could too. You need patience."

"I grew eleven centimeters in one night, but I can't summon a Shadow. Pia said," he paused, "I'm foolish for not training close combat with you as my Lieutenant anyway."

My Lieutenant.

"You achieved Possession," she reminded.

Henry shut his mouth. Pia came to her side, her touch a feather to Henry's burn.

"Ro, what if he can't use his marking anyway? He needs options."

He'd be safe with her.

She trusted Pia beyond question. Giving him training he could use to stay in the White Wings without her direct contact would...

Be liberating.

The corners of her mouth quirked, and she caught Pia's quick nod.

Thank you.

"Roxar expects your marked training to continue. I can't spend more time on close combat, but what you do in your free time is up to you." She inclined her head. Henry beamed. "I expect you in the Webbed room at fourteen hundred hours. Go. Eat. Recover."

"Yes sir, thank you sir."

Pia led Henry hand in hand. Ro's blood bit deeper the further Henry walked away. Ro sank to the ground, willing her blood back to normal, back to controllable. Her mind ricocheted through her skull like a drunk. Instability she hadn't felt in years trickled into her like venom.

"You like him." Will stood over her with a knowing expression on his face.

If only.

"Does Akira know?"

"Like is not the word I'd use," she shook her head. "I need to get out of here."

He offered her a hand up. "Me too, need to swing through the lab."

She took it.

"Wait, did you mean…" Will's color paled.

She squeezed his hand before dropping it. "Don't worry about it."

"If you say so."

Will followed her until she came to a vein. He hugged her fast before she dived.

"Are you… is it happening again?"

"Yeah."

"Is it Henry?"

"Naturally."

"Who else knows?"

"No one, but I'll be fine. You don't need to worry."

She figured he would despite her reassurances. He'd probably tell Pia and Kekoa, maybe Akira. She sighed.

"Ro, we're here for you. Remember that."

"Always. Thanks."

One.

Two.

Three.

Four.

Moments later, her feet touched orange sand. It gave way as she sprinted as hard and fast as she was able. She tore through the Thalweg's thick swells. Feet on sand again, paler and finer than before, she ran to her grove.

The *moment* she crossed that indistinct barrier, her marking vanished. Blind without the pull, she relished the sprint over the beach, through the jungle, to the pool. She splashed into the silver water, floating.

All she knew came from her sight. The water muffled her hearing. None of the plants offered aroma. Her free-floating marking left only her skin to touch.

The sensory deprivation restored her balance within the hour, but her need for sleep left no stamina to maintain it. She dreaded returning to Henry, but mustered the steel in her soul.

CHAPTER THIRTY-THREE

Going back to PT was special treatment after so long in the field. Henry faced the Webbed wall in record time.

"I've had a small discussion with Roxar," Ro began. "Some program changes are in order so that you can access your dormant marking, seeing as you've successfully executed a complete Possession. We are going to start diving," she paused. "Well?"

Henry swallowed. "The diving rule?"

"Suspended for you."

Henry didn't answer.

"Come here."

He came beside her, watched the blue-touched silver slide over her skin.

"We are going to start very, very, very basic."

"Isn't casting a Shadow basic?"

"It is the most basic manipulation of the Web marked Wings can do. It requires our willpower to achieve. All Wings can dive, which requires no will to direct your marking, and since your marking worked in the Web, that's where we're going."

He sighed.

"You promised you wouldn't do that again, right? I trust you," she said.

Henry pressed his fingers against his eyes. He breathed in and out. He stood taller.

"What do I do?"

"Let's lay some groundwork out. You said you couldn't really think when you Possessed me."

"Right."

"The more exposure you have to the Web, the easier that reaction will be to control. That feeling, by the way—like your boiling up, but it feels great, and your mind goes on a one-way trip out the ass—is your Life responding to the Web. No matter how strong you become, the Web will always draw you." Darkness pooled in her irises.

"How do I stop the Possession?"

"Possession manifested because you thought of me. You couldn't know, but to the Web, that only means my Life, so it gave you my Life. Now that you understand the connection between the Web and Life you'll be able to contact people without actually taking them."

Henry paused, a thousand segues pouring through his mind.

"Actually," he faced her. "I don't understand the dimensions. You didn't get into it on watch."

"I'm not getting into it during a lesson on basics."

"Why not?"

"Because I care more about stopping you from Possessing anyone else unintentionally than I do about your curiosity."

"So, when I can control my marking?"

"Sure, then we'll talk. Now, shut up, and listen." She grabbed his hand and pressed it into the silver.

Henry sighed, disappointed she withheld answers again, but focused on adjusting to the heat on his skin.

"Up to the elbow." She sunk her arm in, and the Web glowed around her. Henry mimicked her. His arm glowed too, but without her internal flare.

"That glow is the Web responding to you as a lifeform. Doesn't matter that you're not doing anything, that's just the natural reaction. If you apply your will, then we can change the glow. Watch." The brightness intensified, but the light shrunk to a ball on her palm. "All I'm doing is thinking about my palm. Just focus somewhere specific and allow the natural reaction to happen."

Henry narrowed his eyes on the big crease running across his palm. In and out. Crease. In and out. Crease. He felt nothing, but bright strings shifted. Hundreds of tiny filaments pulsed their way into a new shape. A silver line ran across his palm and up into the Tower.

"Good," she praised him. "Easy right?"

"Yes sir."

She smiled and kept talking. He smiled too, for himself. It was the first step they should have had.

"You look happy," Pia said a couple hours later. "Finally cast a Shadow?"

"No. The Commander changed my training, and it's going better. I'm starting diving."

"Well, well," she smiled big, the kind that cheered people up.

"And Ro lifted remedial."

"In that case, you have some free time. Want to spar?"

"Yes sir."

The next day, his morning PT was almost good. Ro allowed him to submerge his whole body in the Web. She called it floating, said it'd be a good meditation practice. After an hour and a half, he could ignore the Web's hot temptation. That's when Ro suggested more.

"Dive. Go for it."

"Really?"

"I think so."

"Thanks Ro."

She smiled. Hope buoyed his nerves.

"I'll intervene if you need it."

She entered the Web ahead of him. Henry followed her. Brightness burned through his eyelids. The glow was tainted blue on his right. A light pressure on his palm zapped through his spine. Steady. In, out. Ro's fingers interlaced with his. A gentle squeeze. He squeezed back. She let him go.

Henry drew a deep breath. In, Out.

He dived. Diving while already in the Web meant no noise. No pressure. Just movement. The Web burned brighter. Air sped past him. His brain fought the euphoria and won. He focused on Ro's teaching, imagined pushing away from the Web. Just shifting… and his body banked. Right. Then left. Left, down, right, dive, ascend. He kept twisting and turning, mastering the movement. Satisfied he… he didn't know how to stop.

His nerves nuked his brain.

A hand grasped his ankle. His speed reduced, the pressure on his mind vanishing. Two hands climbed his body until her fingers interlaced with his. She towed him from the Web.

"You did fine," she praised.

"How do I stop?"

"This is not at all how it works, but it's a close analogy. When we dive, we don't actually go any faster or slower, but the paths we travel do run faster or slower."

"Speed comes from the Web not the diver?"

"Yes. The most common paths are called threads but they are the smallest and the fastest. They're actually highly unstable, so Wings don't use them. Radials encompass multiple threads, so they're bigger. Lots bigger. That's what Weavers use. Then, there are veins. veins are the largest, and the most accessible, but that makes them the slowest. All Wings access what is called the base vein. Think of it as the vein that requires the least amount of energy to travel on. Now, most Wings can just think of going faster and slower and they have high enough compatibility with the Web that they can move without needing willpower. For us, if your will is strong enough, you can make the deeper dives to get to radials. If you're seriously accomplished, you dive in the threads."

"So how do I do I get to other veins?"

"Practice."

"Then… race me?" he asked.

Ro smiled bigger than ever, but she didn't meet his eyes.

He held out his hand. "I'm not going to Possess you."

Her lips thinned. She took his hand.

"We start inside. First one to the supplementary training fields. I'll flash three bursts then we go."

Henry nodded. He walked her into the Web. She squeezed his hand once—tight and warm. The first surge of brightness penetrated his eye lids.

He focused on the fields. The sunlight. The salty air.

The second flash ignited. Ro let go of his hand.

He focused on winning.

The third burst of light came, and Henry launched. He erupted from the wall outside in two seconds.

She beat him. Ro's arms crossed over her chest, a cocky smile taunting him.

He didn't care. He smiled too.

CHAPTER THIRTY-FOUR

"And after that?" Pia swiped at his head. He ducked under her foot.

"We raced the rest of the time. Nav spec tomorrow." He kicked. She slid around him and slapped against his right ear. He stumbled.

"Next time I won't hold back. Go faster," she commanded.

"Yes sir," Henry grinned. He closed twice as fast, but she spun away from his fist and smacked him in the same ear.

"You're just too easy, Cadet," she cooed.

Henry launched, each punch and kick faster than the last. He got her once, knocking her down. He pressed on top of her.

"Yield."

She kissed him and flipped him.

"Cheater."

She winked.

She towed him to her quarters after. When he made it back to his own, he dreamt of flying through the Tower with Ro on his arm.

"Henry!" Shai punched him in the shoulder.

"Ow!" Henry jolted awake.

"I've tried to wake you up four times now!"

"Fuck," Henry burst from his sheets. He ran to the bathroom and tugged his suit on. Even sprinting, they'd be late. He grabbed Shai's arm.

"Let's dive, it's faster!"

"Against the rules idiot!"

"Not for me. I'll do it," Henry assured him. "C'mon!"

"I'm not covering your ass for this," Shai grinned.

Henry led them to the nearest vein.

"Grab my arm."

Shai held just above the elbow. Henry did the same.

Henry breathed. In. Out. Training fields.

Sound blasted Henry's ears, heralding regret. He hadn't started inside the Web. Last time he went through a vein like this he Possessed Ro. Fear squeezed through the Web's burning. Shai's weight dragged him down. The wind snapping his braids died. The heat on his face lessened.

Henry strained. He fought the Web, pushing himself forward on determination without risking Shai.

A hand came down on the back of his suit. In a breath, they burst into the sunlight. Ro whipped Henry around to face her.

"Explain. Yourself." Her tone seared his ears.

"I am practicing, sir," Henry placated, like soothing a Handakau sandlion.

Ro crossed her arms and hung her head. The brightest light Henry had ever seen grew in the onyx behind her. It grew until the glow condensed into the outline of a woman with milk eyes. A crack in sound revealed the Commander, his marked hand glowing like a torch. Kekoa spewed from the wall a second after. All three looked at Ro. She pointed at Henry. The Commander approached.

Henry and Shai saluted. Henry couldn't stop staring at the shining palm.

"An explanation please, Cadet Harbor."

"Lieutenant Sech taught me to dive yesterday. I am practicing sir."

"And why is Cadet Jukita with you?"

"It was convenient, sir," Henry's stomach kicked itself.

"Ah. Rolyn?" The Commander turned to her.

"I did not give him permission to dive alone, but he did do well yesterday."

"He did excellently," came a gravelly voice. From the light. Henry gaped.

"Henry meet Opal, Opal-Henry," Ro swished her hand between them. Henry's breath caught, and his eyes flicked toward Shai. Shai's chin dipped once.

"Fix his diving technique," Opal suggested. The brilliant light bled from the wall.

"As always, Opal is right, but his manners are flawless. You've truly surpassed yourself," the Commander pet her shoulder. Ro scowled.

"Yes sir," she muttered.

"Cadets. Lieutenant Omika. Rolyn," the Commander nodded to each before sound swallowed him.

Ro shivered, then glared at Henry. "That was really stupid."

"It's my fault, sir," Henry said.

"Let me finish," she held up a finger, "just let me finish." She breathed deep. "Both of you are really stupid. Henry, you just started diving yesterday, and never from outside the Web. Shai, you're a moron for listening to him."

"We told them that they couldn't dive until they became Wings, right?" Kekoa glowered.

"You know what? I think I do remember saying that. Isn't that right, Cadets?"

"Yes sir." Shai's cheeks glowed. Henry sounded quiet.

"I think its suicide-sprints day," Kekoa said. Ro laughed.

"I think so."

The extra PT thrashed Henry. The lieutenants made Henry and Shai race each other up a steep incline carrying double their body weight. Since Henry was lighter than Shai, Ro added an extra fifty kilos on him. They got through their fourth race before Shai puked. Kekoa kept giving Shai shit as he took him to his next torture. Ro gave Henry double sets of PT and three extra rounds of cardio. It took hours that left him exhausted, cranky, and starving.

"You look awful."

"Feel awful," Henry held his sides.

"Webbed room," she commanded.

"Wait, sir," Henry risked. "I never ate. Can we please get some food?"

She relented. She eyed him as he devoured three plates. When he finished, she still hadn't said a word.

"I'm sorry for this morning."

Her lips churned like she chewed her tongue. After a moment, she sighed.

"I could feel you straining. I'm guessing Shai felt like a sack of bricks?"

Henry nodded.

"When you've dived with me, I actively dived with you. Shai just stood there and let you drag him in. Here's the thing. Your dive was pretty stable even if it didn't feel that way. The problem was how loud you were."

"Loud?"

"Well, diving makes… a reaction, we'll call it, when you cross into the Web. You know that loud crack? And the pressure?"

Henry nodded.

"There is a similar reaction while someone travels in the Web, but we all perceive it differently. I kind of feel it like sound. It rings in my blood. Anyway, you dived without an ounce of control. It sounded like a cannon in there," she chuckled and stood. "Webbed room?"

Henry wiped his mouth. "Yes sir."

Ro drilled him with a nav spec, assigning him moving targets to collect. Eventually she put together a course through the tower with dive points and sprints in between. He saw more of the Tower in two hours than he had in weeks.

"Good," Ro praised. He had completed the fifth Web sprint faster than the other times.

"Thanks," Henry gasped.

"So now, we are going to try something a little different."

Henry groaned. "C'mon Ro, I'm dying."

She smiled. "Why fight?"

Henry paused. "Because I'm strong."

She nodded. "Yes. We're going to dive together. Whoever pulls the other out of the Web first wins. Don't lose."

"What?" Henry balked. "Shai was hard enough, and he wasn't trying to be dead weight!"

"Karma," Ro flashed teeth. She grabbed his hand and yanked him into the Web. He strained against her unshakeable grip. He pushed harder. Nothing changed their trajectory. They zapped through her intended portal.

"Isn't that cheating?" Henry demanded.

She shrugged. "Go faster."

Henry blinked, seeing Pia's impish pleasure in her. He improvised. He drop kicked Ro back through the portal and dived after her feet. He dragged her upside down to the nearest portal.

Her feet tugged against his hold and her ankles shifted. Her fist crashed into his face like a battering ram. He flinched, reflexively letting her go. Her hand grabbed around his forearm and she hauled him back through the same portal.

His nose wasn't broken but it bled. Ro's held back a smile.

"Better. And clever. But let's limit the striking, ok?"

"Ok."

"It was a good kick though."

Henry beamed.

CHAPTER THIRTY-FIVE

Henry and Shai had a couple free hours the night before their third mission. Kekoa and Ro had kept them so busy they'd never been awake enough to discuss Opal.

"She's the Gatekeeper."

"So, she has a marking too?" Shai confirmed.

"Yes. But Ro's been vague about it."

Shai rubbed his temples as he paced.

"And Ro said she won't answer your questions until you can control your marking?"

"Yes. And about that," Henry hesitated. "I think someone is interfering with my marking."

"Interfering how?" Shia frowned.

"It started the second time I tried to use my marking. It just felt...different. Like something intentionally prevented me from using it."

"How come you didn't say anything before now?"

"Ro shot that idea down when I told her. Since I couldn't use my marking at all, I guess I went along with her. But now, after the Possession, I think there is something else going on."

"What did it feel like?"

"Like... like the first day, there just wasn't anything there. Everything I tried was useless. Since, it's always felt like I'm pushing against something, like a wall maybe."

"A wall, hm." Shai let his head fall back. "Doesn't sound like much."

"I know."

Shai sighed, "You really think it's intentional?"

"Yeah."

"Who would benefit from you not using your marking?"

"I have no idea."

"Think that's what Opal meant? Ask Ro about this, block, thing?"

"Maybe," Henry considered.

"Speaking of which," Shai's tone grew light. "Akira's been hinting things aren't going well."

"When have you been hanging around Akira?" Henry asked.

"Has she said anything?" Shai deflected.

"You're interested?" Henry faced him.

"Kekoa said she used to date their old teammate and it wasn't weird."

"Really."

Neither could look at each other.

Shai didn't answer for a moment. "Akira's been training with us for a couple days. I'm working on my giant."

Henry whistled. "You gonna do the trial?"

"I want to. Kekoa doesn't think I'm ready. He said maybe when the next round of cadets come."

"Still awesome," Henry congratulates him.

"Thanks," Shai smiled. He sighed. "Doesn't feel like our third mission, does it?"

"Nope." The string of back to back missions during the psych test made it their tenth assignment.

"What do you think we'll do this time?" Shai mused.

"Not sure, but I hope it's better."

"I bet they'll let us sleep this time. They wouldn't give us the same test."

"Why not? It'd validate results."

"No," Shai shook his head. "That's what the academies are for."

"Well… It doesn't even feel like academy, does it?"

Shai frowned at him. "Should it?"

"Not the missions. All of it. The White Wings. It doesn't feel…
strict."

"Maybe for you. You're marked. On my end, it's pretty strict."

"Kekoa is nowhere near Ro," Henry countered.

"Not what I meant."

"How then?"

They were both standing, eyeing each other.

"How? Why don't you go first? How are the White Wings not
'strict'?"

"Diving, today. The Commander, Ro, Kekoa they all warned us."

"And you did it anyway."

"With no punishment?" Henry asked. Shai's mouth snapped
shut. "If I did that the Yard-"

"But this isn't that Yard. And you're a special case. The rules
don't apply to you the way they do to me."

"No. Rank is the only rule. We aren't even White Wings,"
Henry persisted. "I disobeyed a direct order with no real
consequence. Military- the academies- doesn't work this way."
Shai leaned in, but Henry continued, "Even for special cases."

Shai's lips pressed thin. "I got special treatment."

"You didn't break the rules, just records," Henry laughed.

"I didn't ask for it," Shai snapped.

"I know you didn't. Let's focus on the White Wings?" Henry
suggested. Shai slumped on his bed.

"Fine."

"It doesn't bother you?" Henry asked.

"Not really," Shai rolls over, facing him. "This isn't training
anymore. It's not practice. Real world can't be that rigid."

"It doesn't feel right."

"We're soldiers, Henry. We take orders. Not feelings."

Henry's argument withered. Growing up in a military academy
desensitized him to authority. At the Yard, he only played solider.
His true focus lay in his studies. At the Tower, every move was

significant. His usefulness to the Commander was the only measure now.

He remembered Ro's nightmare and told Shai.

"Again, why didn't you tell me before?"

"Wasn't much to tell."

"You mean there was nothing to confirm, but anything between Ro and the Commander is a big fucking deal."

"I… I'm sorry. I should have."

"Yeah. We're teammates, Henry. Santos. As long as we've got each other, it's steady." He clapped Henry on the shoulder and turned toward his bed. Not fast enough. Henry saw the doubt swirling in his expression.

"You believe me now?"

Shai froze.

"Something's up."

"Probably," Shai nodded.

"And you're not worried?" Henry pressed.

"Listen, I trust Kekoa," Shai turned to Henry. "You trust Ro?"

"Yes."

"Then she would have told you if it was a problem, right?"

"Would she? If it's the commander?"

Shai had no answer. Neither did Henry.

"What if—"

"Henry, were you ever going to be anything but a soldier?" A glint hardened Shai's gaze.

"I was accepted to the military programs in the late screenings. For years I thought I'd grow up to be a farmer or a miner."

"Everyone in my family has excelled in the military. I grew up fighting my brothers and sisters. I never did anything but take someone else's orders." He laughed again. "Did you want to be a farmer?"

"No."

"Miner?"

"Definitely not."

"I don't think I would have either," Shai admitted. "But I envy you your childhood."

Shai's eyes pleaded with Henry to read his truth.

Henry thought of the anger that corroded his vision when Taizai revealed the truth about the dimensions. Shai never knew anything but commands and praise his whole life. Henry would never know the kind of bitterness Shai felt at Henry's revelations.

Henry's questions may have unseated Shai's world, but Shai still had his team.

"Shai, you'll be one of the giant Wings."

"I will."

"I'll get past this block, or whatever it is, and I'll become a marked Wing."

"You will."

"We are going to be Santos. Two giants and two marked Wings."

"We will be unstoppable."

"Death, life, and the Web."

Shai shuddered. "Death, life, and the Web."

CHAPTER THIRTY-SIX

Kekoa yawned, "We're going just us this time. No babysitters. This is an escort mission. Get the cargo to the extraction point and turn it over. Security and speed are our top priorities. Relations with the Hibikans are established, but they've come up short on the last three deliveries. We'll negotiate to a point, but the Commander won't press this issue yet. When we land, I'll give Henry a set of coordinates, and we'll start fast. We'll need to cover up to sixty kilometers before nightfall."

"Yes sir," Shai and Henry respond.

"Good."

They dived to a ruined station, scorched earth presaging the abandoned planet. Ro's marking found survivors. She bled onto Henry's palm.

Her blood thrummed to the point of pain against his skin. The pain, ephemeral as it was intense, settled into the vibrations he was used to from the nav spec.

"Instead of focusing on coordinates, think of people."

The vibration focused to a point when he faced his feet.

"They're on the other side of the planet."

"Can't we dive?" Shai asked.

"No portals over there," Kekoa grumbled.

"Can't you just—" Shai flicked his wrist at Ro.

"I could create a new portal in the Web, but I'd be wasted for a couple days. Your legs aren't broken."

In the poor soil, they made bad time, taking almost four days. As they drew closer, an acrid smell made Henry nauseous.

Corpses—charred flesh and bone—piled high, about three deep. Four broken people, still stacking.

The smell stuck in Henry's nose. Ash and burnt meat.

Kekoa pushed forward, his medical gear in hand. Ro stood by, waiting for instruction. Henry and Shai mimicked her with revolting stomachs

A chemical spill in the main hub had started it; the arid atmosphere fueled the inferno. Nine of them made it out of the lab. Nine out of thirty-one. Those nine used the resources in the mobile labs they could salvage to combat the flames. They beat it down to a smolder. For four days, they kept it at bay. On the fifth morning, rain extinguished the embers. Five escaped the fire. One died from her injuries—fell over carrying a woman's body and never got up. Now, she lay in the pile too.

The fallout imprinted on Henry's retinas. He couldn't see past the burn scars on the survivors' limbs. Nothing permeated the carnage clinging to his nose.

The main hub had collapsed, burying Santos' cargo. Ro assigned Henry and Shai to dig it out.

Henry and Shai stared at the rubble.

"I wanted to talk about the Commander."

"So did I."

Shai turned wide eyes to Henry.

"I can't."

"Me either."

The debris, dense from six floors above and below ground, provided release from the death around Henry. Henry didn't speak through his labor.

That first night, the inescapable smell stuck no matter how far out Henry and Shai staked their campsite. When Ro arrived, she carried an armful of firewood. Henry swallowed bile. He couldn't start the fire that night.

"What happened to the bodies?" Shai's voice cracked.

Ro dumped the firewood and stretched, her shoulders drooping with exhaustion.

"I gave them peace."

"You buried all of them? In one day?"

"I did."

Shai traded looks with Henry. Henry shook his head. Shai rolled his eyes. He crossed the space to her.

"You doing ok?"

"Yes. Why?"

"You sound… wiped out. Death is hard," Shai fumbled his words.

"I certainly didn't kill them."

"Of course you didn't. You were responsible for their ending."

"To me that's not dealing with death. It's about respect."

"Fine," Shai gave her space. "I'll do the fire," he mumbled.

Ro stared at his back as he bent over the firewood. Gratitude warmed her eyes, and Henry stiffened at the way she kept looking at Shai's back.

Kekoa came back hours later. They had eaten already. Kekoa skipped an offered plate and hugged Ro.

"Okay?"

"Like lieutenant, like cadet," she smiled at Shai.

Shai and Ro annoyed each other the rest of night. Kekoa interrupted a few times to mediate. When night came, they took individual guard shifts. Henry took the last. He watched over his teammates until the sun rose. Shai grumbled about the light, burrowing into his sleeping bag. Kekoa kept snoring.

Ro woke. She moaned, her voice husky. She stretched. The sun glinted on her lips when she yawned.

"Morning."

"Morning," Henry mumbled back. Her eyes brightened, a soft smile clearing hazy eyes, before she left to relieve herself.

The morning air relieved death's odor, and Henry smiled after Ro.

Ro helped Henry and Shai clear the remaining debris. Instead of a shovel, she molded her blood in a giant cradle spanning both arms. Her marking-made shovel carried more than Henry or Shai. Henry pushed himself harder every time she passed him with a bigger load than his.

They found the onyx before sunset. The waited three more hours until Kekoa finished treating the wounded. They dived back to the Tower. Some lab rats took the onyx off them.

"I'm going to Roxar about the lab," Ro said. She dived on the spot.

"I'm going to let Hettar know about the wounded and send an evac team," Kekoa left too.

"So, what now?" Shai asked Henry.

"Now, shower."

CHAPTER THIRTY-SEVEN

The brush with tragedy overhung Henry and Shai. It took a week to settle back into routine, chatting, laughing, and teasing. Neither Ro nor Kekoa pressed them about it.

"Don't you think that's weird?" Shai asked.

"No."

"But it is!"

"It's not weird to be quiet about death."

"But—"

"You're reaching," Henry smiled.

Shai resumed pacing. "I'm not used to questioning everything." He paused. "We don't really know anything about Ro or the Commander."

"Not really. Listen, I don't mean for you to get wrapped up in anything you shouldn't."

"You mean in a markings thing? So what? Kept something else from me?"

Henry hesitated. "No."

Shai laughed. "Is it that bad?"

"I don't know," Henry caved. "That first watch, she never clearly explained what Life or Death were, but she said the Web was more than another universe that we can travel. She said it's a literal web between all life forms. Marked Wings could use it to Possess people."

Shai blinked. "Then what are Death and Life?"

"Exactly."

Shai frowned. "Henry, you mentioned three abilities once. Was the Commander's Possession?"

"Yes."

"What's hers?"

"Blending?"

"What could Blending do through the Web?"

Henry stilled. He'd never asked that question. "I have no idea."

"If there really is something going on between the Commander and Ro, you're already caught up in it, especially if one of them is involved with the block."

Henry froze, his mind churning through consequences he hadn't thought of. "We need answers. Fast."

"A lot faster. You have to talk to her."

"I—" Henry stammered.

"Let's go find her."

"Now?"

"Yes, now. What else are we going to do?" Shai demanded.

"What would we say?"

"If she won't tell us what the dimensions are, or about the block, then we press about the Commander. I'm all ears if you have a better plan."

"I don't."

"I know," Shai gloated.

"Fine. Only if she's alone."

"Fine," Shai held out his hand, and Henry heard the tremor behind his next words. "Death, life, and the Web."

Henry took his arm. "Doesn't mean the same anymore, does it?"

"Still teammates."

"Then, Santos."

Shai grinned. "Santos."

They sped through the Tower to a private sparring room. Ro battled an immense Atal with spiked up hair. He stood over three and a half meters, but his intelligent eyes intimidated more than his wingspan. He and Ro were stripped to essentials. He was muscled like a beast; her lean definition looked normal next to him. His scars stood out compared to her unmarred skin.

Both disengaged the moment Henry and Shai interrupted.

"Is this serious?" Ro turned toward them. Shai's jaw dropped at her sweaty, bared body.

"Not really, but I'd like a go," Henry eyed the monstrous Atal.

The Atal's laugh rumbled. "Who's this?"

"A Cadet who's going to get his ass out of here."

"Next time?" Henry pressed.

"Out!" Ro shouted. Henry and Shai left but lingered.

"Who was that?" Henry asked.

"She's unbelievable," Shai blurted.

Henry deadpanned.

"I'm sorry. She caught me off guard."

"Have you never seen tits, or something?" Henry grumbled.

"I've never seen hers," Shai emphasized.

"Whatever. Who was that?"

"Never seen him before. Bet Kekoa or Pia'd know."

"Let's try Pia."

Shai shrugged so Henry sent the comet off. They found her in the mess, louder, happier, and more crowded than normal.

"What's going on?" Henry asked.

"One of the Majors got back."

"Major? Never seen that rank before," Shai frowned.

"You wouldn't. They're all stationed off base and they go solo. No teams."

"No teams?" Shai sputtered.

"That's right. Majors are rare. There are only nine active majors in the Wings right now, and that's a high number compared to previous years."

"What do Majors do if they don't have teams?" Shai pressed.

Henry leaned in. He couldn't fathom what a single Wing could do that a team couldn't.

"They are kind of like the special forces of the White Wings. Their missions are heavily classified. I have no idea what they do."

"Is this Major a big Atal with—"

Pia interrupted, "You met Turtle?"

"Who?"

"It's actually Major Wade Rake, but I've never heard anyone call him that. He prefers Turtle."

"Weird," Shai crossed his arms.

"Who cares? He does advanced hand-to-hand combat when he's around. Ro and I trained under him when we first made Wingman. He's not around much anymore," she lamented.

Henry's unease accelerated through his logic. Instead of getting answers, the knowledge that Majors existed made him more cautious. He hoped to catch Shai's eyes but the giant brooded.

That night, Pia kicked him out instead of cuddling.

"No. I'm tired. Go away."

"That's not what you said an hour ago," Henry teased.

"Shut up," Pia grumbled.

"All right, fine."

She pressed a kiss to his lips before he got out of bed. As he was about to leave, Pia came up behind him. Her arms wrapped around him and she sighed into his back. He leaned into her warmth.

"Everyone's happier. Is it because Turtle's back?"

"Yes," she breathed into his skin. "We don't have too many things to celebrate."

Henry closed his eyes. In that way, the Tower was the same as the academies. The military lacked individuality. It was necessary. So, anything bright shined, especially in the Tower's darkness.

Henry guided her back to bed and tucked her in.

"Good night, Henry," she smiled.

"Night, Pia." He leaned down to kiss her because she shined too bright.

CHAPTER THIRTY-EIGHT

Shai made him promise to ask Ro during PT. She beat him to it.

"Why'd you find me yesterday?" she asked after cardio.

"Still want—to know—about—dimensions—" He said with each sit up.

"Keep going. Stop talking. Listen. You have questions. I have some answers, but I'm not an expert. Not just that, but I told you that it was only different for marked wings. Until you earn that, you don't need to know."

"Not fair—might help—"

"Keep talking and I'm upping your reps."

Henry shut his mouth and kept crunching.

"It wouldn't. If I thought knowing would help you control your marking I would've told you on day one. This is all on you."

Henry stared at her but kept silent rep after rep.

She rolled her eyes. "What?"

"If I don't—make it—not fair—gimme chance—"

"A chance?" she blinked. "Actually…" she jogged to the wall and a flash darted from her fingers. "You can stop. If I hear back soon I'll give you your chance." She smiled.

Henry groaned and lifted from the grass to join her.

"Thanks Ro."

"I'll remind you that you thanked me for this when you get your ass beat." Silver swam toward her.

"Sure," came Turtle's deep voice.

"You still want a go?"

"Definitely."

"Good. Beat Turtle and I'll tell you about the dimensions."

"What? But he's a major! That's not—"

"You asked for a chance. Hasn't Pia been giving you extra hand-to-hand?"

Henry glowered at her.

"This isn't fair either."

"Take it or leave it."

"Let's go," Henry said.

Ro led him to the private sparring room. He jogged in place until Turtle arrived. The Major pulled Ro into a hug. She squeezed him back.

"So I'm testing your pup?"

"He's all yours." She backed away.

"Come here son," the Atal boomed. Henry obeyed. "Let's go ten minutes. Show me what you've learned."

"Yes sir."

Henry stepped forward and focused. He steadied his breath. He had one chance.

Turtle took the offensive but Henry dodged it all. Turtle held up a hand.

"You've worked with Pia too, haven't you?"

"Yes sir."

Turtle laughed. "Good man." Eager eyes appraised Henry with new focus. "Ro said this was a bet, but I've got no stakes. May I add my own?"

Ro shrugged. Henry nodded.

"If you beat me, I'll make you a combat Wing."

Henry froze.

"You don't have that authority," Ro scoffed.

"The Commander owes me a favor," Turtle shrugged. He pointed at Henry. "If you're as good as I think you could be, then you'll get there anyway on your own."

Henry couldn't breathe.

"Would I still be Santos?"

"Up to the Commander."

"Yes." New determination surged through Henry, making him tremble in his boots.

"Good. Give me all you got. Don't hold back."

"Yes sir!"

Henry charged. Turtle's style was similar to Pia and Ro, but Henry couldn't anticipate his moves or his speed. It made Henry get creative.

"That's time," Ro stepped into their field of vision.

"What?" Henry exploded. He'd only begun processing Turtle's skills.

"It was a strong effort," Turtle nodded to him.

"But—"

"Next time."

"Next time?" Henry repeated, looking between the two.

Ro sighed. "Sure, why not?"

"And you?" Turtle turned to her. "Last night was not enough."

"'I can do tonight. I'll ask Pia if she can. Alberio won't be here, left three days ago for Sharshun."

"All right. Tonight then." Turtle hugged her again before he left.

"Does that mean you and Pia are going to spar?" Henry asked.

"Yes."

"Can I watch?"

"I'm sure you won't be the only one," she huffed.

"What do you mean?"

"Turtle's probably the most experienced combat soldier in the Wings. He only trains Pia, myself, and another Horn on team Tayir. He singled us out as the best in the Tower, so whenever two of us train together, especially when he's around…"

"How many people watch?"

"I don't know. Never focus on them."

"Oh. So, when can I spar with Turtle again?"

"That's up to him," she waved his question off. "You'll get your chance Henry. And until then…" she offered him a hand.

He took it. She hauled him to his feet.

"No more questions, huh?"

"That's right Cadet."

They met up with Shai and Kekoa at the mess.

"I hear you're sparring with Pia tonight," Kekoa's eyebrow arched.

"Who already knows?"

"Everyone," Kekoa snickered.

Pia ran through the mists straight for them. Several people hollered at her. More people chanted Ro's name.

"Tonight? Really?" she exclaimed.

"Mhm," Ro nodded.

"Going to beat you this time," Pia beamed, sitting next to her friend.

"In your dreams," Ro bumped against her shoulder.

"Kekoa, how much are you betting this time?" Pia thrust her chin at him.

"Betting?" Henry turned to Shai.

"Apparently they bet liquor. I didn't even know they had moonshine," Shai grumbled.

"Are you still upset about that?" Kekoa chuckled, looking over.

"I can't believe you won't share," Shai scowled.

"You're not a Wing yet," Kekoa shrugged.

"Gonna be," Shai muttered for Henry alone.

CHAPTER THIRTY-NINE

Bodies plastered Henry and Shai to the wall of the sparring room. At least sixty others crammed into the tight space. Ro walked in first.

"What the—"

Noise muffled her frustration.

"No!" she bellowed. Everyone shut up. She crossed her arms. "You're all ridiculous. We'll take it to the arena. If you bet on me, you're sharing later."

Cheers deafened Henry as he and Shai followed the horde out. A mass of comets lit the way. Shai found Kekoa's head and pulled Henry toward him. Kekoa chatted with Akira about their bets, both on Ro.

The crowd came to a massive misted door. On the other side, they stood in a giant pit. The domed ceiling illuminated a thirty-meter arena below. Turtle, Ro, and Pia already stood in the center.

"Welcome!" Turtle's voice canceled out the noise. "While I don't mind spectators, I'll remind you if you distract my pupils from their work, I'll throw you out myself."

The people next to Henry quivered in silence. The crowd hung on Ro and Pia's every move. Pia roved her corner, restless. Ro didn't move but seemed to grow. Henry doubted either listened to Turtle's instructions.

"Three rounds. We'll use a tournament point system. Ten points per round. Do you have your suit specs?"

Both nodded.

"Good. On my mark…" Turtle's hand swung.

Ro leaned in to Pia's hair-raising smile. Henry concentrated on their whirling strikes. He gleaned their familiarity with one another. Pia's smile grew as her movements sharpened. Ro's icy resolve didn't yield, her movement economic. He'd never seen people of this caliber fight.

Henry couldn't help but feel cheated. Pia never gave him the chance to reach this level in training. Ro never focused on hand-to-hand with him at all. Yet, both were masters. Henry seethed at their half-assed training.

A timer went off before either of them get a solid hit. Turtle broke them apart. They breathed deep but not hard. Henry watched them walk about, switch out their wraps. Pia's smug gaze. Ro's frosty confidence. Henry's aggravation ratcheted when he realized they had only warmed up and were now ready to begin.

Both entered the second round with the same bravado: Pia's glee and Ro's chill. Turtle's hand swung, and they flew across the floor toward each other. Viciousness earned each a critical hit in the first thirty seconds. The next minutes taxed their limits, both women increasing their blows in speed and strength. The timer sounded when both had reached nine points.

"Draw!" Turtle bounded between them. They disengaged, but unlike the last break, neither broke eye contact. The side of Pia's face purpled. Ro didn't put weight in the leg Pia tagged. The tension grew in the silence around Turtle's observance.

They took the floor again. Steel replaced Pia's ego. Ro's blank eyes didn't see Pia across the ring. Henry grew nervous.

Turtle's hand swung. They almost blurred in Henry's vision. Flashes of red showed him Pia. Pia's stumbles showed him Ro. Both took damage, but neither let up. It took minutes of brutality before Henry saw Pia slow down. Just a fraction. Henry wasn't the only one to figure it out. Some around him slumped, their quiet heavier to hold. Pia looked nothing like them. She punched and kicked and blocked until she couldn't dodge one in time. Ro's heel slammed into the back of her head. Pia sank to the ground.

Turtle moved to Pia's side. Two medics followed him. They busied over Pia's body, unconcerned.

Silver splattered Pia's skin. Red oozed from her ear, making her hair clump. Her upper lip split open like a plum. Dark marks swelled on the bits of arm and leg Henry could see. The medics removed her wraps. They gentled her purple broken-skinned knuckles.

Ro stood at the edge of the arena. Silver and red splashed her suit. The bloody mix smudged below her left eye. She cocked her right foot off the ground. Medics tended her, but she didn't seem to notice. One of them pulled the boot off her foot. Her body flinched. Her eyes didn't.

Two other medics arrived carrying metal buckets filled with gray slime. Henry could smell it from where he stood.

"First time smelling slime?" Kekoa asked.

"What is it?" Henry pinched his nose.

"An organic compound we can only get in the Merganan system. It's Web compatible—like onyx—but it's effect is regeneration. Trust me the smell is worth it. Watch."

The medics dunked Ro's foot into the bucket up to her knee. With gloved hands, they rubbed it into her skin from her toes up her calf. For Pia, they submerged her whole head.

The medics removed their gloves and moved their suits over their hands. The placed both hands on the slime covered skin. Silver sparked inside the gloves. They sat there, just touching their patients. After five minutes, the slime on Ro's ankle turned from grey to glowing blue.

They brought out another bucket filled with viscous, hot pink liquid. It smelled worse than the slime, like comparing bad eggs and chemical waste. They trickled the liquid on Ro's slime-covered ankle. The slime hissed, fermenting into a lumpy, rosy lotion. The medics massaged it into her skin. They washed the remnants away by dunking her foot in a bucket of ice-water. When they pulled her leg out, Ro's red skin had no bruising or swelling.

It took fifteen minutes for the slime on Pia's head to turn silver. The icy water made her shudder awake.

One of the medics broke away with Turtle. Turtle nodded at him and went to Ro. The medic came to Kekoa.

"I can't force Ro to spend the night. She doesn't really need it, but…it was a hard fight."

Kekoa nodded. "I'll keep an eye out for her."

"What about Pia?" Henry blurted.

"I'm keeping her overnight to monitor her brain activity but so far so good."

"Thanks."

The medic nodded and rejoined the others. They took Pia out, and Henry caught a forlorn flicker stiffen Ro's shoulders.

CHAPTER FORTY

Kekoa clapped Akira on the shoulder and walked to Ro and Turtle. Akira turned to Shai.

"I'm hungry. Want food?"

"Sure."

"I'm in," Henry said.

Akira and Shai discussed the slime. Henry kept quiet, stewing in his worry for Pia and his anger at both lieutenants for holding back on him. Kekoa joined later fuming.

"She's intolerable sometimes," he grumbled.

Akira chuckled. "What'd she say?"

"She didn't want to talk to me. When I left, Turtle was still arguing with her."

"She wanted to keep sparring?"

"Of course."

Akira shook his head. "That's my girl."

"That's nuts," Shai frowned.

"That's Ro," Kekoa rolled his eyes.

"I'll check on her later."

"Fine by me.

Kekoa left to finish his data analysis. Akira and Shai returned to the Wings' trade agreements with the Merganans, the civilization producing slime. Henry had no interest in intergalactic trade so he left, claiming he wanted to visit Pia.

"Tell her Ro said good match if she's awake," Akira asked.

Henry nodded. He went back to his quarters, but he sat on the edge of his bed, pulse racing.

If Ro wanted to spar, he'd oblige. His anger simmered under his skin. He drew a circle on the wall and thought of her. She surprised him.

She was in the infirmary. She ducked into a dark room when someone else approached.

Henry paused. She probably visited Pia. He had already intruded on her privacy once.

But he gambled she wouldn't be naked this time.

Ro walked down a long hallway, full of plants and soft light. Peaceful.

She found the seventh room on the left. She took a breath before the mist. Her shoulders sagged. She smiled on the other side.

The patient, an Atal, male, beamed when she climbed onto the bed like she'd done it a hundred times. He wrapped an arm around her. They kissed each other's cheeks. They talked. They laughed. He sometimes rubbed circles on her thigh. She played with his fingers when his hand fell in her lap. When she left, the man pulled her close. She held him back.

The sight brewed jealousy alongside his frustration.

The Atal had to be a teammate. Someone Henry probably replaced. An ounce of satisfaction replaced his envy.

She exited the infirmary and dived. He lost sight of her. He pressed his palm to the wall, igniting silver. His nav spec focused on her. A pulse, like an electric jolt, lit a path through his arm through the Tower.

Ro had left. She dived outside the eastern boundary.

She couldn't have offered him a better chance. Henry sprinted for the nearest vein. He pushed his speed, only diving for four breaths.

The Web pushed Henry out, soaring over orange sound. His own moon-muted shadow grew as he fell. He landed feet first and rolled out of it. His momentum shoved his knee caps into the bridge of his nose. He cursed and punched the sand by his feet.

Outside the Tower, his nav spec couldn't find Ro, only coordinates. He'd have to track her. Henry scanned the sand. Right foot, left, left hand. Shoulder, back, butt, launch. Her footprints bounded forward twenty meters until the orange dunes flattened into a beach. The sand darkened where the waves surged. Ro's footprints deformed at that line.

Henry searched the horizon. Layers of purple fog cupped the water. A chance wave, a shift in the air. Henry made out a lump hovering in the black curls.

Henry plunged into the water. The ocean tore at him, savage and strong. He gasped before water crashed into his face. Weariness set in after two hundred meters. He pushed. He made it to a rocky outcropping jutting into the surf. He crossed behind it, and the water lost its grip. Gentler current moved him toward shore. He treaded the last shallows and dragged himself on to paler sand.

Henry gulped air, rolling to his back on the shore. The sky bound his sight. Big Red, home of the Horns, shadowed both moons. He perceived swirls and eddies in the atmosphere that warped the stars' shine. He lost track of time recovering under that magnificence.

He didn't know when she brought him back to earth.

"Why did you follow me?"

Henry tilted his head back. She stood at the edge of the rainforest bordering the beach.

"Kekoa said you wanted to spar."

She came forward and sat next to him. "You're angry with me."

"Of course I am." Henry didn't turn.

"Still want to spar?"

He didn't. "I wish you'd train me in combat."

She sighed. "Your marking comes first."

"I'd be loads better if you had trained me like that from the beginning."

"You got there anyway with Pia."

"I'm not there." Henry jerked up. Ro sat with her chin on her knees. She was unbruised, unmarked, but her eyes were empty. His frustration melted.

She didn't answer. Henry appraised the void. He hated she could mask her emotions from him. A sudden contraction in her pupils exposed doubt.

"Why did you start calling me Ro?"

"Pia suggested it."

"She's clever."

"Yeah." He paused. "How can you fight her like that?"

She shrugged. "We've both had good training."

"That wasn't sparring. You fought her. Really fought her."

Pain shaded her blue eyes. "We're soldiers Henry. I didn't use my marking. For Pia, that's about as equal footing as I can give."

Henry didn't answer. Darkness grew through her irises until her pupils dilated, but her voice kept even.

"Would you like to see where I was going?"

"Yes."

Henry offered his hand. They pulled on each other to stand. She jogged into the tress. The sand grew firmer; she quickened. Henry kept pace, winding through, over, under, and sideways through vegetation. She ran surefooted through the trees. Henry aspired to her agility. He hit the huge rubbery leaves where she swerved around them.

Henry liked running here. The salty air energized him. The firm footing gave enough traction.

Henry's eyes picked out the thinning in the trees ahead. He surged forward to be neck and neck with Ro. They broke through the trees into a nearly perfect circle. The boundary between jungle and soft, short moss was too abrupt—man-made. A pool in the center of the clearing mirrored the star-lit sky above, except for silver colors.

"What is this place?"

"My grove."

CHAPTER FORTY-ONE

Henry peered at Ro. Something bright banished her darkness—joy.

"Your grove?"

She nodded. "I used to come here when I first got stationed at the Tower. I couldn't live in there after my first dive. I couldn't control my marking at all, and the pain, the distraction, the disorientation… it all drove me crazy."

Henry's shoulders crept up his neck. She sat. Henry copied her. The damp moss surprised him with warmth.

"My marking is very different. All of you have true markings—concrete parts. Your eyes, Roxar's arm, Opal's body. All flesh and bone. Those markings have shape, dimension, space." She paused, her face wrinkled. "My blood is liquid. My body is solid, though."

Her clinical tone silenced Henry. He locked eyes with her. Her breath shuddered, and she turned to the pool.

"Being blood marked has its upsides. I can release my blood from my body, as you've seen. Under the right circumstances it has militant applications." Her fingers plucked at the moss by her boots. "The downside is steep. My blood flows through my body, however the Web pulls it. It's never been bad enough that my blood has completely stopped flowing like it should. I'd be dead then," humor cracked her frozen mask. "But it—" her face lost its lines, emotions, everything. Her fingers still picked.

"What do you mean the Web pulls it?"

"I mean my blood physically moves through my body toward the Web. That's how my 'radar' physically works."

"That's not possible."

"Tell that to Taizai. He's the one that figured out what was happening to me."

"That's… how?"

"My blood moves to the part of my body closest to the strongest part of the Web. Well, guess what? The Web is attracted to all Life and the Tower is embedded in the Web. It's just… it's everywhere. It feels… it's… I'm ripped in a million directions from the inside."

The imagery made Henry imagine. Ro, smaller and shorter, untrained and ignorant, always coming second to her marking, always fighting herself, body and blood. There would have been no escape, no place where her marking yielded to her will. He cringed picturing those silver veins pulling through blue skin.

"When I did my first dive, my blood went all over the place. And… you know how my marking connects with Life. All those people walking around. All Wings or lab rats. All people the Web is doubly attracted to. The lab was especially bad. And Opal. And Roxar…. Now that my will is stronger, it can be useful sometimes. But back then—" She stopped again. Her story splintered, like an addict remembering the crash.

"The pain was unbelievable. No one knew how to help me. I couldn't control it. So Roxar made my grove, away from the Tower and away from people…" acid filled her tone. "I owe him."

Her venom recalled her nightmare Henry had overheard. He grew wary.

"Why do you hate him for it?"

Her finger froze in the moss. Round eyes stared at him.

"You can tell me."

She flinched.

"Please."

She stammered but no words came out. Blank eyes begged him. Henry put his hand over hers.

"I trust you. Will you tell me when I become Wing?"

She didn't answer.

"You owe me that, Ro."

She flinched. "I told you why Possession is so dangerous. Taking another's Life is as bad as killing them. But, when you're really good—and Roxar is the best—you can do more. You can Possess parts of the Web itself."

Henry frowned.

"Is that how the Commander made this place?"

"Yes. The Web could only exist here by touching me. The rest of the life here isn't connected to the Web. It's called Unthreading."

"But… the Web is everywhere—what binds us all."

"I know, and it is. Except for here. I don't know how to do it. Possession isn't my strength. But Roxar…" her mouth screwed up. She turned away from Henry.

"Why won't you tell me?"

"It's not your fight."

"Why are you fighting the Commander?"

"We're both marked Wings, no matter our rank. He'll always be my rival, and I'll always be his. In the Web and out of it."

"So what am I?"

Sadness lifted the corners her lips. "You're not a marked Wing."

Lightning intuition uncovered Ro's darkness.

"It's us, isn't it? Our markings. You're in pain because your marking is pulled to the Commander and me the most."

Ro froze.

"It's awful around me, isn't it? That's what you meant on Optra."

"Yes."

"I'm sorry I ruined your grove."

"Don't. Here it's easier. My marking is focused only on you and not every other Wing in the Tower. I barely notice this."

"I don't want you to hurt."

"That's not your problem."

They stared at each other.

"We shouldn't be teammates," Henry admitted.

"That's not your call."

"It makes sense. I inhibit you."

"No," she snapped. She stood, glaring down. "You give me an arsenal off-base. You'd increase Santos' primary advantage."

Henry stood, looking down at her. "You were good before I came here. You said so yourself. You don't need me."

"Fine! Is that what you want? Transfer? Roxar would do it if I asked."

Henry hesitated. "It's the right thing to do."

"But not what you want, right?"

Henry remembered the sunrise illuminating her sleepy eyes, her soft smile—how the ash and charred meat faded.

"No."

They stayed quiet. Ro paced around the pool; her stride radiated frustration. Henry watched until she sighed.

"You're not responsible for my marking. Don't burden yourself with it."

They stood on opposite sides of the pool. Her resolve pressured him even across the space. Henry nodded.

"Thank you." She smiled again. The real kind. "Let's go home."

They ambled through the rainforest back to the beach. Henry couldn't speak. His guilt churned. He wanted Santos more than he wanted to spare her.

Ro stopped him when they reached the water.

"You're lucky the Thalweg didn't sweep you out the first time. Lucky for you, we won't be swimming back."

She pulled a switch blade from her boot and sliced along the cut on her finger. Silver trickled out. She twisted her fingers and the blood suspended between them.

"Pick up your foot."

Henry obeyed. Ro swept her palm over the bottom of his boots. Her blood followed, sticking to the treads. She did the same for his other foot.

"Because I Blend, I can atomically bond my blood with compatible substances. Water is easiest compound. Apply the property of surface tension to my blood and…"

She stepped on to the water. She didn't sink.

"You can walk on water…"

"You can too, just with my help," she winked. "Race you!"

She sped across the surf toward the Tower. Henry, awestruck, didn't catch her. She laughed when he found her at the base of the cliffs.

"You can walk on water," he repeated.

"I can. One sub-civ planet—I dunno, maybe two years ago?—Kekoa had the hardest time with negotiations because they thought I was a goddess come to conquer them. Your face looks just like theirs."

"You just walked across the Thalweg."

She chuckled. "So did you."

Henry shook his head. Ro leaned in and hugged him. Short. Soft. Henry held her back.

"Good night, Henry."

"Good night, Ro."

CHAPTER FORTY-TWO

Pia. Her best friend's injuries healed, but Ro's guilt rode hard.

When the medics took her back to the infirmary, Ro followed. She snuck into Pia's room. Ro only had minutes since they gave her sleeping drugs.

She whispered, "Hey."

Pia's head lolled toward her. She sighed, snuggling into her pillow. "Good win. Snuggle?"

Ro crept under the covers, scooting close like when they were kids.

"Good fight."

Pia's words slurred, "Getcha nextime. Gladu come finme."

"Of course. Always will."

Pia dropped into sleep smiling. Ro stayed for a minute more—warm, wanted, and weary. No matter Pia's forgiveness, no matter Pia's loyalty or love, her marking carved through her veins toward Henry.

Ro cracked. Her fears yawned, clawing through her with more desperation than her marking.

She craved comfort that could speak sense. She squeezed Pia tight before finding Ham. She needed his humor and a hug.

Wistful angst tainted how he held her, made her laugh. When she left, she craved stillness—numbness—and the frequency she'd needed it rekindled doubt. She sped to her grove... and Henry ruined it.

In her dream, shadowy fingers and ominous eyes terrified her. She remembered the power of his fingers clamped around her forearms, her marking gnashing through her will at his touch...

It has to be Roxar.

There was no other explanation for Henry's power if he couldn't use it.

She groaned. She held her head in her hands, sealing her lids against tears. She could at least force those away.

I have to know if Henry's his pawn.

Or his spy?

She wandered the Tower, cometless, purposeless, her paranoia, fear, and survival pushing each step forward while her marking careened. Mist appeared in her drift—Roxar's door.

She entered.

Roxar stared at a beat-up journal, somewhere in the middle of the book. She always found him in those pages when she came unannounced.

"Rolyn, what a surprise." He nodded to a spot closer to his desk.

As she walked toward him, her marking tore between Henry and Roxar, drumming her blood into a frenzy.

"To what do I owe the pleasure?"

"Henry has no power of his own, does he? Did you force a marking on him or something?"

"Oh? This, again? You rarely disappoint me Rolyn, but this…" Roxar shut the book and stared her down.

"Not even you can deceive the Web. I know what I feel."

Roxar smiled, flexing silver fingers. Ro's marking flinched, and she set her defenses, uncaring if Roxar sensed them.

"Henry has his own power. I had nothing to do with his marking."

"Have you Possessed him?"

"No."

"Then what did you do?"

"I will make an assumption that I hope does not offend. Between his and mine, you can't handle us both, not at the same time anyway. Especially not since he Possessed you, too."

Ro grimaced.

"I know you too well, Rolyn. Your pain is a gift. Embrace what it's telling you."

"I'm fucking confronting you, aren't I? I know what my marking is telling me."

"Apparently not. How many times have you needed to run to that island? How many more times until you recognize what's happening to you?"

Shit.

"I know you better than anyone else here, Rolyn. I'll always know. Your control is slipping, your will losing. When you will admit what you know and move on?"

"Move on? From what?"

Roxar sighed. "You've always been stubborn. Fine—you'll force my hand. Promotion."

Ro guffawed. She couldn't stop the weird sound.

"I don't kid Rolyn."

Giggles erupted through her nose.

"Enough." Roxar's arm snapped up, bright palm suppressing her. All her defenses crumbled against a smashing force, Roxar's ace. He robbed her of control, of choice. A dark emptiness swallowed her reason. Fear overtook what she had left of herself.

No, no, no, stars please no.

Run.

I can't.

"Promotion. Blink if you understand." His Possession loosened on the muscles controlling her eye lids.

She blinked.

"I anticipated this since you came to me after his Possession. You are stronger than you realize, but the nature of your marking does hold you back. It's not your fault—don't look at me like that." She hadn't made a face, but he sensed her response under his Possession. He quieted for a moment, glaring at her. "You were right to question me based on those events. Your doubts made me question my own motives in your training. I admit, I've ignored what you needed too. I didn't want you to leave, but you've needed something different for a while now."

She stared. She couldn't blink.

When I've needed something different? Is he serious? What could I... Santos is all I have.

"Blink, Rolyn."

She didn't.

"Don't think I misunderstand you. You feel your life is turning to pieces, your last foundation, your Team, the last hiding spot."

I won't leave my home.

"And still, you've never needed others for strength. You still don't. You don't need my shelter."

Shelter? It's my home. The Tower is where I live, where I train, where everyone I care about comes home too.

"You need freedom."

She couldn't move, but she hardened. She blinked.

"Rolyn. The Tower is your arsenal, not your home. Your freedom is out there. You run to the grove just to get away from Henry and me."

She blinked. It felt like closing the door.

The pressure vanished. A breath—*finally*—from her own lungs. Anger, frustration, and self-loathing collided with her marking's spasms in her returned body.

Roxar's hand stretched out, silver but without the shine—a poisonous offer. It extinguished her courage.

"Take the promotion. So much more awaits you out there."

She choked on the words. "What rank?"

"Major."

Why again.

She took his silver palm.

"Initiation will start tomorrow; keep that confidential. We will be observing them as you progress through the typical routines. We will tell them Initiation has begun on the third day. You will complete three missions, culminating with a specialty exam. The following day they will officially be accepted as Wingmen and your term as Major will begin. Six days from now, you will become my tenth Major. Report to me after the specialty exam for your first assignment."

He let go. Numbness descended, drowning out the jolts where his skin had touched hers, even Henry's tugging.

She shuddered. She couldn't say a word in the void.

"Leave now, Rolyn."

She turned without hesitation.

CHAPTER FORTY-THREE

She dived to her room, craving silence. Akira waited for her.

"Hey."

"Hey."

Akira patted the bed next to him.

"I thought you'd be asleep, so I was worried when you weren't here. I sent a comet, but—"

"I went to my grove."

"I guessed as much."

Ro didn't answer. Akira didn't push. His arms offered familiar warmth, and she let him lift her into his lap. She pressed into his neck, inhaling the subtle spice that drove her wild. She started. She hadn't felt desire since Henry had arrived.

We haven't… I haven't…

Guilt quashed the tendril of sensuality. "I'm sorry I haven't been myself lately."

"You want to talk? You've been… ever since you lost Ham, you've been shutting us out. All of us… but me especially."

He kissed her. She pulled from his comfort.

"Hey, hey, hey, what's wrong?"

"He promoted me. Major."

Akira blanched. "Major?"

"I'm leaving in six days."

"Ro—"

"I haven't been here for you and I was actually here."

"It's ok, just—"

"I can't make this work."

"Ro, that's not it. You've taken a beating and it's not letting up—I get it. But I'll be here. I don't care about the distance. I love you."

"Akira, it's not just the promotion. I can't… Henry—"

"Look, I get it. You don't need to explain it to me. You're worn out, and no one else can lift that load for you. I don't care. If you come back and all you want is to sleep? Fine. I'll sleep next to you. If all you want is to eat then sleep? Fine. I'll feed you and then sleep next to you. It's not about the sex, though you are really spectacular at—"

"Please, not now."

"Fine." He stood, pulled her in, enveloped her.

"I mean it. I love you. We can do this."

"You probably can, but Akira, it's not… it's just—"

"Just what, baby?" He smiled, tucking hair behind her ear.

"My blood pulls me to him. It's bad. You remember that first weekend? He accidentally Possessed me when we dived. Akira, it was unreal. I've never felt that much freedom since I was marked."

"So this is about Henry?"

"I guess, technically."

"What do you mean?" Akira pulled back, caution pulling his smile.

"Since the moment we came out of the Web… all my marking wants is that… that freedom. It's fucking terrible. When we're in the same room? My blood only pulls to him. I don't notice a single other Life, it's that bad. It's… it's worse than it's ever been."

"Are you kidding me?" No warmth colored Akira's tone.

"No."

'This makes no sense Rolyn. Pain's never stopped you before. Stars, you're the youngest lieutenant ever."

"And now the youngest major… or will be."

"So, won't that be a good thing? You'd be away from the Commander and Henry both. You'd only be in the Tower for a few months a year."

Is that what Roxar meant? "I think that's why he offered it."

"Wait, offered? You could have declined?"

"Well, no, but—"

"You chose to leave?"

"No! He made me take it."

"Did he order you or did he offer?"

The doubt in Akira's tone triggered Ro's irritation.

"He used his marking."

"That's not answering my question."

"I didn't have a choice!"

Akira's eyes lightened to yellow, his fingertips elongating into talons. He shook his head, forced rigid legs to sit until he calmed. Ro gave him space until his eyes returned to their normal hazelnut, his nails trimmed. He didn't look at her. She didn't look at him. Mutual frustration at the other's lack of understanding charged the space between them. Ro started pacing.

"Is this some part of your delusional anti-establishment crusade against the Commander?" Akira said.

"No. He. Made. Me. Do. It."

"I don't believe you."

Ro snapped. "I never asked you to! You said you wanted to be here, right? Well, this shit with Roxar is part of the package, sweetheart."

Akira made eye contact. "Does it actually hurt? So much that you—Rolyn fucking Sech—can't learn to handle it?"

"Yes."

"Even right now?"

"Yes."

"Prove it."

She cut along her finger. Silver dripped, caught in her other palm.

"One hundred percent of my will." The blood hovered above her skin, shapeless and shivering.

"Fifty." The blood arrowed toward the floor.

"Ten." Her blood hit onyx, blue growing in the silver swarming the black.

Akira's tone lost emotion. "Where's it going?"

"Henry." She stiffened as she reengaged her will. Grinding her blood to a halt made her eyes white out—but her marking came back.

Seeing her blood so strongly manipulated without her control... Akira knew, and she saw it in his downturned head.

"You seriously can't make that any better? Turn it off or something?"

"No." She paused. "Henry couldn't either—or can't as far as I can tell."

Akira frowned and stood.

"So that's it. You don't want to try."

Ro swayed on her feet. "I can't."

"I loved you, Ro. I thought you were the one."

"This has nothing to do with how I feel about you."

"Yeah. Ok."

Akira left, his empty words echoing the hollow, hopeless blue in the onyx behind her.

CHAPTER FORTY-FOUR

Shai lay awake when Henry returned.

"You where a while. How's Pia?"

"Pia? Shit, Pia! Do you know how she's doing?"

"You weren't at the infirmary? I assumed you were still with her."

"No, I wasn't. Have you heard anything about her?"

"No. So where were you then?"

"I…uh…I was with Ro."

"Figures. Did you learn anything?" Jealousy constricted Shai's words.

"Hey, relax man."

"Sorry," Shai slumped into his pillows. "I just—" Shai shook his hands at the ceiling.

"That bad?"

Shai sighed. "I guess."

"And what about Akira?"

"We're friends, but—she's just—"

"Did you know she can walk on water?"

"What? No. But that's exactly it! She's just… she's incredible."

Henry chuckled. "You're an idiot."

"Why?"

"Because you like attention more than she does, but she's hotter and better than you are. It'd drive you insane."

Shai scowled. "She's already driving me insane." He shook his head. "Whatever, man. What'd you find out?"

"Nothing for the dimensions, but a lot about her marking. Her marking literally moves in her body relative to the Web. Being around the Commander and me, because our markings attract a lot of the Web, is basically torture for her."

"Really? So why does she—"

"I tried. She told me it's not my problem and asked me to leave it alone."

Shai's eyes lit. "Think she's a masochist?"

Henry shook his head. "C'mon man, focus. Remember the nightmare she had after the seizure? I don't think pain alone would warrant that kind of distrust. Not from her."

Shai shook his head.

"But, whatever is between them, Ro has to be biased about him. About both of us, really."

"Agreed."

"She did say they were rivals because they were both marked, regardless of rank."

"Shit. That's not good. Do you—you don't think it's mutiny right?

"It's the worst-case scenario."

Shai clenched his eyes. "First the dimensions, then your block, now this."

Henry shivered.

"This isn't what I signed up for. I wanted to fight Rahni. I wanted to defend my country. That's what I've been fucking told my entire fucking life. And here I am, top post in the military, and we haven't even seen a Rahnus. We don't even try to go after them." Shai's anger was all too familiar.

"They lied to us."

"They've lied to all of humanity."

Henry and Shai stared at each other, sizing up the other's values.

"I can't let that go. I won't betray my country, but I can't... I have to change it."

Shai's ambition charged Henry. "You won't do it alone."

A tense silence passed as their words created dishonor.

"Where do we start?" Henry's commitment didn't hide his grim understanding.

Shai's brow set. "We need to separate Ro from everyone else and make her trust us enough to clue us in. She may be biased, but we can't move forward without knowing her information. Same with the Commander."

"How do we get close to the Commander?"

"Through Ro. Along the way, if we find the person blocking you, we'll deal with it too."

Shai stood and held out his arm. Henry grasped his forearm. Shai returned the grip.

"I'm trusting you, Henry."

"I'm trusting you, Shai."

Both paused. Years taught their tongues to speak the dimensions.

"Brother," Shai said instead.

"Brother."

They didn't sleep. With their strategy set, tactics 5consumed them.

"What's with you two?" Pia asked at breakfast.

"Just tired," Henry shrugged.

"You look like someone died," Pia smacked him on the arm. "Lighten up!"

"Sorry," Henry grinned.

"Won't be around later," Pia brushed her hand up Henry's thigh under the table. "Moved our departure up to today, but I'll be back in a couple weeks."

Henry frowned. He and Shai had planned on tapping Pia for more information about Ro. Henry had hoped to ask her that night when they were alone.

"Have fun," Henry told her, squeezing her hand.

Shai smacked him on the head. "Stay safe. Man, you're stupid at the wrong times."

Pia giggled. Only Henry heard the strain in Shai's tone. On the way to PT, Henry and Shai adjusted their plans to pressure Ro then rather than after they were part of Santos. Neither thought it was good timing, but Pia's departure left them few options.

"I doubt that's it. The dimensions have to be metaphorical. How else could death be a dimension?" Shai's voice carried to where Ro and Kekoa stood.

"Unless it's physical," Henry picked up the script. "Death would fit then."

"Too literal. The Web can't be physically quantified at least."

Kekoa and Ro listened with grim expressions.

"But Life is physical. You can't prove the Web isn't physical."

"That's a loose argument. Metaphorically, though, Life is the vaguest. It could be anything."

"Did you two rehearse this?" Ro asked. Henry flinched but Shai's tone was smooth.

"Hardly. Henry posed an interesting question about the dimensions with regard to his marking. I contend they are metaphorical, but he thinks they're literal, like actual different dimensions. Tell him he's an idiot," Shai swept an arm over her shoulder.

Ro shook him off. "You're lying. Out with it."

"Henry and I want answers."

"To which questions?" Henry had never heard Kekoa sound so firm.

"We're not sure. It's just… it was over our beds. You remember right?" Shai widened his eyes, softened his shoulders.

Henry forced himself still. Shai could pull it off, and he wasn't going to ruin it.

"You were never curious at the Yard?" Kekoa demanded.

"No."

"So why now? It's not above your beds now, is it?"

"All the more interesting," Shai countered. "Isn't this where the Yard was supposed to put us? Why drill that into our heads if it's not worth something?" His cheeks grew hot. "Did you never tell me because I'm not marked like Henry is?"

"Don't be stupid," Kekoa rolled his eyes, but the tension dropped. Henry was shocked Kekoa bought Shai's arrogance so easily.

Ro squinted at Shai, then put her hand on Kekoa's arm.

"Neither of you have a right to those answers. Your markings don't deserve them."

Shai's indignant mask was perfect. "But we're your teammates! And it does matter. You're marked and Henry—"

"Fine," she sliced her hand through the air. Shai quieted. "You're not my teammates, but if you do become—"

"We will."

"If you do," she spoke over Shai, "then I'll tell you whatever you want to know. Teammates trust each other, right?"

"We're only going to make Wing because of you two. Of course, we trust you."

"Cheeky brat," Kekoa muttered. "Absolutely frustrating. Extra laps?"

"Triple laps," Ro glared at the cadets.

CHAPTER FORTY-FIVE

The lieutenants pushed them through hell and back. After four hours of PT, Ro took Henry to spar while Kekoa took Shai to the range. Turtle greeted them in the sparring gym.

"Turtle!" Ro hugged him. Her arms couldn't reach all the way around. One huge hand stroked her head, down her hair.

"So, he's finally ready?"

"Well…" Ro trailed off. She turned to Henry. "Here's that next time."

"Show me how much you've grown, Harbor."

Henry grinned. They sparred over two hours. Turtle took time to work with him. Henry learned from every minute with him. Ro watched without interrupting.

"Enough," Turtle waved Henry down. Henry walked himself out, panting.

Turtle faced Ro. "You're missing out. Henry's got exceptional talent."

Henry stopped, beaming.

"Yes sir." She fidgeted.

"You should match Pia's efforts," he insisted.

Ro crossed her arms. "His marking comes first."

"The Commander is not so unrelenting," Turtle took her hands and pulled her up. "You know that."

She leaned into his huge frame. "I'm not a major. I don't have the luxury of calling orders unrelenting."

"He loves you like I do, duckling. You would grow just as much as Henry would," he let her go. "Harbor, next time I'm around, let's train again."

"Yes sir. I'll practice," Henry grinned. The Atal slapped Henry across the shoulder before leaving, like an anvil to the traps. Henry grinned at Ro.

"You're snuggly around him."

"I never get to see him."

"Why not?"

"He's a major."

"Come on, what does he do?"

"I told you, I don't know. We never find out where they go, what they do… anything. About once every seven times or so one of the majors will suggest a new planet to scout. Those recommendations make up less than forty percent of the new planets we scout. Everything else is found by Roxar."

"I had no idea."

"There are only nine of them."

"So few?"

"Only one in four Major promotions survive their first year."

Henry paused. "How long has Turtle been Major?"

"Fourteen years."

Turtle's longevity dumbstruck Henry, and Ro didn't bring it up again.

"Let's try something fun."

"Ok." Henry doubted her idea of fun.

"This will be a diving and tracking test. I'm evading, you're catching. Got it?"

"Easy enough."

"If you say so." She snapped her fingers and her suit flashed brightest silver. "Made you look." She vanished in sound.

Ro played dirty. She used tricks Henry never conceived of to confuse her trail. She didn't hold back on speed either. It took him eighteen minutes to catch her the first time. The next two times he got faster. On the fourth, it took over an hour.

"Damn that stamina," she panted, afterward. "Thought you'd give up ages ago."

"Thanks," Henry gasped. "Should have fun more often."

"Come on, you must be wrecked."

"I am starving."

Ro lit a comet toward the mess. "Think Kekoa and Shai are done yet?"

"They probably finished hours ago," Henry teased.

Kekoa and Shai had finished earlier. Both lieutenants packaged their food to go, claiming they were knee-deep in data analytics.

Shai and Henry returned to their quarters.

"I'm not happy with how that turned out. We needed Pia."

"I know," Shai's irritation infected Henry's calm.

"I don't think there's any way out of this."

"Though there is one silver lining," Shai stopped pacing. "She promised she'd answer our questions." He gestured between them. "At least now we don't have to depend on you making it through the marked trial."

Henry stilled.

"No offense," Shai added.

"None taken." Henry frowned. "She was adamant I didn't find out until I was a marked wing. I don't think she'd make that mistake."

"Then why did she make that promise?"

"I don't know." Henry stared at the floor.

"It's not about you. Don't worry, you'll make Wing. I doubt that's the problem."

"Maybe. I forgot to mention. I sparred with that major today. He said something weird to Ro. Something about how the Commander loves her just like he does, so she should ignore orders and train me."

Shai started pacing. "They're highly classified, right?"

Henry hummed.

"Think they're like spies?"

"That's a possibility."

"Think it has anything to do with the dimensions?"

Henry considered it. "That'd be a farfetched connection. Especially since none of the marked Wings are majors."

Their questions couldn't keep their sleepless night at bay for long. They drifted off mulling over mysteries.

Kekoa and Ro made reunited them for joint PT, and tripled everything again.

"Why are you still punishing us?" Shai complained.

"Yesterday was immediate consequence. Today is unforeseen consequence."

"That's some burnout shit," Shai muttered to Henry.

Training returned to normal after that, except three notable faces kept popping up, even when they split into sparring and shooting. The next day, Kekoa and Ro upped their PT again, but they joined in this time. The four ran all over the compound. Henry set a ruthless pace under Ro's command. She and Kekoa ran them through PT again at the end of the day. Henry's body hadn't ached so much since his first few days under Ro. That whole day, those three strangers observed them.

"I hurt," Shai whimpered over dinner. Henry's head lay next to his empty plate.

"Stop whining," Ro chided.

"You haven't had your ass kicked for three days!" Shai snapped.

"Watch it, or I'll wash it," she warned.

"Only if you do the rest of me," Shai slipped into smooth too quick. He smiled at Ro's annoyed huff.

"Enough," Kekoa interceded before Ro could. "You two. Bed."

CHAPTER FORTY-SIX

When Ro woke, the cold bed matched her loneliness, her marking's wails. Kekoa found her before breakfast.

"Want to explain why Akira's hungover?"

"Did they flash you the instructions for initiation?"

"Yeah. What happened?"

"We broke up."

"Why?"

"Let's talk later in my room."

Kekoa understood she meant when she could use her marking to muffle their conversation.

"If you insist."

Kekoa lost his patience after completing evaluation interviews with the captains. He paced the entire time Ro weaved thread around them to distort their voices to meaningless tones. Ro understood. She shared his frustration after such a high intensity day.

"Ok. Akira, now the cadets are acting really strange, and you've been cold all day. Seriously, what is going on?"

Ro sighed. "A lot. I'll start with the easiest. I'm getting promoted. As soon as initiation is over, I'm leaving."

"Well that's... unexpected." Kekoa sighed, sagging into a chair. "Is that why you broke up with Akira?"

"Mostly. Henry's marking is driving me insane. This honestly... might be for the best." *Admitting it feels good.*

"Stars, Ro, you should have said something." He moved over and she squeezed onto the armrest. "How long this been going on?"

"I've gone back to my grove a few times now."

"How many?"

"More than a few."

"Why didn't you say something?"

"Nothing you could've done I wasn't already doing." She leaned into him. He wrapped an arm around.

"Teams," he squeezed, "bleed together."

"Please don't. I'm too tired for that."

"Hard not to."

She flinched. He let go.

"Moving on. Why are Shai and Henry asking questions?"

"I need to be honest with you—"

"Oh stars, Ro, you know I believe you, but—"

"No, listen, Henry's marking doesn't work. Not the way mine or Roxar's do. I think that's because Henry isn't really marked at all. Roxar pushed the Web to mark him and is using Henry to…"

"To what?"

"Well, I don't know that part yet, but I'm telling you—"

"No. Stop it. Just tell me why you think they are asking weird questions."

"I'm trying to explain. I don't understand what Henry is asking. All Roxar or Taizai ever trained me for was how to use my marking, not dimensional theory."

"So, why is he asking?"

"I don't know, but I bet Roxar does."

"Or Taizai."

"Sure, but Taizai's not marked."

Kekoa sighed. "So, what are you planning to do?"

"Well, Henry also asked me about the majors. Could be they're involved too."

"Couldn't it just be because he noticed them today? New faces stand out."

"Maybe, but if I'm right Roxar's using him, then…"

"Did you ask Turtle?"

"I would have. He vanished after assessing Henry."

"Well, you're out of luck and time. You've got five days left, now."

"Yeah."

"Promise me you'll stay safe out there."

Ro gulped and nodded.

"You know we're here for you."

"Always, thanks."

"Are you telling anyone else?"

"Stars, no. I couldn't stand saying goodbye to Pia."

Kekoa sighed, put his hand over hers. "I know how this is going to sound, but that's your past talking. She deserves to know, as does everyone else who cares about you."

"It's not even official yet."

"But it's going to happen. At least give them warning when you can."

"You should feel lucky I'm even telling you."

"Yeah, well… Santos." He squeezed her hand.

"Seriously, don't make me cry."

"Sorry, Ro. Can't help it." Kekoa's eyes were wet. "Five days left."

"I won't be gone forever."

"Yeah. Ok."

Kekoa squeezed her hard before he trudged through mist toward his own bed. His words remained, hooks descending through memories she couldn't avoid.

Why again?

Her memories seared the backs of her eyelids, mirrored the isolation she now craved from her grove. A child huddled at the base of roots four times her size. She whimpered.

It's not the same.

Her family feared more than loved her. She was glad they didn't stop her when she ran. Years later, that boy found her, and the hive-mind revealed that same fear, strengthened by age and awe at her survival.

I never belonged. It's not the same.

She made a place to belong. Fought for a home that wanted her. Lived for people who needed her.

Her marking, the thing that severed her from her family, now cast her from the home she made for herself.

It's not fair. It's never, ever fair.

That night, she learned to let go of everything she'd built herself. It hurt, a thousand times more than before, but it was not hard.

I've done it before.

She never voiced the goodbyes clogging her throat. She wouldn't repeat the shallow ritual she'd needed when she was six.

Now, she needed the rigidity she'd learned from service. She needed detached precision. She needed unbiased focus.

She needed to remember the girl who ran, from her home, from her family, from her pain, twice. She needed to remember the survival instinct churning her feet fast and far.

Ro let her feet carry her from her quarters. She roamed the Tower, remembering running through darkness with Ham and Kekoa, and letting those memories go. She filled their remaining emptiness with cold resolve.

I will become stronger than him, with or without Henry.

I will take my home back.

And I will make him pay.

CHAPTER FORTY-SEVEN

A flash woke Henry early.

"Escort mission on Ajejouzhan. Accompany onyx shipments to extraction location. Coordinate with team Gotham. Depart at oh five hundred." Opal's voice sent a chill down the back of Henry's neck.

"Why didn't they tell us last night?"

Shai shook his head.

They got to Kekoa and Ro as quick as they could.

"Hurry and get some food. This is going to be a long haul," Kekoa urged.

"About that. Why didn't you tell us we had a mission coming up?" Shia grumbled.

"It's not exactly a mission. This is your initiation."

Henry froze, gaping.

"This? An escort mission?" Shai stammered.

"Well, today is an escort mission. Tomorrow is recon for a new planet. Day after is cargo delivery through hostile territory." Ro didn't look at either of them.

"Did you know it was starting?" Henry asked.

"We both did. And technically, it started that first day we upped your PT," Kekoa answered.

"Those three people from yesterday. Are they the ones running it?"

"Thought you'd notice," Ro said. "They're majors. You don't recognize them because you came after their rotations started. Nalani was gone the longest. Seven months I think? Anyway, go get breakfast."

Henry and Shai walked away fuming.

"I can't believe they didn't tell us," Shai griped.

"At least it's starting now. We won't have to wait much longer."

"I guess." Shai didn't look mollified.

All three days flew by. The escort mission was easy to the point of boring. Shai took a major role the second day. The planet didn't have civilized life, but the dominant carnivores were territorial. Shai sniped anything within a hundred meters of them. The third day, Henry and Ro took the entire cargo and hauled ass. Shai and Kekoa, unburdened, maintained defensive artillery fire. Being hunted terrified Henry. Knowing he needed his team and they needed him thrilled him.

When they dived back to the tower, the Commander and Taizai waited with Turtle and the three other majors. Two Kau, and one Horn.

"Quite the performance," Taizai praised.

"Fast," the Horn said.

"Good marksmanship," the taller Kau noted.

Silence hung. Everyone waited on the Commander. He only had eyes for Ro. She wouldn't meet them.

"Harbor. Jukita," he still kept on Ro, "report for specialty testing."

"Harbor!" Turtle called.

"Jukita!" the tall Kau ordered.

"Yes sir!" Henry and Shai moved.

Kekoa and Ro stood at rest. Kekoa smiled at them. Ro avoided Henry's gaze. Turtle gripped Henry's forearm.

"Dive to the arena."

"Yes sir," Henry obeyed. His fingers didn't make it around Turtle's forearm. He dived. The packed arena greeted them with cheers.

"What is this?"

"The final exam in initiation. A panel of judges will evaluate you. Get as many points as you can in fifteen minutes."

Henry blinked. "Not marked?"

"Ro put in a good word. I gave her less credit than she deserved." Turtle raised his hand high. The crowd quieted.

"Give the Cadet your respect! Don't cheer. Don't applaud. You're here to watch, only."

"Yes sir!" The chorus rumbled through Henry's chest.

Turtle turned to him. "Get ready, Harbor."

Henry drew his focus from the crowd to Turtle, to himself—to winning.

Henry considered some of the tricks Ro used. He could use his nav spec to track Turtle's movement, eliminating any surprises. That would allow him greater speed and technique. He shifted the onyx in his suit to reinforce his shins and knuckles. Each hit would strike a heavier blow. He did the same on his forearms for defense. Satisfied, nervous, and exhilarated, he nodded to Turtle.

The crowd gasped.

"Scary," Turtle whistled. He flicked fingers toward his eyes, then at Henry.

"Glowing?"

"Like stars."

Henry stood taller. "I'm ready."

"Let's go."

They took their starting stances.

"Start!" a disembodied voice rang.

The nav spec tactic sped up Henry's response time and sharpened his accuracy. He didn't have the weight right in his reinforced zones but regulated as he moved. Turtle still exploited Henry's speed and adjustments.

"You've been practicing."

"I have."

A fire grew in Henry's chest. He wanted to knock Turtle flat. Wanted to be stronger. Wanted to be faster. Henry pushed. Everything—faster. Everything—harder. Turtle still blocked every strike, so Henry forced his body further. Henry hit his physical limit. He knew it. His drive exceeded it.

Henry launched into one of Pia's favorite combinations. Turtle, recognizing it, flowed in defense, but Henry saw his opportunity. He accelerated one punch, his fist powering into Turtle's jaw. Bone crunched. Henry's didn't stop. Neither did Turtle.

Turtle introduced a new level of skill. Fast didn't come close. He struck Henry in the IT band four times in thirty seconds. Henry staggered. He couldn't stand on his leg, but he stayed up.

"Enough. You're done." Turtle straightened. He turned from Henry.

Henry couldn't hear or see. He tasted bitterness. Frustration. Loss.

A flash skidded to Turtle's feet. He flicked his fingers. The silver swam from the onyx through the air to his hand. Turtle held the ember to his ear. Silver smoke wafted from his fingers.

Turtle swung his arm wide. The crowd silenced.

"With a total of fourteen points...Harbor, welcome to the Wings!"

Cheering engulfed Henry. He teetered on his good leg.

"I made Wing?"

"You did." Turtle walked over, sliding an arm under Henry's shoulders. He helped Henry toward two medics while the onlooking Wings roared. Henry listened, stupefied, as a medic ran a gloved hand over his thigh.

"You're not damaged enough for a full slime. A few minutes with the patch should do." She swiped up his leg to reveal his skin. Another medic brought her a black sticker that reeked. She stuck it on Henry's thigh then moved her hand to drag the onyx over the whole area. "Let that sit for five minutes then you're good to go."

Henry sat with his leg outstretched. The medic moved to Turtle.

"Still smells gross," Turtle muttered as she slathered his jaw. "I'll pay you back for this alone."

"Yes, pleas." Henry grinned.

Strong arms wrapped around his neck from behind.

"Good job, White Wing," Ro said.

"Thanks." She felt warm against his back. She squeezed before letting go. She turned to Turtle.

"It's about time you took a real hit. Henry, you've made many jealous today. Wish I could've done it. Better you than Pia, I guess."

The medic came back to Henry and removed the sticker. She poked and prodded him.

"All done."

"Great! Come on, Henry."

She took his hand and towed him at a run. As the exited, shouts and thumps assaulted Henry's back. Ro tugged him clear, laughing. When they were free, she let him go and lit a comet. She took off fast.

"I'm sure you could have guessed, but Shai made it too. Apparently shattered the record for the marksman exam."

"Of course he did."

They celebrated in the mess. Later, alone, Henry and Shai relived each other's trial rounds. A sudden silver circle silenced them. Kekoa emerged into their quarters.

"Good you're still awake. Let's go,"

"What? More?" Shai protested.

"No idiot," Kekoa scoffed. "Party."

CHAPTER FORTY-EIGHT

Henry had passed. Shai had passed. Ro's duties ceased. She dived to Roxar's office.

One.

Two.

Three.

Four.

Five.

Six.

She exited with a straight spine.

"So reluctant to see me Rolyn?"

"Reporting for duty sir."

"Lieutenant Rolyn Sech, do you accept your post as Major of the White Wings?"

"Yes, sir."

"Do you swear to uphold your duty through all you encounter, all you doubt, and all you learn?"

The unorthodox question caught her off guard. Anger crept from her control.

"Where are you sending me?"

"Accept, Rolyn."

She bit out, "Yes, sir, I accept."

"Thank you, my Rolyn." Roxar sighed over the tension. She did not respond. He flicked his silver fingers. Black oozed over his left palm. He held his hand out to her, and she took it. Weight sank through her suit, taking up space alongside her other spec.

"What is this?"

"Sneak: the only spec limited to major. It's necessary I'm afraid. Majors' lives are too precious to me and too sought after by others."

"The Rahni?"

"Stars forbid it. Other Web-capable species know the power someone like you holds. You will no longer be able to run home when danger finds you. You'll need it before long."

Sneak wasn't the heaviest spec she carried. She flexed her marking and spread the spec over her whole body.

"I can hardly sense you. Forgive the pun, but it suits you."

She shrugged.

"Truly."

She refused to answer. Roxar waited but all she wanted was to rid herself of him.

"All right, all right. Major Sech."

"Reporting, sir." *Just end this.*

"Your mission is singular. Leave. Explore the unknown. Come back when you have found power of use of me."

"A roving mercenary."

"No, an opportunity. Fly, Rolyn. Grow. I have only given this chance to thirty-two before you. Nine have stood to the task. I have no doubt you'll soar above them all if you wanted to. Go. Join the ranks of the strong. It's been time for a while."

"Yes, sir."

"Until we meet again, Rolyn."

She ran from him. She hid in her quarters. She flashed Kekoa. She didn't know what else to do.

"Ro?" he exited from her Webbed wall. "What's wrong? You're missing all the fun."

She moaned wordless sorrow.

Kekoa held her. More than that, he dried her tears. He encouraged her to see everyone one more time.

She shook her head. "I've already said my good byes. Besides, got enough of a buzz earlier. Want to really sleep it off."

"It's really time then."

Fresh tears made her head ache. Kekoa squeezed. He didn't let go until she breathed steady.

"Come home soon, ok?"

"Yeah, I will."

Kekoa left her with a hug.

Not thirty minutes later, Akira found her sniffling.

"Ro, I came to talk."

She pursed her lips. She could smell him from across the room.

"I know you're pissed. I've been an ass all week. I get it." He held his hands up.

Uh oh.

He walked forward. She didn't move.

"You're drunk."

"Yes, sir." He cupped her jaw, his thumb tracing her bottom lip. She put her hand on his arm.

"This is not a good idea."

"I know." He moved both hands to her hips.

"I'm leaving in the morning."

"Then kick me out."

She hesitated. He grinned.

"I still—"

She sealed her lips over the words, refusing to hear them.

Later, her breath came shallow and her chest heaved. Sweat dripped off the end of her nose. His climax drained from her body, and she ignored the slow, hazy contentment sliding into place. Her fingers found his cheek before she pushed herself off.

"So, I wanted to say… well, I still—"

"Come on Akira, neither of us would be here—"

"I still want to try."

She snapped her jaw shut.

"Not what you thought, huh?"

"No."

"Well, I mean it," he lounged back, his tone growing cocky. "Besides, can't say you were thinking about Henry during that, can you?"

She sprung from the bed. "Back the fuck up. This was never about sex. You said so yourself."

They fought harder than ever before. She said some of the worst things she ever had to him, and he called her names that made her skin glow hot. They tore into each other for half an hour before Akira threw himself back onto the bed.

"You're crazy. You dumped me for a masochistic fetish without the benefits."

"My life is falling apart at the seams, and it's a little overwhelming, and you dare make this about sex? I'm not fucking Henry!"

"Everything has to be about you doesn't it?"

"Oh, I'm sorry, is your ego lonely without someone else to stroke it?"

"Fuck off!"

She sank to the floor, exhausted, angry.

Why is he's such an asshole!

Dried out eyes cried stinging tears.

Akira stopped. He picked her off the floor by both shoulders.

"Cut it out."

"I am, really am, sorry Akira."

He let her go. He hung his head. When he spoke, his voice rasped.

"I do still love you, Ro," his voice cracked, "but I just can't listen to this anymore. You're shedding your whole life for an illusionary vendetta."

Rejection rang in the hollow room. In the silence, their anger simmered fresh. She watched him walk away stone-faced. She blinked.

She grieved, and she stopped.

She fetched a towel. She wiped at the spot where her eyes leaked. She straightened the bed, erasing Akira from everywhere she could. It took little time. She had been thorough when they broke up. All that was left was the smell on her skin. She headed to the bathroom, towel left in the pile with the dirty sheets.

She stayed in the shower for a long time after she washed. The pounding in her head, the waves of rare tears, the linger of booze, all thundered loud enough to distract from her marking's pull. Ro sat under the water, waiting for her head to subside. When she started to nod off she accepted only sleep would erase that night. She blundered toward bed, and her marking nagged against the thud in her skull.

And just like that…

Her marking slammed against her so hard it shattered the headache away. Henry was there.

I didn't want this goodbye.

CHAPTER FORTY-NINE

"Ok, get in there initiates!" Kekoa pushed them through mist.

Shai and Henry stumbled into a packed room. People lounged, talking and drinking. Everyone held cups.

"Welcome to fucking initiation!" someone yelled. Everyone cheered. Ro brought two cups filled with clear liquid. Shai took one.

"Is this it?" He sniffed.

"Moonshine," Ro smirked.

Shai locked eyes with her and downed the whole thing. He shrugged. Her smile grew. Shai shuddered and started coughing. Kekoa and Ro laughed.

"You're such an idiot!"

"What a noob!" Kekoa agreed.

"Here," Ro shoved the other cup in Henry's hands. He sipped. It tasted horrible and burned his throat.

"Your turn," an Atal from team Bardos, Second Lieutenant Petra Felt, thrust cups at Kekoa and Ro.

"Another?" Ro groaned.

Felt giggled, raising her drink. "To your Wingmen!"

"Santos," Ro held her cup toward Kekoa.

"Santos," he bumped his cup against hers, sloshing into each other's. Like Shai, they downed them and spluttered. Kekoa pulled Ro into a tight hug. Her face screwed up like she was going to cry.

"Hey, hey. We're celebrating, ok?" Kekoa held her at arm's length. "They got through. We got through. That's all that matters now."

She nodded, sniffing. Pia, red-faced and laughing, bounced to her side and kissed her quick on the mouth. Henry saw Shai gulp in his peripherals.

"Lighten up!" She bonked Ro on the nose. She flitted to Henry. "And you… catch up!" She bashed her cup into his, kissed him fast, and chugged. Henry stared at her. She finished, laughed, and ran to get another drink.

"Dude, what have we been missing?" Shai asked.

"I'm gonna find out." Henry drank the rest of his cup and choked at the end. "Stars, that's bad."

As soon as Henry finished a drink, someone pushed another in his hand. Eventually he just kept an empty cup. He met a ton of new people congratulating him on his round with Turtle. Like Ro said, many drank with him for landing a real blow on the major. Even she came by to say so again.

"You really were amazing today." She leaned against him, shoulder to shoulder. Henry liked the warmth.

"Thanks," he bumped against her. "Means I could take you, right?" Her laughter was short but gleamed, like a bubble.

"Maybe next time." She lay her head on his shoulder. "I actually have to go."

Henry lay his head on top of hers. "S'okay. G'night, Ro." They untangled and she stood.

"Goodbye, Henry." She squeezed his arm and she left. She hugged Kekoa her way, and Shai followed her out. Henry chuckled.

The night carried him from person to person. At some point, all of Sekhmet sang to him and Shai. Pia stole Henry for half an hour that he wouldn't remember. He drank more. He talked with anyone around. He found Shai was the funniest. When he started to grow tired, he kept to the corners. Akira came over.

"Lo!" Henry saluted with his cup. Akira bumped his cup but didn't drink.

"I've got bad news. I didn't think she was going so soon, otherwise I wouldn't bother the way you are now."

"Was dat?" Henry blinked. Akira sighed and took a swig. He pulled a mean face.

"Ro is leaving."

"No, no, no she already left." Henry smiled.

"No, Henry. Someone is replacing her on Santos."

"That's nice." Henry nodded. "Geometrically speaking, I was wonderi-"

"Henry, you're plastered. I get it. But this is serious."

"Was serious?"

"Do you like Santos?"

"Yeah! I made Wing," he hummed.

"Yes, you did. Do you want Ro to leave Santos?"

"No."

"Well, Ro is leaving Santos."

"Wha?" Henry slammed his empty cup down.

Akira sighed. "I… I don't think I can give you many details."

"But I don't want that!" Henry complained.

"Yeah, well, me either. I've already tried to talk to her. I think it's pretty shitty she didn't tell you." Akira looked sick.

"I'll go convince her not to!" Henry announced.

"I bet she'd love that." Akira drained his cup.

"You think so?"

"I need more." Akira indicated his cup and slouched off.

Henry staggered and stumbled after his comet to the nearest vein. He dived. The speed made his head spin. He tumbled on to a cold floor and lay groaning. He dragged himself to sitting, blinking around the dimly lit room. He faced a wall that wasn't black or silver or even blue—red. Hot, violent red. If fury had a color…

Brightness behind made him whip around. Ro stood backlit in the mist to her bathroom. Even drunk he could make out every brilliant speck of her eyes, but the colors spun. He jerked his eyes down to stop the nausea.

And everything else snapped into focus. Towels and sheets piled in the corner. Steam creeping into the room. The puddle forming around her feet. Her bare skin, dripping. Every muscle taut as she darted forward, gripped his chin, forced his eyes up.

"What are you doing in my quarters?" her nails dug into his jaw. He stared at those swirling colors, unable to look away. Blue, blue, blue spinning all too fast.

"Ro I'm sorry, I'm dr-"

"Sir," she snapped.

"Lieutenant…I'm… I'm…" he couldn't hold it down. He yanked away from her and collapsed to all fours, vomiting. The acrid smell made him heave again.

"Shit. Shit. Shit!" Ro retreated to the other side of the bed, snatching a dirty sheet she hoisted around her.

"Oh god, I'm so sorry Ro… you have no idea… I'm drunk, and Akira and I were… we were talking, and he was telling me… about everything, and I… I just want—" another wave cut him off. When he looked back up, wiping his mouth, Ro was rooted to the ground, her eyes unfocused. Anger jarred her features, but Henry had never seen that kind of ire, like watching someone implode.

"He told you? Everything?"

"You can't leave us, Ro. We're a team now."

She hitched the sheet higher around her shoulders. "We'll talk about this tomorrow, but right now that shit smells awful. Get out of my room, and go to the infirmary, they'll fix your headache." She fled to the bathroom.

Henry knelt in front of his mess, confused and guilty and horny. He had fucked it up. He didn't convince her of anything.

He seared the image of her naked body on the backs of his eyeballs. He'd always remember the sheen on her curves, the lilt in her hips, the dance in her eyes. He didn't know how he got to his own quarters, but when he did, he was alone. He took advantage of the privacy, consumed by shades of blue.

CHAPTER FIFTY

"Figured you two would be hung over."

The voice hammered through Henry's skull. He thought he might puke again.

"Go away," Shai groaned. "I'm dying."

"Maybe now, but not after this."

Even through shut eyes, the light ached through Henry's skull. His hope for relief eased the pounding as he opened his eyes. Kekoa passed him a large pill.

"It's chewable."

Henry popped it in and lay back on his pillow.

"How long?"

"About ten minutes. Shai, stop it."

Henry rolled over. Shai whined from his cocoon of sheets, huddled against the wall.

"Just eat the damn thing!"

"Leave me alone."

By the time Kekoa wrestled Shai free, Henry's head didn't throb. His stomach settled. He got out of bed and stretched. He felt fine.

"What is in that pill?"

"What else? Slime. I meant to give it to you last night, but I honestly forgot."

Henry blinked. Last night. Ro.

"Where's Ro?" he blurted. "Akira said something about her leaving."

Kekoa's smile died. "She did. She left." He rubbed his face. "She told me that this was her chance."

"What do you mean?" Henry asked.

"You two don't get it. Haven't seen her when it gets real bad. The hard thing is…part of it is Ro's always lived on a tether. Her marking. If she could get free, she'd—I told her to go for it." Kekoa's eyes searched the ceiling. Henry wondered if he'd been to Ro's grove too.

"Where'd she go?" Shai demanded.

"Well, that's classified. She got promoted."

"When?" Shai's hands shook.

"Rank?" Henry dreaded.

"Last night. She's a Major."

Silence shared their unspoken fears.

"When will she be back?" Henry broke.

"I don't know."

The next two days, Henry trained with Shai and Kekoa. Training under Kekoa, too similar and too different, hurt and comforted Henry. The third day, they received a mission from Opal.

"Well, it begins," Kekoa sighed.

"Who is Captain David?" Shai asked.

"You've probably seen him in the mess a few times. Atal. Average height, thick bodied. His hands are huge."

"Why him?" Henry asked.

"They are testing us. Seeing whether to add another Wing, separate us, leave us alone. Who knows. It depends what they are looking for now that Ro is out of the picture."

"More damn tests. How the fuck is this useful?" Shai grumbled.

They went on mission after mission, cycling through the captains without ever getting feedback. After the third, all three of them soured every time new orders came skidding to their boots. On their days off, Kekoa continued to drill Henry and Shai. Without Ro to push him, Henry had given up drilling himself in front of the unyielding onyx, but he still kept eyes and ears open for the blocker. Weeks passed into months without any change in their stagnant routine until one evening.

"You still have more to do?" Kekoa frowned.

"Yeah," Akira sighed. "I swear that shroud of death with be the actual death of me."

"Sorry, the what?" Henry interrupted.

"It's this phenomenon the Commander found ages ago. Taizai made a breakthrough last month, so now we have to apply his findings to all the research we completed last quarter up through now. Everyone's doing double shifts until we clear the backlog."

Kekoa sympathized while Henry and Shai traded excited looks. They scarfed the rest of their meals and dived to Henry's quarters.

"Did he really say the shroud of death?"

"Yeah. The night I met Taizai, we were in a room filled with weird grey smoke. I didn't think anything of it at the time, but I wonder if that was the phenomenon Akira meant."

"Seems like Taizai has the Gatekeeper's answers."

"Sure does," Henry grinned.

"Think you could ask him outright?"

"Doubt it; not if she warned me to stick to Ro."

"All right," Shai's mischievous grin matched Henry's, "I'll go to the shooting range for the sake of appearances. Don't get caught and let me know as soon as you're back."

"Thanks, man."

Sharing adventurous thrill, they split into darkness, and Henry ran to the lab. His feet carried longer than necessary. When he'd counted three minutes without change in the black, he stopped and pasted his hand on the wall.

The black didn't glow under his touch, an eerie slate devoid of even onyx's luster.

"Who are you?" Henry's voice thundered through emptiness.

Henry sharpened his sight deep in the dark surface. He couldn't see light, but his marking thrummed.

He breathed twice, before stilling to his most extreme focus. He recalled his Possession, the way his image overlaid Ro's, his light enveloping hers. He pushed out.

The unknown emptiness weighed more than onyx did. Henry put his other hand on the wall and heaved, his will shuddering under the mental strain.

Thread creeped from his fingers up the blank slate. Henry could only increase it a few centimeters with each exertion. He knew he couldn't keep it up, but elation soared even as the emptiness swallowed his light.

He narrowed his will to a pinpoint, more focused than he had ever attempted in training. He shifted his hands so that he braced against one spot with all his weight. He shot his marking through the contact, a singular beam puncturing the emptiness to reconnect with the web.

A shimmer of noise fractured black shards under his hand. The mask fell from the wall's surface, revealing the gleaming black and ravenous light. The fragments that blocked him turned to ash and disappeared.

A familiar brightness lurked near him. Henry grinned through his panting.

"Well now, hello Opal."

Opal approached the surface, her marred features nearly discernible.

"I'm not the 'block,' as you call it."

"Don't lie to me."

"Yes, this, just now, but I'm not the one stopping you from using your marking."

"Why should I believe you?"

"I can answer all your questions soon, but I'm shielding you from his probing. I won't last long here."

"The Commander?"

"No."

Henry appraised her brilliance, her timbre of sincerity forcing his belief. He lit a smolder in the wall and cupped the light.

"Meet me back at my quarters." He let the ember go.

"Does that count for me as well as Wingman Jukita?"

"No. You'll come with me."

"As you wish." Opal glided alongside his comet, staying just ahead of Henry.

"How much energy are you expending shielding me?"

"Enough that I'd be disadvantaged if the base was breached right this moment."

"Rahni? Here?"

"Perhaps."

"Will you be able to maintain it until I get back?"

"Yes."

"And?"

"And I'll answer your questions when you're safely back where you're supposed to be."

Henry nodded and jogged back in silence. Shai waited for them.

"What in stars' light is she doing here?"

"She said she has answers."

"Really?"

"Really." Opal moved to the ceiling, and her light morphed into a shapeless glow that radiated less. "Now," her voice echoed, "ask."

CHAPTER FIFTY-ONE

"Who is blocking my marking?"

"I can't tell you."

"What?" Henry demanded through Shai's spluttering.

"That really is the only answer I can give you."

"Liar," Shai accused.

"Why can't you tell me?"

"Following orders."

Henry's jaw snapped shut, and Shai sunk onto Henry's bed.

"Whose orders?"

"I can't tell you."

"Shai, ask her instead."

The radiance overhead flared.

"Who ordered you?"

"Sochiban Taizai, Second Commander of the White Wings."

"Tai...Taziai?" Henry managed. "But he—"

"Is every bit as dangerous to you as Roxar or Sech."

Henry snapped toward Shai's blinking face. "Ask her what the full orders were."

"What did Taizai order you to do?"

"To monitor the splice planted on Henry without telling him what I was doing."

"But telling me in front of Henry is still okay?"

"I am literally obeying his orders."

"Can I ask you about the splice?" Henry interrupted.

"Apparently, since the command didn't override my speech patterns."

"What?"

Opal shrugged.

"Ok, well… what does the splice do?"

"It intercepts your will so your ability never manifests."

"Why can I still dive?"

"Diving is a passive use, reliant on your interaction with the Web instead of you to source the power."

"Then what about when I Possessed Ro?"

"I don't know for sure, but I think you could because you were outside the Tower. Here, Taizai's marking taps into Roxar's ability, but outside he's just another lab rat."

"Taizai can use Roxar's ability? How?"

"I… can't tell you."

"Is that a different order?"

Opal remained silent.

"Who gave you that order?"

Again, the shimmer above kept quiet. The hush settled on Henry's darker fears, but he swallowed the ramifications for later.

"Why did Taizai do it?" Shai's dour tone shared Henry's revelations.

"Henry's marking is useful, even if not for himself."

Henry shook the military gloom from his mind, "But how?"

"Do you understand Sech's reaction to you?"

"She gets a power-boost."

"In a very basic sense. The same applies to Roxar, but without your active use of it, he can dip into more than normal."

"Stars, Henry, you're his battery."

"Sound like it," Henry shook his head. "Why? Why not use me, for real? I can—"

"We don't need more super soldiers. We need power." Reality crisped Opal's tone, leaving Henry's ears ringing.

"Who is we, exactly?" Shai asked.

"Roxar, Taizai, myself, and the majors."

"I knew it," Shai glared at Henry, who rolled his eyes.

"Yeah, you got one. Opal, why isn't Ro part of that?"

"For the same reason you're not."

"She doesn't have a splice, though."

"No."

"So how is he stealing her power?"

Opal's silence spawned awful questions.

"Does she know the answers you can't tell us?" Shai's hope buoyed Henry.

"No."

"But does she know about Henry's splice?"

"No."

"Is that why you told me to stick with her?"

"Yes," Opal smiled—a flare above their heads. Henry traded grins with Shai.

"She could remove the splice, couldn't she?" Shai asked.

"No."

"Who could?"

"Roxar, Taizai, or Henry."

Henry stammered, "I could?"

"Indeed. The splice is made of the same material I used to prevent your progress through the Tower earlier. Do you remember its weight?"

"I could barely lift it, but I did break it."

"When you found it, the Tower helped you. That material acts as a cloak from the Web, and the more of the Web you draw, the blinder you are to its presence. You have the strength to break the splice, but you'll never find it."

"What is that stuff?" Shai's wonder paralleled Henry's.

Opal kept quiet.

"You can imagine the questions I have left. Think you'll be able to tell me more?"

"No."

"Figures," Shai grumbled.

"What can you tell me?" Henry asked.

"You still haven't finished your second lesson."

"I know, but Ro isn't here."

"She isn't," Opal emphasized.

"Oh," Henry muttered, "all right, I'll talk to Akira."

"Close."

"Kekoa."

Silence.

"Pia?"

Opal beamed. "If that's all?"

"Guess so," Henry said, while Shai flopped on to Henry's pillow.

"Good night, Wingmen."

The onyx faded, leaving Henry and Shai forlorn.

"So," Henry rubbed his eyes, "I'm Roxar's battery, Taizai is helping him do it, he's got Ro somehow, and the majors are protecting him from everyone else. That's pretty much the worst-case scenario."

"And unless you're ready to take on the Commander I don't know how that splice is coming off."

"Yeah," Henry sighed. The relief at catching the block confirmed more fears than it yielded satisfaction. Sweat spent nurturing his instinct that someone opposed him, someone needed him to fail, bore only betrayal.

"Come on, Henry."

The anger Henry had deferred swelled.

"Henry?"

"This is Taizai's fault."

"Right, but what can we do about it?"

"Confront him."

"Stupid and wasteful."

Henry didn't answer.

"Henry, you have to try to break the splice."

"You think I didn't try that? Every day in front of that burnout wall and I never broke through anything."

"But now you know what it is."

"Not what it looks like, what it's made of, or how to track it."

Shai's persistence stilled. Henry summoned a comet.

"Please, don't blow this. You're a Wing. Ro may be gone for now, but when she comes back we know where to start."

"They've lied to us, all our lives."

Shai didn't deny it.

"What they're doing is wrong."

"What you're implying—the big picture—is wrong, too. I'm not rebelling against my country."

"My country didn't turn me into a human power supply. They did."

Shai dropped his eyes from Henry's. Henry left and followed his comet toward the nearest vein. When its brilliance filled the tunnel, Henry heard panting growing behind him. Shai whizzed into view a moment later.

"I'm counting on that special treatment of yours." He held out his hand.

Henry grinned and took it, diving them toward Taizai.

CHAPTER FIFTY-TWO

The dive spewed them into the lab. Henry's comet darted down a familiar path. Henry stopped short ahead of the alcove with the smoke.

The Commander turned first, Taizai refusing to face them.

"Wingmen."

Henry and Shai snapped salutes.

"Good evening, sir."

"At ease."

Henry gripped his hands behind his back to quell his trembling fingers.

Taizai didn't turn from the box. "Why are you here, Wingman Harbor?"

Henry didn't answer, staring at the Commander.

"You aren't interrupting, Wingman. Please," the Commander's glowing hand swept toward Taizai's back.

"Thank you, sir, but it is nothing urgent. I can come back another time."

"I am free now, Harbor," Taizai said.

"Yes sir," Henry stalled. "I, uh... had some ideas—no, questions—about the first dimension."

"Which are?"

Henry stuttered but didn't manage deception under the Commander's frown.

Taizai turned, "If I may ask you some questions, then?"

"Yes sir," Henry stiffened.

"Why drag Wingman Jukita into this?"

Henry measured his words. "Into what, sir?"

"I thought I plainly said each Wing makes himself here."

Henry stared at the floor, "Yes, sir."

"Now. You're here about the splice?"

Henry stopped breathing as his stomach turned to stone.

The Commander held a hand up, "Excuse me?"

"I spliced him."

"Did you, now? When?"

"Shortly after he arrived. He visited me one evening for assistance."

The Commander's eyes widened, his jaw went slack. His surprise fed Henry hope, but no rebuke came.

"Well done."

"Thank you."

Henry's eyes dropped to the floor, the back of his neck hot. Shai bristled next to him, spiking Henry's tension.

"I wondered when you'd notice," Taizai said.

"You've placed a limiter on the output, haven't you?"

"Naturally. It was the only way to prevent him from spending himself to death."

"Sir," Henry cut through their rambling. "Why?"

Taizai snapped, "By now, I thought you would have realized we overheard your conversation. You already know: power source."

The Commander snapped silver fingers. A window appeared above their heads, the image sharper than anything Henry had produced.

Henry swallowed bile. "Then you know why I'm here. Will you take it out?"

Taizai didn't respond. The Commander's quiet pressed against Henry's ears. Anger stirred.

"Please, sir."

Moments of silence passed, revving Henry's frustrations.

He appealed to the Commander. "Sir, please remove it."

"No."

"Why not?"

The Commander snapped his fingers again. The Tower's brilliance coalesced overhead in individual luminous columns. "All Lives contain power, some more than others." Half the beams dimmed while the other half grew brighter. "No matter the power, the Web still brings them all together." A silver filigree connected every beam to one another. "So, if we use the Web's power just right," the Commander's fingers drew together, and two beams merged, exuding unprecedented radiance, "a single Life can eclipse all others." The Commander's hand fell, and the light splintered into darkness. "The splice funnels the power of your will—in essence, the strength of your Life—to me."

Henry struggled to keep his hands pressed against his back. "And Ro?"

"What of the Major?" Taizai asked.

"Why not use her like you're using me?"

The Commander's frown deepened. "Why do you assume I'm not?"

"She doesn't… there's no splice, so—"

"A splice works on an amateur who can't tap into his own marking, not a fully-fledged Wing," Taizai said. "You remember, don't you, that you couldn't use your marking before the splice? You failed to that very day."

Fury itched Henry's remaining control. "So you made it harder for me?"

"If you can't overcome this yourself, then you truly don't deserve the power you have," the Commander's finality stung Henry's restraint. "Wingman Jukita, unless you have something to say…"

"No, sir," Shai's voice was quiet.

"…Then I recommend you both leave. Wingman," he stared Henry down, "I won't resist any effort or progress you make, and won't retaliate if you do surpass your inabilities. Until then… remember your place."

Henry and Shai saluted and ran. Henry dived them to his quarters, his grip unsteady on Shai's arm. Shai shook too. When they emerged, Henry screamed.

"They're probably still watching," Shai lamented.

"I don't care!"

"Henry, you—"

"I can't do anything about it!"

Shai exploded, his features turning beastly. "So what?"

Shai's heat startled Henry from his tantrum.

"You giving up?" Shai demanded. He shoved Henry in the chest.

Henry's temper boiled, and his aggression spewed over. He wrestled Shai back and kicked him into the bed frame. The giant toppled but scrambled to stand, new logic in his eyes.

"Wait, just wait a burnout minute. Shut up and listen to me."

Henry's anger cooled. He nodded as Shai's pupils dilated back to their human color.

"Yeah, you got dealt a shitty hand. I'm not denying it… but you are a Wing. A fucking White Wing. You're strong enough to beat this."

"But if it isn't just the splice then—"

"Then nothing. You're a soldier. Marked or not, we fight."

"We fight because we're strong." Henry envisioned blue.

"Right. The Commander and Taizai haven't acted illegally, and what they did is fucked up, but… wouldn't you do the same?"

"What day you mean?"

"If you were the Commander, and you had access to someone like you, wouldn't you use him too?"

"Not like this. We're supposed to be on the same team."

"No, we're not. He leads our team; he's never been part of it."

"Well, maybe—"

"Maybe nothing."

Henry nodded, sighing into his hands. Shai's logic prevailed over his vengeance, and Henry hated it. Years of indoctrination sweetened the acceptance Henry now swallowed. He was on his own, but not alone. "Thanks, brother."

Shai smiled, "Always, brother."

From that night on, Henry faced onyx walls every day he had in the Tower, determined beyond what Ro ever inspired in him. He confided in Pia about the Gatekeeper and her lessons, but not about the Commander, not until he could talk to Ro first. She and Ro had never discussed death as a dimension. Between Henry and her, neither could unravel what Opal intended. Months melted past, leaving Henry bone-tired from training or numbed to indifference touring with the captains. The night before their second mission with Gambare, Henry failed in front of the wall again and caught Shai and Kekoa on their way to the mess. He was listening to Kekoa's briefing for their mission when blue drew his eye.

CHAPTER FIFTY-THREE

The flash hovered at Ro's feet. "A Major so young."

"Where am I going Opal?"

"I don't recognize these coordinates."

Ro scooped up the smoke. The onyx on her palm hummed, processing the data. A weak direction pulsed against her marking.

Good… good… she wiped her cheeks. *I'm leaving now.*

"Good bye, Rolyn." Opal's light dimmed, leaving Ro alone.

She clenched her jaw. She left. The coordinates took her to a planet on the edges of scouted territory.

She had never operated outside scouted territory. She didn't know how to find the unknown.

She slid back into the Web, trusting her marking more than her knowledge. She set her will to explore the Web's vastness beyond her. Though normalized to its allure, she still reveled in the Web's wonder.

She noticed a niggling, like the sense someone watched her. The pulse tugged her marking at an angle Life never did. She listened to instinct, a deeper clarity where doubt couldn't live.

This is Roxar.

She refocused. The winds of the Web stirred around her. Her marking sung in her veins, harmonizing with the Web. She spread her arms wide as her will contracted.

Not Roxar.

Her ability shattered the peace, and she pitched full tilt into the Web's depths. After a few breaths, she recognized free space. She perceived the shift in the planets flashing past her consciousness rather than in the Web itself. They turned unsullied, like snow without footprints.

She guided her dive toward a random planet. She halted before making contact, observing. The Web hugged the planet, but no threads leaked from its surface.

A true adventure.

Words from long ago, a memory she shared with no one.

But not my good bye.

She activated sneak. The spec encased her with its own, untouched thread, masking her as filament of the Web. Its weight hung from her shoulders, but resolution could bare it for a few hours. *I hope.*

She pushed the Web hard with her will, unseating a thread. She concentrated on her Life to fuel a new portal to the planet. The Web obliged, and Ro dived to the surface.

It rained. Not warm soothing rain like Syllen—cold, whipping sheets of water. Wind pulled at her braided bun. Another pressure, above her, made her look into the rain. Across the dark, stormy sky, a thin silver line touched each horizon as far as she could see.

Another seam?

She had only seen three of them before, the biggest one on Norvin where she fucked up in the first place. She grimaced. Seams operated on the same principles as portals, but on a global scale. The only difference was a seam only originated in the Web and breached into reality, never the other way around.

If it did, maybe I never would have ended up here.

The seam on Norvin had been big enough to aggravate her marking enough to disturb her will. This seam's radius was smaller, but its luminosity explained why this one sent a throbbing spike on pain through the top of her skull.

She sighed, blocked out her marking, and turned to task. She applied her will, sweeping her marking across the whole planet.

Wow. Fast.

The seam quickened her scan three-fold. The planet was small. She could probably run around the whole thing in two days if she wasn't using sneak.

With or without sneak, that seam will compensate for what I used to create the portal. Worth it.

She stood mid-calf in water. Lots of life, mostly marine, and mostly small game. Limited plant life. Definite intelligence in some creatures.

Lucky there's water.

She bent down and retrieved her knife. She reopened the cut along her finger. She bled ten drops into the water by her feet. She applied her will, forcing her marking to Blend rapidly with the water. She inhaled deep and ignored the world around her.

Cohesion.

Her marking lit within the molecules of water, refracting the light from her ability through every drop of water on the planet. The shine died in a second leaving Ro with radar that didn't require her active ability to run. She scanned the predatory animal life and approximated a three-meter radius would be enough warning. Again, she blocked out all distraction.

Guard level one.

Her marking facilitated a low-level sentry ward around her marked perimeter, her blood leaking from her suit. She rolled her shoulders with the lighter weight. She flexed her will and pushed more blood out to coat her feet. She stepped up to the surface of the water. She took a few steps and her ward moved with her. Satisfied, she raced off toward the closest intelligent lifeform.

She raced for under an hour. She reached a group of six beady eyed, scaled humanoids. They screamed at her approach from the top of bedraggled ruins.

No weapons. No projectiles.

She pushed off and funneled her Blended water into a spring under her feet. She launched into the upper level of the ruins. She pressed offense without using her marking and dropped all six in seconds. Only one stood back up.

"Leave."

No comprehension. The humanoid rushed her. She punched it in the face, and it collapsed.

She dumped the unconscious bodies into the water, making sure they were propped up. She waited, watching her radar. The whole time, no other intelligent life came near.

It took forty minutes for the ex-defenders to wake up. The one that lasted the longest rose first.

It came to, shrugging its shoulders and gingerly touching its nose. Ro cleared her throat. It jumped away from her. She breathed deep and settled in to wait it out. After minutes of inaction, its eyes darted to its companions. The ex-defender let out low growls. Two of the others came to, rubbing sore spots. Together, they carried the other three away. Ro watched them turn north and scanned ahead of them. Pockets of humanoids littered the next twenty square kilometers.

Ro waited longer, monitoring them. No one came near for another thirty minutes. Skirting boredom, she summoned her Blended water and worked it around the nearest few kilometers in close detail. She tracked larger lives looking for a meal. The fourth animal she found was large enough. She tightened her will, her marking snapping around the fish's body. Her Blended water forced an eel toward her. She scanned the fish, checking its biochemical makeup.

All edible. Yum.

She dried out some sea plants by Blending with the moisture within them and sucking it out. She materialized her flint from her suit and managed a small, smelly fire. She cooked the meat, pinching her nose when the fat sizzled foul oil. She ate it anyway. It worse than it smelled. She rested for thirty minutes before setting off again, her stomach sitting heavy.

She collected her Blended water again. It took more time since it spread far during her nap. She took off at high speed, locking onto the nearest cluster.

In two days, she took over half of the humanoid's territory. She hadn't killed any one of them. They fell too easy to warrant force. She realized within her fourth fight that all these humanoids had three things in common.

First, she far outstripped their physical faculties. Taking on twenty wouldn't make her sweat.

Second, they were territorial with each other.

Third, all of them ate only one kind of animal; everything else was algae-like plants. The animal resembled a frog, but it tasted like Atali frosted caviar.

On her sixth day, she waited fifteen minutes out from the largest ruins she had found. Over a hundred humanoids huddled and squabbled under the broken shelter, and none of them would stand a chance.

She knew when they spotted her. She sensed a life creeping close and heading back. Closer. Retreat. Closer. Retreat. She stopped counting after the tenth advance. It took seven hours for them to reach her. They entered her field of vision crouched, each bearing a seaweed basket on its back. The baskets brimmed with edible plants and berries she didn't recognize. One basket held five eggs with glittering shells. They converged on her, slow and steady, until the one bearing the eggs stopped in front of her.

She didn't hinder her marking, and her brilliance shimmered blue against its grey skin.

It flinched but prostrated before her.

CHAPTER FIFTY-FOUR

Ro turned away, shutting down the glow in shame. Her oldest nightmare raged within, confronting her with worse than this water-covered world.

Blood. Bodies. Faces... faces I know. Is this where that road starts?

"Get up."

The humanoid quaked but stayed down.

"I said get up," she kept her voice free of inflection.

The creature pressed its forehead lower.

Ro sighed, materialized a frog leg, and extended the meat, "Get up. Here."

The others keened in unison, each bending to bow.

"No, fucking get up you burned out pieces of sh—"

The egg bearer pushed its basket toward her feet. Ro wrung her hands and picked one up.

"Fucking happy now?"

The humanoid burbled and back away, its head gyrating. Another humanoid approached, its basket full of sweet-smelling algae. Ro blinked, but didn't reject the offering. The humanoid burst in chitters and scuttled away to be replaced by another, then another. The last three baskets held three slabs of stone with crude shapes hewn into them. The humanoids set them in front of her and one remained.

It keened and pointed.

The first slab showed several humanoids, each bowing before a circle. In the center of the circle, a humanoid didn't bow, but filled the space and reached for the edges.

Fingers motioned to the next slab, its croon shifting. That sadness pierced into the softness the military hadn't beat out of Ro—irrevocable loss.

A humanoid held hands with a beast, both encircled. The humanoid cried; the beast howled.

The hand signaled to the last slab.

The humanoid and beast walked away from one another, the circle split into two parallel lines between the opposed bodies.

Or are they threads?

Ro traced the two lines on the third slab and pointed to the seam above.

Every humanoid's head gyrated, their chittering confirmations raising the hair on the back of her neck.

Could this be one?

She'd never seen a Rahnus, and doubted the storied black flames from legends.

"Show me."

She stood, and all but three humanoids resumed bowing. She rolled her eyes and motioned the standing three onward. Their progress lagged because her guides kept walking backward every few steps, watching in awe as her feet stayed above water. Her tolerance lasted minutes before she insisted on applying her blood to their feet too. They squealed when she sent her Blended water to wrap around their feet, screamed when she levitated them to coat the bottoms of their sandals. They stumbled away when she lowered them, exclaiming when they realized they shared her power. In turn they came to her feet, pressing their foreheads to the tips of her boots.

Ro couldn't breathe through their venerations. Kekoa had always stepped in front, postured as her apostle or her herald or whatever was needed to keep them at bay. Alone, wordless, and trembling, she fought the subconscious fears gaining momentum with each mumbled thanks upon her feet.

I am not her.

The lure of her nightmare only subsided when the three urged her to follow once more. She applied her marking to scanning the planet, over and over, to keep her mind from playing out its pitfalls.

Hours passed until she noticed an oddity. She never would have noticed it had she not used sneak. With every scan, she started to notice a blank spot, like a pixel on a map that didn't align on one side.

Emptiness.

She knew that one spot was unthreaded, how though scared her. She held her hand up, and the three stopped. She pointed northeast, where the unthreaded part lay. The humanoids chittered.

"I can take it from here," she closed her fingers into a fist. All three humanoids splashed through the shallow water, shouting surprise. Ro turned from their splutters and flexed her will. Her blended water started to draw back from its sprawl, flowing into her suit. "Thank you, but...I'll be back."

She took off, allowing her suit to assist her speed. She regretted the impact it would have on her guides, but she couldn't stand their gaping much longer. The more Blended water she took on, the faster she could go. She covered half the remaining distance before nightfall. Few animals roamed that far north, making dinner difficult and distasteful. Ro mustered appetite for double her normal ration. Instinct prepared her for a long day tomorrow.

She rested easy despite the unknown. That battle calm, the hum that drove instead of her frontal lobe, surpassed her emotions.

Morning drew her eyes open and her marking out. She resumed running after a light meal. Midday, she left behind life-baring land. She rested enough to recharge her stamina and started scanning. Her marking combed the terrain as she walked methodically closer to the emptiness. All day, her marking didn't burrow into a point disconnected from the Web. As darkness fell, Ro retreated to where wildlife felt safe.

The next day, Ro sped toward the emptiness and pored over the landscape. She even released the blood covering her boots refine her focus on just finding that unthreaded spot.

Her marking, for once, failed her. Enough times to tease, she would sense the aperture just ahead, then her marking would veer, dragging her the opposite direction.

Her tracking skills were useless in the water, but she refused to give in. Night didn't affect her determination. Morning saw her sitting above the water, her blended molecules spread for five square kilometers around her, her focus trained on listening over looking.

Where are you...

The sun hung above her head when she finally found something. Her marking spread equally, but in one minuscule pocket, she felt her blended molecules overlapping one another. An irregularity masked in her own arsenal sounded alarms, but she breathed past reactionary panic. There was no tug—no manipulation—of her marking, just a fold in what she could see.

Ro steeled her will, condensing her Blended water around the cells huddled on top of one another.

Ro bent her will, dragging her marking apart to reveal a cavernous void. The chasm opened beneath her, the water, sunlight, and her body careening into darkness.

CHAPTER FIFTY-FIVE

"You're...you're not Kyndor. What are you—no, no, she didn't...don't tell me...she's alive, right? I mean, she must be, if I...why? Why, why, why didn't she come? Please, I'm dying. You have to bring her—"

Ro slammed the frail man back, his shaking hands clinging to loose jowls.

"Please, you have to bring her! I can't do it—it was too hard, I should have listened! Please—wait, are you..." divine hope lit manic eyes, "you take it. Take the Gate." The man extended his hand—brilliance like a star in his palm—and a circle haloing his figure.

That's no thread.

Ro backed away from the supplication. "No, I'm not a Gatekeeper."

"You have to—"

"Stay away from me," Ro held her hand up, the cut along her finger welling with silver.

The madman's eyes zeroed in on her finger. "Luizen touched you! You must take it!"

He ran at her again, but Ro pulled her marking's shield back. In all her life, Ro had never felt her marking pull toward anything like that. Instead of magnetism, her blood roiled for sacrifice, and its need terrorized her.

I'm not stronger than that.

Ro snapped her marking in tight; she needed to preserve her strength and carrying the Blended water in addition to her specs would drain her stamina. Ro drew her suit back from her arms and legs and knocked the Gatekeeper out with one blow. The place where she collided with his head smoked; the skin covered in embers. Ro released Blended water to soothe the burn, holding it in a bubble around her calf.

Nowhere near as good as slime.

Safe for the moment, she inspected the bland purgatory of the Gate. She stood in a dimensionless, grey void, the Gatekeeper's prone body the only object to add depth. Neither the circle nor the star remained in his unconsciousness.

Her marking spread in infinity, but unlike in the Web, her brilliance reflected only her own Life. Not even the Gatekeeper bid her marking toward him.

That Gate though…

Weighing her chances, Ro pushed her marking around the Gatekeeper's body. Navigating his anatomy challenged her without her marking's attraction to pull her through.

Her Possession paled in comparison to even Henry's, especially with so little energy to spare. She counted on his debility.

She applied her marking's sensory pull, elated when she could define the boundary between the Gate and its keeper's Life. Ro locked her marking around the man's hand, sealing his will from activating the Gate.

She waited. Ro's restlessness surged as the Gatekeeper recovered. Her adrenaline kept spiking her will, draining her stamina wastefully. She chastised her lack of discipline, only to be interrupted by another irregular rush.

Time had no foothold in the Gate.

The man woke long after exhaustion drooped Ro's lids. Battle training whipped her to standing, her Possession steady.

"You hit me."

"You attacked me."

"I—" fearing eyes trained on the blood coating his skin. "Yes, please," he sobbed. "I can't take it anymore."

"I'm not taking the Gate. I'm keeping you from using it, too."

"Then…" he looked down into his palm, the bright curses appearing. "Bring me Kyndor. The Gate is overtaking me. She needs to bring another Keeper, otherwise—"

"I don't know Kyndor."

"You…then how did you find me?"

Ro flexed her will, her marking shining through her skin.

"Luizen called you here," he nodded. "Maybe it doesn't need her if you—"

"I told you, I'm not taking that Gate." Ro didn't allow frustration to leak through, but the weight of her marking sapped her endurance faster than she could stay awake.

"Please listen, you need to—"

Ro clenched hard on her will, shocking the man's system back to unconsciousness. Ro slumped, panting. She didn't fight sleep but withdrew to a primal part of her mind. Her will maintained Possession as her body broke around it.

Ro woke to the man eyeing her, resentment carving every wrinkle in his face.

"Whatever you've done to me, stop it."

"No."

"I can't even move."

"I don't trust you."

"I—" The man sighed, glaring. "I can't force the Gate on you anyway. You have to accept its burden, otherwise it will spit you back out."

"Where?"

"How would I know?"

Ro didn't answer. Opal always knew where the Web connected to the Tower's Gate, but Ro reflected that was only in Roxar's domain.

"Who are you?"

"My name is Ro."

"That's a boring name."

Ro kept quiet.

"I'll call you Bore instead."

Ro didn't answer, but her eyes narrowed.

"Well, Bore, why are you here?"

"Your people sent me to rescue you."

"What?"

"Grey skin, eat eels, weak punch."

The man grimaced. "Oh, great prodigal Bore, should I be bowing to you like my brethren? I'd genuflect before your great water-walking magic but—"

"You saw?"

"Of course I saw. I'm the Gatekeeper."

"Not for long, sounds like."

The Gatekeeper flinched in Ro's grip. His fear brushed against her marking, a hungry vacuum.

"I've always known it was coming, but…she said she would be here."

"Why?"

"To turn the Gate over to another keeper before Luizen's wrath prevailed. She said she would guide me through to the other side."

"Who is Luizen?"

The Gatekeeper's voice caught, "How did you find me, Bore? You seem unaware of…everything."

Ro kept quiet.

The Gatekeeper stilled, his soul resting against her Possession without purpose. "I only ever met Kyndor. I never guessed one could inherit Luizen's touch without understanding."

"Who is Luizen?"

"Bore, you're leagues behind that question, no matter your strength. Even if I gave you the Gate, you'd be swallowed whole."

"That, I did already know."

"Maybe you're not as lost as you seem."

"Try me."

CHAPTER FIFTY-SIX

The Gatekeeper snorted. "No, distrustful Bore, let me go first."

"I refuse."

"Then we will wait for Kyndor. Either she will come or I will die, and neither bodes well for you."

Ro resisted the bait. She tightened her Possession between the Gatekeeper's legs. She raised her brow as his breath shallowed.

"I lost lust a long time ago."

"But not pain."

The Gatekeeper blinked first. "Fine. Let me earn my freedom then. If you like my answers let me go."

"Better answer all my questions then."

The Gatekeeper huffed and closed his eyes. "Now. Let me begin. I was born Jinh, and was born again as Keeper. War gave me glory in my youth, but my soul outlasted my body. Kyndor led me here, to the Gate of Kerm, and explained my fate. I took the Gate from the old keeper, whom she led through. She promised she would return to safeguard my own death, and so I've waited, watching my family flicker and expire, guarding the Gate."

"Is there only one Gate on your planet?"

"I am Kerm's sole keeper."

"But there is only one entrance? Only one access to this world?"

"No, Bore, Luizen's wrath pierced the sky long ago. I merely control this Gate."

Ro assumed the wrath was the seam, hoping that meant there was only one Gate this keeper maintained, unlike Opal's thousands.

"Ok, I get it. So, who is Luizen?" she tried again.

"Oh no, Bore, we still have to talk of Kyndor, my angel."

"Ok then, who is Kyndor?"

"Touched by Luizen, but she has lived eons longer than I have watched. She knew Kerm's age and valued our Lives."

"Touched like you or like me?"

"Touched like you, but you and I share Luizen's gift."

"Wait, the touch and the gift are different?"

"Indeed, Bore, as I said, wait until you learn more of my angel." Jinh licked his lips. "Kyndor's light stuck in her smile, fascinating and forbidding. She told me of other angels but described none like you. She told me of her sisters, one with lips of light, one of silver-tongue, and the brother conquerors; what they see, they take…"

Ro stopped listening as imagery reeled through her mind.

What they see, they take…could Henry have been on his side the whole time?

"Are you listening?"

"No, I'm sorry."

"Contrition undermines a torturer."

She shrugged. "Don't be dramatic."

"For my own benefit, I'll repeat: Kyndor warned me of the brothers' greed, but assured should her sisters find me first, the brothers would already be too powerful to stop. So which future do you herald, Bore?"

"Excuse me?"

"Do you side with the brothers or the sisters?"

"I have my own side."

"Yet, I take it you know these brothers."

"Yes."

"Well?"

"One is amassing power; the other just inherited Luizen's touch."

"How much power?"

"I can't beat him."

The Gatekeeper blanched.

"Not yet, anyway."

"You have a chance?"

"Depends on what a chance means. What did Kyndor warn you they would do, specifically this time?"

"Well," he paused, and Ro settled in. "To explain that, I must tell you a story told to me. Before time measured Life, one was all, and all was one; then, the first angel, Kyndor's eldest sister, cast time, and all fragmented to some, and one splintered to half. Luizen, who only knew death, breathed in Life, and madness descended. Three angels, my Kyndor among them, cleaved Luizen from Life, but the madness grew to wrath at the turn of their betraying wings. The wrath hungered for their wings, unyielding and relentless in pursuit, and pierced through time to find them, leaving an altar of Luizen's light in its every passing. These altars tore through space and time, defying Death and Life, and giving passage to Luizen back to Life. Kyndor found the first strong enough to bear the altar's light, and so the first keeper gained Luizen's gift. The keepers have preserved this lore with Kyndor's help, as she still finds the keepers to prevent Luizen's return."

"I, uh, I'm not much of a religious type…so, uh—"

"Ask, Bore."

Ro scratched her scalp, the raking distracting her from the nonsense tempting her derision. She closed her eyes to hide scorn, trying for confounded. "I still don't know who Luizen is."

"Luizen is the one who only knew death."

"Right, but who is he?"

"Luizen only knew death, then the first angel cast time, and—"

"Oh, yeah, right, that's, uh, that's right." Ro pinched her lids shut, grinding her teeth. "Why are you dying, then? Your story didn't mention that."

"Those strong enough to bear the light sacrifice their Life to that Gate. Though unburdened by the limitation of a body, Life can only burn so long against wind. When a keeper's Life winks out,

Luizen's wrath leaks through the Gate. An impure Gate will consume the Life of the planet housing it, unless another keeper can reclaim the altar's sanctity."

"I thought it was Luizen himself that came through?"

"Only Life has gender, Bore."

"Oh, ok. Sorry."

"The wrath is Luizen as much as the light is. A keeper can never reverse the wrath, only halt it."

"Never reversed, but halted. Great. How much needs to leak before it explodes?"

"Not an explosion, Bore, an implosion. A Gate reflects all the Life that called Luizen to begin with. When the wrath consumes a Gate, the planet remains. All Life returns to the first dimension."

"The…first dimension?"

"You truly know nothing Bore."

"You mean Death."

"I do mean Death."

"Can I go there?"

"Of course. You can die, can't you? Or are you immortal, Bore?"

"Far from it."

"All with the gift must be, otherwise our sacrifice is meaningless."

Ro opened her mouth, but settled for nodding. She understood fractions of Jinh's story, and clarifying it was more frustrating than listening to it.

"Well, Bore, will you let me go?"

Ro released her control over his nerves, allowing the electric impulses to flow again.

Jinh gasped, "You're really a natural, even if you're a dunce."

Ro sighed, "I, unfortunately, have a lot more questions, but first let's get out of here."

"I'll never go home. My only way out is through, Bore, and you couldn't manage that even if you wanted to."

Fair enough.

Ro couldn't afford sympathy for the people who sent her to recuse Jinh, though she warmed knowing they'd remembered his loss even through generations. "If I find Kyndor, she can help us both."

"If you found Kyndor, you wouldn't bring her here first though, would you?"

"Dive me out, and I'll bring her back to you first."

Jinh laughed.

"I keep my promises."

"You'll—"

"Won't take the Gate, will bring your angel."

Jinh averted watering eyes. "Thank you."

"Where am I going?"

"All I can manage is to send you back through the wrath. The rest is up to you."

"I'll come back soon."

"Goodbye, Bore."

A portal sliced through the void, sound screaming through Ro's ear drums. The messy dive tumbled her into the Web, but her marking chugged in relief. Her will resumed control, her body slowing from its tumult.

Ok. Kyndor time.

CHAPTER FIFTY-SEVEN

Ro bent her marking toward the Web, thinking only of that name: Kyndor. Except she didn't move. The Web left her hanging, no wind, no rush. She reached out again and again, but her marking never took hold in the Web. Wherever Kyndor lived, Ro's marking couldn't stretch far enough to find her.

Ro hadn't anticipated finding another marked person would be easy, but she expected something. Anything. She floundered with her marking, unsure where to go.

In the space between focus and feeling, in the periphery of her senses, Ro's marking did find something.

Touched. My touch.

Jinh's planet bore her claim. Ro reached out. The blended molecules she'd left on the planet stretched for her will. She didn't have the strength to summon the water through the Web or control it, but a new expanse grew within her sensory information.

Is that what he meant by growth?

She had every reason to believe Roxar only used her for personal gain, which would not explain why he'd urge her to accumulate her own territory. Distracted from Kyndor's mystery, she worried as the idea clung to darker implications.

I'm missing something important, something big.

In a snap decision, she banished all thoughts except two.

Untouched. Water.

Her will flared, fanning her marking out as she flew through the Web. She marveled at the spread of planets the Web offered, each an untouched soaked landscape.

She dived faster than before, hurtling toward the nearest planet. She arrived land-side the next breath. She activated sneak and scanned the planet. No major life forms nearby. No people.

Rocky, red, and a burnt sky. The atmosphere pressed on her, the sky too close to the surface to be comfortable. She looked for descent. Her marking pulled her north and she moved leisurely. She understood how thin air could suffocate.

It took only minutes, but when she came to a cliff's edge her breath came fast and shallow. She urged the suit to cover her hands with silver-spikes. Smaller, rougher spikes covered her elbows and knees. With her marked claws in place, she climbed down the jagged face. The lower she climbed, the more the air thickened with humidity. It took over hundred meters descent before she could breathe easy. She used her marking again to scan in finer detail for life. She found producers, but no consumers.

A new planet, just starting to form life.

She continued her climb down, ignoring the cramp in her forearms. It took three hours on her internal clock, but the planet's cycle had turned twice already, throwing her into dusky darkness and forgiving light. A pleasant day, even if short by her standards.

She never came to ground. The cliff face extended into deep water. The smell of salt pinched her nostrils. She sliced along her finger and dripped blood into the lake.

Am I claiming land again?

Shame shuddered along her spine, waking her oldest nightmare.

Blood. Bodies. Faces…faces I know. Is this where that road starts?

She stilled, observing the silver dripping from her finger into the water.

By growth, what if he meant…that.

Ro refused to follow that thought through to its conclusion.

I will never kill for him.

Dazed but determined to move forward, she willed her marking to Blend, making the dense water hers, molecule by molecule. She dropped from the cliff, pulling her Blended water up to catch her before she crashed. She manipulated her Blended molecules so the salt wouldn't damage her skin. The denser water pushed her form back to the surface. She contracted her suit under her skin and floated.

Why would he benefit from my growth now?

Roxar quit training her personally when he promoted her to Lieutenant. She'd relished that time with her team, so she never questioned why he claimed she'd learned enough.

What changed?

Henry.

Every fear that drove her paranoia of the wingman resurfaced, without her marking's masochism to interfere with her judgment.

If he wanted me to be stronger so I could control Henry then he would have taught me Possession, not sent me away.

But if…

She faltered.

I'm thinking about it the wrong way.

She closed her eyes, and let time align her ideas.

He ordered me to leave, not so I can get stronger than Henry, but to keep me away from Henry.

Instinct pushed her.

To keep me from using Henry against him.

Relief seeped from her spine. She relaxed; unaware she'd held her muscles so taut. Growing both her and Henry's strengths separately insured he could tap into either of them without fearing their collusion.

I'm such a burnout. Why didn't I see that sooner?

She didn't spare more self-pity, instead trying to find a silver lining. Without knowing his end game, she couldn't develop a counter strategy besides working Henry over when she did go back to the Tower.

Ro's thoughts stumbled a second time.

But I can't go back now. He ordered me to explore the unknown and find…power of use to him…something he can't find himself?

Possibilities flew through her brain. Several related to the Rahni, several didn't.

If she concluded right, something eluded Roxar and Taizai both. No matter their schism, she knew Taizai's loyalty surpassed his personal feelings. Many of her Rahni theories evaporated. Taizai did not have a strong hand in the war. Still, Roxar had increased draft requirements for the last two years.

She remembered the pillar of smoke—colorless, shapeless, and beating like a heart, and definitely very wrong.

Urgency recalled her marking. Ro peeled her Blended blood from the water, making sure she didn't leave any of herself. She opened a portal underneath her body and sank into the Web. The winds welcomed her marking, the light drying her skin. Facing the immensity of the Web, she hefted all her attention on her memory of that hazy anomaly.

Ro lurched forward, the Web pushing her through veins faster than she could have achieved before.

CHAPTER FIFTY-EIGHT

Ro halted the dive the moment she sensed she headed back into Roxar's territory. She adjusted her will to exclude Roxar, but the Web still pushed her toward one of his planets.

Could he sense me?

Ro reached out to Jinh's planet. She sensed her touch, her blood left behind, but nothing beyond herself. Ro circled the planet she faced, scanned with her marking from afar, and found nothing beyond Roxar's touch. The neighboring planets were untouched and unremarkable.

Ro gambled. To be safe, she engaged sneak still in the Web, and plummeted. No wind, or light, or warmth, a void swallowed her in free-fall until she disengaged sneak.

She burst back into warmth and light, the Web seeping under her skin with welcome.

Did I just go outside the Web?

Filing that question for Taizai, she dived to the planet, activating sneak as soon as the Web spit her out.

Roxar didn't come.

No Wing came.

No trap sprung around her.

Sighing, Ro scanned the planet. She found no life, but unlike the last planet, the dearth didn't indicate potential. Lingering decay hung in the doorways of small houses. Baskets and bowls cluttered the street, gathering dust. Shriveled plants stirred in the wind.

Ro walked through the abandoned buildings but found no sign of what happened. She left the skeleton village behind and followed her marking. It guided her for hours past several more abandoned villages. Ro found no clues to what had happened to the people.

Ro knew when she drew close to the smoke. Her marking reverberated off of it like sonar. Ro frowned. Her marking's strength relied on Blending with the Web or with Life; she'd never encountered something that denied her marking.

Ro crested a hill and sought out the wisp reaching to the sky thirty meters away. She surveilled the area with her marking as she approached. No life or Wing interrupted her.

Ro came to the base of the pillar, the smoke rising a few meters before petering out in the air. The ground around its base ruptured and cracked. Burn scars marred the dirt in every direction.

Ro observed the smoke for an hour without change. She decided if Roxar knew she'd returned, he would have found her by then. Still keeping sneak active, Ro bled on the ground and sent her marking burying deep. The smoke had no anchor in the earth. She recalled her blood, the silver rising to circle the smoke's perimeter.

Ro focused her will, listening to her marking. The smoke still pushed back against her.

What do I do?

Ro avoided Blending. She tried every technique Roxar taught her about Possession, but still the smoke repelled her.

Hours facing the smoke yielded no results.

I'm just like Henry.

She smiled to herself. She stretched her hand forward. The blood in her veins pounded in refusal, but she touched it.

Frost burned her skin, and she retracted her fingers cursing.

A ghostly palm touched the smoky barrier from the inside.

She forgot the blisters forming on her skin as the other hand patted at the smoke, as if reaching for her. A few tense minutes passed before the other hand faded back into the smoke.

Ro sank to the cracked ground, aghast and awed.

When the wrath consumes a Gate, the planet remains. All Life returns to the first dimension.

Is that a Gate to the first dimension?

Ro touched the blisters on her fingers, remembering the chill that burned her. Instinct told her this planet had imploded, its Gate broken, its people dead.

I wish I had listened to Henry.

Ro tapped into the minimal store of slime she kept in her suit, enough for small cuts and bruises. She grimaced as the slime stung her burn, missing Kekoa's deft skill.

As she regenerated her skin, she kept eyes on the smoke. No other souls came to the surface. Once healed, she opened up the cut on her finger. She held her blood in the air, forming a waist-high ring around the smoke.

She constricted her will. Her marking wailed, but she forced her blood nearer and nearer the smoke. The moment her blood made contact, electric current zapped through her, an intense cold leaving her breathless.

Ro staggered back, the ring of blood collapsing into the dirt.

A hundred hands clawed at the smoke, but the swirls of grey never parted.

Ro gaped as the dead reached for life; she would not help. Caution outweighed pity.

The hands didn't fade for ten minutes. Ro feared their disturbance would alert Roxar, but still no one came for her.

She breathed deep and held it in. She mourned, a pang of helplessness and sadness and anger without outlet.

No one should die like this.

I won't let Jinh down.

If Kyndor meant to prevent this, I have to help her beyond Jinh.

Steadied by conviction, she didn't agitate the smoke again. She wouldn't learn anything more from it. She cleaned and returned her blood and left the smoke behind.

If her marking failed to find Kyndor, only three other people might know.

I won't play his games anymore.

But if he knows anything about this, I have to work with him. I owe Jinh that much.

Ro resigned herself toward home, heart heavy.

CHAPTER FIFTY-NINE

The Tower welcomed her home. Her marking lunged toward Henry, biting at her skin with fire she hadn't felt for months.

I've needed something different for a long time.

Instead of leashing her marking's writhing, she engaged sneak and drew more power from the Web. Sneak quieted her power surge and her will held firm.

Her marking whipped her senses, but she didn't lose ground to it.

Finding the stamina to regulate the influx of power from the Web would challenge her, but she'd figure that out later.

For now...

One.

Two.

Thr-

She slid from the Web before Roxar.

That was fast.

Roxar blinked, "Rolyn?" He closed the journal and stood. "Remarkable," he gaped. "Your skill with sneak surpasses most of the other majors already, and in only months."

Ro sucked her tongue before approaching the desk. She set her hands down and leaned in. "I'm not here to talk about my strength or my marking or any of that. I'm done playing the games you've set for me."

Roxar sat again, a piqued curiosity about his face. "You think this has all been games?"

Ro didn't let him distract her. "You're stronger than I am. My marking is bigger, we both know it, but the Tower is an asset I'll never have." She fought back bitterness. "I need your help."

Roxar hummed, appraising her. "Uncloak yourself."

Ro obeyed.

"Raising the amount of Web stored in your body is risky."

"I know."

"If you've grown this strong, then you don't need my help."

Ro ground her teeth but maintained composure. "I don't need strength from you. Do you know Kyndor?"

Roxar froze.

"Who is she?"

"Did you meet her?" Wonder softened Roxar's tone.

Whatever Kyndor's relationship with Roxar, Ro never expected that vulnerability in him. "No. I need to find her."

Roxar sighed. "I've been looking for her for a long time."

"Who is she?"

"Why are you looking for her too?"

"I met a Gatekeeper who told me to find her."

"And you agreed why?"

Ro hardened. "I don't have time to play politics with you."

"You are my Major."

Ro took a deep breath, "I'm going to find Kyndor and you're going to help me. If it means I have to resign, so be it."

Roxar laughed.

Ro didn't respond.

"Resign? You thought I'd believe that bluff?"

"I have no team. Ditching rank means nothing."

Roxar paused. "This still is your home."

"Your Tower."

"Rolyn, whether my Wing or not, I won't help you find Kyndor."

Ro repressed a shudder. "I wondered what it would take to make you say that. You never hesitated to use me to gain power, but you won't let me near it for myself. I can respect that."

Roxar didn't answer.

"If you won't help me, will you stop me from looking for her?"

Roxar ground his teeth, "No."

She'd hoped the possibility to find Kyndor through Ro's efforts would tempt Roxar to a truce. "Good. Then I'll make you an offer on the condition neither of us interferes with the other: give me Taizai, and I promise I won't use Harbor."

Roxar's smile betrayed anger. "Think you've figured that out, have you?"

Ro held her hand out. "I don't have time for games. Do you agree or not?"

Roxar slumped into his chair, his eyes calculating. She didn't crack under his scrutiny.

"I want to go one on one. It's been, a year?"

Ro's hand fell. "That's all you want?"

"You've been gone three months, come back more refined than I thought possible, and with knowledge you shouldn't have. Of course I want to test the rest of your skills."

"You want to see if you really can still beat me."

Roxar's smirk translated his hunger.

Ro sighed and extended her hand again. "Give me a week with Taizai first, then you can test me however you want."

Roxar took her hand, and her marking screamed at the contact. "Deal."

She turned on her heel and dived on the spot through the floor.

One. I fucking nailed it.

Two. I fucking nailed it.

Thr-

She slid from the Web into her quarters. Her Webbed wall bubbled in sunrise shades.

"Relax." She drifted fingers through the mist.

She took her own advice. She cleaned and lavished her body with cold and hot water. Her towel smelled like grass and sunshine. Ro giggled into her pillow as onyx cloth ghosted over her skin without adding two hundred kilos. Lying on clouds of fiber and comfort, Ro surrendered to the bubbling in her chest.

I'm home.

She woke in an hour, her rigid routines overcasting home's warmth. Refreshed, she routed to food.

Real, hot food. She quivered in line as she picked out fresh fruit and simmering meat. She groaned when she took the first spoonful. Rich flavors—*stars, salt is good*—shocked her tongue. She sucked her spoon for the lingering spice.

"That may have been the hottest thing I've ever seen." Masera sat down next to her.

"Welcome home." Charles sat across from her.

"Ro!" Her best friend pulled her into a hug. "You damn spoiled brat, why didn't you tell me? I can't believe you didn't tell me."

Ro laughed, hugging Pia back.

"I am happy you're home."

"Me too."

CHAPTER SIXTY

Ro joked with Pia and Sekhmet like no time had passed. It warmed Ro deeper than soup could reach.

Pia grinned. "You haven't even touched your food. I have to run. Dinner later? How about twenty-one hundred?"

"Sure."

Pia hugged her before Sekhmet left for debriefing. Ro smiled as she finished her cold soup.

Her marking prickled when Henry's will focused on the mess. The pain ratcheted with each footstep that brought Henry closer. She sucked in more of the Web to match. She kept still when Henry, followed by Kekoa and Shai, walked in.

Her blood zinged up along her back, shoulders, arms, neck, scalp, and back down again. Her marking palpitated with his heart, wrung her veins into tiny threads and burst them to enormous size. She abandoned the added power from the Web and locked her marking into the smallest cage—being this close still hurt too much.

I did it with Roxar. I can do it again.

"You're back."

She steeled herself and looked Henry in the eye. His gaze savaged her. She remained stronger.

Huge, familiar, missed arms encircled her.

"Stars, you and Pia both." She held Kekoa back.

When they sat, Shai pulled her in. Henry had sat across from her. Even the half meter of distance helped. Her marking fawned over the added space, and she couldn't resist meeting his eyes again.

His marking seared her, and her blood fizzled.

He's grown too.

"You didn't say goodbye," Shai accused without heat.

"I certainly did. Both of you were very, very drunk."

"You didn't tell us, though," Shai squeezed her shoulders.

"As I said, both of you were very, very drunk."

"You should have seen Shai the next morning. It was hilarious," Kekoa added.

She laughed and asked him about the selection process. They fell into a comfortable pattern.

I missed this.

"So, you promised you'd tell us about the dimensions," Shai interrupted her reflection.

Shit.

Henry's gaze searched her, scorching her face.

"My bargain to you," she pointed at Shai, "was when you became my teammate. You are not. And my bargain with you," she pointed to Henry, "was when you make marked Wing. Still have a way to go, boys." Her heartbeat sped at Henry's tension.

"That's weaver shit!" Shai fumed.

Ro shrugged. "That was the deal."

"But—"

"You once told me if I could beat Turtle, you'd tell me."

The hair on the back of Ro's neck stood. "I did."

"Well, you're a Major now. What if I beat you?"

"Is that a challenge, Wingman?"

"It is Major." Henry and Shai traded grins.

"Nope," Kekoa shook his head. "We've got departure in five hours. We are going to bed."

"Oh, relax." Ro nudged him. "Like you weren't going to stay up with me anyway?"

Kekoa glared at her. Henry laughed.

"She wins."

"Half an hour," Kekoa demanded.

Ro huffed. "Two minutes."

Henry spluttered. "What?"

"Deal." Kekoa beamed.

Kekoa and Ro chatted the way to the sparring gym. She stretched when they got there. Henry bounced from foot to foot.

"Don't hold back, Henry."

Henry nodded.

"All right. Whenever you're ready."

Henry gave it his best. She pinned him in an arm bar in thirty seconds.

"Yield," she commanded.

Henry tapped out.

"Stars, that was good," Shai praised.

"That didn't even take a minute," Kekoa shook his head.

Ro released Henry's arm and rolled up to stand.

"Let's go again." Henry rubbed at his elbow.

"No time. I've got other people to see."

"But—"

"I'm back for a little while. I'll take you on any time, after your mission."

"But that's not fair," Henry whined.

Ro sighed. She hugged him. Her marking burst at the proximity. She stayed put, earnest to see how strong she had become.

His arms came around her, and she focused every fiber of her body in resisting her marking's seizing.

I am stronger.

And she was.

"I missed you guys." She smiled. "Come on, Kekoa." She left, taking her friend with her.

Ro went with Kekoa back to his quarters, and she curled up in her favorite blanket of his.

"I missed this." She nuzzled the soft fur.

"You should get one of your own and take it with you. A little bit of home."

…Home.

"Hey? You okay?"

"Yeah, sorry, I blanked out. It's been awhile since I could really relax, ya know?"

"Or sleep."

"I don't know if I can knock out for more than an hour. I'm so used to—" she waved her arm, trying to mime the time apart between them.

"Here," he pulled a bottle from a drawer. "Take two. You'll sleep like a baby."

"Thanks." She sent the bottle through the Web toward her quarters.

Kekoa peered at her. "What did happen out there?"

"You know I can't talk."

"Sure, but you came back in three months. No major comes back in three months."

"Stuff happened, and I had to come back."

"Stuff?"

"Stuff."

Kekoa nodded. "You're not going to be around that long, huh?"

"At least a week."

Kekoa blew out a big breath. "We'll barely see you again."

"Hey, if I made it back in three this time, I'll do it in two next time."

Kekoa smiled at the floor. "Yeah."

"I'm going to meet Pia for a late dinner. Want to come?"

Kekoa joined them. Ro used eating to keep quiet, listening to Pia's exuberance bounce off Kekoa's humor.

This is home.

"Hey Ro?"

"Yeah?"

"You must've got stronger, right?"

"Some."

"Is it enough that you can manage Henry now?" Pia's wishful eyes pushed Ro's only regret to the fore.

"Not really."

"Oh."

Kekoa kept smiling, but Pia couldn't shake dejection.

You idiot.

Ro nudged Pia with her boot. "Hey. Even if it was, Roxar won't put me back in rotation. Things are different now."

"Yeah, but—" Pia sniffed. "I hoped that…you know."

"I wish."

Pia shared her mournful smile.

I wish I could stay home too.

A flash of smoky hands jerked Ro out of her reverie.

Things are different now.

Kekoa left first, though he stayed longer than she expected. Pia talked Ro's ear off until she started to droop at the table.

"Seriously, Ro, have some self-respect," Pia scoffed.

Pia walked with her back to her quarters. Ro took Kekoa's pills and snuggled into bed. Pia lounged with her until she couldn't keep her eyes open any longer.

But some things won't ever change.

CHAPTER SIXTY-ONE

Henry never expected Ro would pin him in under a minute. That surprise surpassed his guilt at not asking her about the dimensions. He awed at how much she had grown.

She left with Kekoa, leaving Henry with an envious Shai.

"Let's go to bed," Shai grumbled.

"You at least remembered to ask."

"I don't want to talk about it." Shai's voice deflated. Henry didn't mind keeping quiet so Shai could cool.

"Think she's going back to Akira or get a new lay?" Shai still sounded peeved.

"Do you ever ask Kekoa this shit?" Henry deflected.

"Fuck no. Their relationship is totally platonic."

"My relationship with her is totally platonic."

Shai laughed. "Honestly, you've never thought about her?"

"Hard not to after seeing her naked." It slipped out. He winced, checking Shai's reaction from the corner of his eye.

Shai glared. "What'd you say?"

"Initiation night."

"And you didn't tell me? How the fuck did that happen? Did you...you didn't—"

"No, no. Of course not. Akira told me she was leaving, and I drunkenly thought I could talk her out of it. She was in the shower when I got there."

"That's it? Come on man. What did she look like? I mean, c'mon!" Shai flung his arms.

"I don't have a picture."

"Ro naked," Shai wondered aloud. "That'd keep me hard for night." Shai's spite tempered his heat.

"Dude, drop it." It hit too close to home.

Henry had trouble sleeping. All he could think of was Ro. She hit harder than he remembered. Faster. He tossed and turned through the night, contemplating their next round. How he'd outmaneuver her. Outpace her. Stand over her.

Shai's mood had not improved the next morning.

Henry muttered low enough so neither Kekoa nor Gambare could hear. "Come on, get over it."

"Why didn't you tell me? You know I…"

A flash stopped Henry's exasperation. Opal confirmed departure. Gambare transferred coordinates to Henry and they linked arms. Henry accessed his nav spec and focused on the point of direction. He dived.

Henry pushed them into a faster vein from the start.

Force heavier than Ro's fist smashed into his face, reversing the dive. Shai's grip vanished. Henry's body shuddered under the pressure of his dive being knocked off course.

Henry fell, hurtling blind into brightness. He fought against the chasms of the Web but his will couldn't find purchase.

The Web spat him onto land. A squelch absorbed his back, the pressure pushing the air from his lungs. He gasped, vulnerable, forcing his panic down. He rolled over rotting fruit and slime molds. He gagged on the acidic stench. He pulled onyx over his face into a helmet. The air purifier relieved the odor and blocked hazardous chemicals. When he recovered his breath, his breathing still felt tight like a foot pressing on his back.

He closed his eyes and searched his nav spec. It worked, three team signatures tugging at him. He moved toward the nearest, only able to walk at first. Parasitic vines creeping up thick trees and swampy conditions hindered his progress. Behind him, yellow spores fluttered from the disturbed marshes.

In half an hour, the terrain inclined. Once free of the mud, Henry could run. Exertion gave Henry an outlet so he could think instead of worry. Something had derailed the dive. Something had hit him. He had no idea where he was, and the other signatures weren't moving.

The incline shot up, making Henry scramble the last half kilometer. He cleared the ring of tree growth, seeing past the canopy.

The Web glittered above, silver against midnight, a rip stretching the sky, horizon to horizon. Henry's eyes throbbed so he looked away. He still felt the pressure in his lungs, constricting, electrifying. He shivered. He'd never felt the Web affect him like that.

He pulled himself over the lip of what turned out to be a crater, almost ten kilometers in diameter. He scanned with the nav again. He faced north and took to the empty plains. Open, flat space. Henry, starved for reassurance, consumed the distance. It took minutes to reach Kekoa.

"Henry!"

Kekoa was dirty and bruised, but unbroken. Henry's tension bled enough to let his fear show.

"I don't know what happened. One moment we were good, and the next we… I don't know. I—"

"It's not your fault. I know it wasn't." Kekoa took his arm, his voice sinking into a deeper register. "That's never happened. Never. You have no idea. I was terrified. I don't have Nav, I don't think any of us do besides you. Thank the stars you're unhurt."

"You too."

Kekoa's grip pinched. "I wish we had Ro."

Henry gulped.

"Can you still find Shai and the Captain on the nav?"

Henry checked. They had grouped together further away.

"Sixty some kilometers west."

"Let's go."

Henry breathed easier with a teammate at his back. He lapsed into a pace that pushed Kekoa.

Ro. His throat grew tight. If she were here, she'd know if they were okay. She could open a portal straight to them.

He cleared his mind. Wishing would only distract him. Each stride carried his brain back to trouble even though he avoided blue.

Nothing he knew of could stop a dive. It had to be Web-compatible. He ruled weavers out. White Wings weren't powerful enough.

Marked Wings were. Reality crashed his consciousness. Henry fought to keep his stride even.

If either Ro or the Commander sabotaged them, it was an ambush.

Ro wouldn't.

Ro didn't trust the Commander.

Henry reasoned the Commander had nothing to gain from attacking his own. If Henry and the rest were lost, the Commander would have to replace four White Wings, one of them a Captain. Morale would plummet. Teams would have to pick up the slack. It didn't make sense.

Henry wanted Shai's perspective. He sped up.

Half way there, the flat plain undulated. Trees sprouted, dark and smelling of mint, unlike the rubbery jungle in the crater. They had to detour around another crater. It added an extra hour.

"Lieutenant! Wingman!" Gambare waved them toward a large tree.

Shai lay behind it, a blanket draped over his leg.

"What happened?" Kekoa's color paled as he took in Shai's slack jaw.

"Broken leg on impact. He went out right after I moved him. Get to work."

Kekoa knelt and steady fingers pulled the blanket back. Shards of bone made Henry stop.

"Kekoa, do you have enough slime for that?"

"No. Go away."

Gambare motioned, and Henry turned to authority for structure. He needed a firm tether before his nerves imploded.

"I lost communication coming through the atmosphere. Do either of you have a connection?"

"No, sir."

Gambare sighed. "I know your marked training isn't complete, but I need a marked Wing more than anything. What can you do?"

"Nothing, sir. I Possessed once, but that was inside the Web."

Gambare pointed at the sky. "That's a seam. Major Sech has reported it's an immense phenomenon. Can you feel it?"

Henry found the seam, analyzed the throbbing in his retinas.

Ro had asked at the first if there was a change, something different. Pain was new.

Pain was how Ro felt it too.

"I can."

"Okay. Okay," the Captain stammered. I've never even worked with her…We've all seen the blood thing. Anything like that?"

"No, sir."

Henry didn't stop looking at the seam. "If I could touch it, it'd work."

"Stars, Harbor, touch it?" the Captain blanched. He rubbed fingers through his hair. His eyes lit. "Hold out your palm, Wingman."

Gambare gave Henry a new weight that settled in his bones.

"I gave you my transmission package. It connects to the nearest one of our satellites, but because it runs through onyx it has to go through the Web. It might be enough with the seam."

Henry pressed his palm toward the seam. Needles pricked the backs of his eyes, but he didn't flinch.

"It's responding, sir."

"Try diving. If it works, come right back."

"Yes, sir."

Henry, whipped by fear and need and duty, reached for any vein he could find. Rumbling grew above. Sound struck, and silver lightning engulfed him, flinging him into the Web.

CHAPTER SIXTY-TWO

Henry tumbled through chaos. The dive tugged and jerked him, the wind battering in every direction.

Henry extended his will behind. The dive collapsed around him like sand filling in the gaps he pulled through the seam. He scrambled against the Web, fighting for every inch back, back to his team.

His will caught an edge in the Web. Henry reached forward and grasped what pulled on his will. The Web suffocated him. Light blinded him. Henry didn't let go. He stretched the Web's fabric.

It ripped. A poisoned cough spat him on rotting fruit and slime molds. The spot where he landed was singed—lightning had cleared his path to the ground. The smell made him gag. Henry checked his nav. His team stayed clustered to the west. Henry breathed easier. If they hadn't moved, he hoped he hadn't missed much.

He sacrificed stealth for speed, splashing through the muck. He crested in the crater's lip in twenty minutes. Alone, he flew over the plains.

"Harbor!" Gambare's voice broke his running rhythm an hour later.

Henry stopped in front of the captain, saluting. "When I dived back, I landed in the same spot, sir."

"I don't know enough about the creation of portals to understand why that was the case. Can you get us back?"

"Yes, sir." Henry remembered pulling Shai behind him the Tower. "I'd need yours and Lieutenant Omika's help managing Shai if he's still unconscious."

"He's awake, but he can't move." Gambare paused, gauging Henry. "Did you have any issues returning?"

"Nothing like the first time, sir. It was hard to come back through the seam."

"How so?"

"The pressure, sir. It got worse the closer I got back."

"The transmission package bounces between satellites until it gets back to Old Home. Do you think you were fighting the package?"

Henry considered it. Unlike his nav, the transmission package wouldn't be affected by his will. His dive would have opposed its direction.

It wouldn't affect the Web, though. No spec or package did, and the pressure hadn't been internal.

"No. I don't think any spec or package could have done that, sir."

"Harbor. This discussion stays between us. Report all of this to the Commander as soon as we get back, and no one else. Understand, Wingman?"

"Yes, sir." Henry swallowed other words. The captain's fear opened dread's door. Gambare withheld something and it made Henry's stomach churn.

Gambare nodded, eyes bleak, and turned. Henry followed him to where Kekoa stitched Shai's leg. Shai growled, eyes savage orange.

"How long have I been gone?"

"Long enough," said a voice so rough the familiar words were alien.

It appeared, right between the four of them. A ring of black dust—ashes of onyx—burst a meter off the ground. A portal snapped wide for one moment before disintegrating. White hair, a beastly body, and silver teeth.

Henry's eyes could follow but his brain would have never reacted fast enough. In a fraction of a second, the beast lunged toward Shai and Kekoa. Its arm lashed out. Shai's lips peeled back howling. Henry's body started to move, was catching up to his mind. The beast smashed into Kekoa's head. The giant staggered.

Henry's kick generated enough speed to blur. The beast crashed into the nearest tree, its cry a shrill whistle that erupted into cackles. It twisted and scuttled up the tree's trunk.

"Stay put!" Gambare snapped.

Henry froze despite every instinct screaming to pursue.

"We need a defensive perimeter to protect the injured—"

Kekoa thrashed, slicing his hand across his throat, pointing at Shai and doing the same.

"Why?" Gambare demanded.

Kekoa held a finger up. The fingernail elongated into a four-inch talon. He pointed at Shai and mimicked blowing up.

The giants slipped into their beast forms if they suffered bad injuries, but without control. A wild giant would demolish them.

"Omika, go giant." Gambare ordered.

A ring of onyx, just like the one that had spewed the beast, blew from Kekoa's center. Kekoa disappeared for a moment. He reappeared four and a half meters tall, thick bodied with legs like trees. The chocolate fur on his tufted ears offset electric yellow eyes and long fangs.

"Harbor," Gambare grabbed his arm and thrust his toward Shai. "Get Jukita out of here. Get the Commander. Tell him everything. Bring reinforcements fast, three defensive teams, two evacs, and have medics on standby. Go!"

Henry faced Gambare's back. He knew it was a mistake. He knew that if he left, they'd lose their only way off this planet.

Henry didn't even know if he could make it back to this planet.

Shai was losing his fight to stay human. A strangled cry distorted into snarls. The sound sent Henry toward him instead of where he knew he should have been.

"I'm picking you up. Don't scratch me."

Shai bellowed when Henry lifted under his leg. Undeterred, Henry heaved Shai over his shoulder and locked an arm around him. He concentrated his will. Lightning gathered. It struck faster than before. Henry surged into the blaze, his desire for home pulsing through the Web.

Shai's weight dragged Henry like an anchor. Henry tightened his grip and strained into a faster vein. The wind on his face increased, increased the strain Shai put on his back. Henry pushed harder.

He hoped it didn't take as long as it felt.

They emerged in the empty portal bay. Shai groaned. He gripped his reopened leg wound with talons.

"Don't transform," Henry yanked Shai's hands away, but the damage was done. Shai's talons stripped more flesh. He snarled but locked his furring hands above his head.

Henry pressed his palm on the ground. "Medic!"

A wave of light rippled from Henry's hand, canvassing the entire room. The brightness singed Henry's eyes. He blinked. Air ripped around him.

"What's going on?"

"Who's hurt?"

"Why am I here?"

"Henry?"

"Frist Lieutenant Frank!" Henry called in relief.

The woman from Gorain approached.

"Giant with a broken leg! I need—"

A Horn with graying hair bustled forward, snapping at two other Kau. "Second Commander Romirez. Chief Medical Officer."

Henry moved out of her way. He pulled Frank aside. "I need the Commander. Captain Gambare and Lieutenant Omika are stuck on that planet with an unknown hostile. I need three defensive teams, two evacs, stars, make that thee."

"Harbor, you're a Wingman." Henry wanted to shake her until she saw sense.

"Captain's orders, not mine. Please, First Lieutenant."

She opened her mouth but frowned instead of retorting.

"And Medics on standby."

She glowered but nodded. She popped into the Web. Thunder split behind him.

"Henry!"

He whirled. Furious blue eyes found his.

CHAPTER SIXTY-THREE

Falling asleep to Pia's comfort with Kekoa's drugs kept Ro asleep, snug and dreamless, far longer than she wanted. So much sleep made her groggy when she woke. Her marking didn't writhe so hard.

Right, Henry's gone.

She lounged in bed, relishing the minimal pangs through her body.

I am so much stronger.

She had slept late, and sloth infected her motivation. She leisured in the shower, enjoying the cold water seeping through her scalp.

The Web hit her. Henry's dive crackled through Tower and set a ferocious storm through each of her vessels.

It's been hours since they left...

A blast whipped her mind and body. Her marking tattooed pain across her vision. As her blood rampaged, Ro pushed her will into the Web. Henry's residual power still snapped at her, but she ground her teeth and dug in. She traced the blast, found Henry, found Shai, identified Henry's blood lust, felt Shai screaming.

She revved her will and wrenched pain aside. She leapt from the water and tugged her suit over wet skin. She ran to her Webbed wall and dived.

One.

A stentorian clap. She emerged headfirst and sideways, parallel to the floor. She rolled to her feet, adjusting for the slip of her sodden suit. She surveyed the scene in an instant. Henry's marking hammered through her. Shai shook on the floor in pools of red.

Romirez and two other giants pinned him to the ground. A few others milled around them, anxiety and fear keeping them inactive.

"What happened?"

"We were ambushed!"

Kekoa. "Where is everyone else?"

"Kekoa and Gambare are still back there. We need to go back, now."

"Give me the coordinates."

"There aren't any."

"Explain."

"When we dived, something happened, stopped the dive. I had to bail, and we landed on a planet we've never scouted. I think I can follow my dive back there, but I can't track it."

Someone stopped the dive…

"Only marked Wings can establish a com link on planets we haven't scouted, and since I wasn't there to begin with I won't be able to establish one. An extraction team relies on their comm. We need a combat team, not an extraction. How many targets?"

"Just one."

One?

A primal urge flared inside her. Only one target crafted the perfect scenario to get rid of Henry and an entire team.

What could Roxar do in that aftermath?

"I can handle it. Let's go."

"No! You'll lose!"

She spun to see Shai pushing off the bloody floor. He turned giant fast, but remained human enough. The desperation in his voice made her tremble.

"We will wait for back-up," Henry paused, "but we will go."

Turning to Henry felt like knives against her corneas but her will rose above the pain. If Henry wanted to go, she would have backup.

"We won't need any, not together."

Henry's head jerked to Shai and back to her. "Please, just wait one minute."

She huffed in frustration and scanned the Tower for whatever teams headed their way.

None. Not a single other White Wing was coming, but Roxar was, and closing.

She dropped sneak entirely and pushed her marking through the Tower. She forced her marking concentrate on him, using her blood pull to sift through his marking.

She felt Roxar powering up by the step.

He's coming for a fight.

She knew enough to guess his motives. Roxar would only fight, *really fight*, in the Tower if there was a direct threat to his power. She was sure of it. If leaving to go back for Kekoa and Gambare met that condition…

Whatever attacked Santos scares Roxar. If he's truly scared of it, then he knew they would die.

Her fury cried foul, and her will roared. She charged her marking up in kind, counting the steps until Roxar came through the mist.

I'll pay him back sooner than I thought.

"Pay close attention," she directed Henry. She sliced her wrists. She pushed her will out, urging her marking into the air.

Roxar pushed through the mist, his eyes on her. Roxar's voice boomed, his arm glowing like a solar flare.

"Wingman Harbor you have no authority to endanger the lives of my White Wings. Do you understand me?"

My turn.

She flexed her will. Her ability congealed blood, thick and viscous, condensed from thin air. She shot it at Roxar. Her blood hit him in the face and she forced it down his throat. His wracking coughs barely made it through her thickened blood. Flecks and chunks hung from his lips.

"Not another word."

"Stop, Ro!"

She faced Henry. Her control faltered, and the blood expanded in Roxar's throat.

Oops.

"Stars, Henry, can't you feel it? He means to abandon them by fighting us here!"

The Wings milling in the portal bay, stunned by Ro's attack, started to hum like a hive of bees. She had little time.

"Let him go." Henry's marking lashed against hers, his sudden fear palpitating in his stare.

"He's leaving them to die!"

"Major Sech, stop this at once!" Taizai shouted. He struggled to hold Roxar up.

"Please, Ro." Henry tugged on her arm.

Henry's eyes seared through the back of her neck. She turned to him. It was that look, the same one Roxar wore years ago when he Possessed her for the first time.

Absolute desperation.

"Take us, right now, and I'll leave him."

"This is mutiny!" Taizai screamed.

"He is letting them die!" she yelled back.

"Now, Ro," Henry urged.

She yielded, and her blood withdrew from Roxar's throat. She surrendered, allowing her marking to pull rampant toward Henry. Her blood glowed like when he had Possessed her, but she never felt his marking contract around her.

The sound of Roxar trying to recover sent a trickle of mirth through her spine just as the Web consumed them.

CHAPTER SIXTY-FOUR

Wind buffeted rather than blew. The heat seared and cooled at random on her skin. The dive, despite Henry's steady grip and Ro's aid, crumbled around them. The vein's jagged construction jerked on Ro's marking.

Ro marveled at the corruption in the Web, caution beginning to backpedal her urge to save Kekoa.

It took ages. Time had dragged by after she felt Henry catapult beyond the remnants of his last dive. The rough path they had traveled through the vein just ended. The Web squeezed on her from all sides, trying to sever her connection to Henry. Dauntless, Henry pushed through. *With excellent form.* Henry, bushwhacking through the galaxy.

The Web spat them out on something yellow, squishy, and moist. As soon as she landed, she hauled her marking back. With Henry here, she'd be unstoppable for a short period of time, maybe a couple hours. She had to store all the energy she could.

She staggered. Pressure above indicated a seam, but she'd never felt one this strong.

And man-made.

She knew, same as she could recognize Roxar's territory, that the seam above was created by a marking. She couldn't tell whose, but she guessed.

Her marking hurt, distracted by the Web flowing above her, even if she couldn't yet see it. She dropped to one knee. She snarled, and she fought. Of course, thanks to Henry, she had to earn her keep twice over.

She picked herself up. Her back was straight. Her blood gyrated against her veins with power—the good kind of pain. The kind that sometimes came with winning.

"Ro, what you did—"

"I don't have time for regret, not now." She grimaced. "Please."

Henry bit his lip but nodded. Relieved, she scanned the planet, but her marking encountered no life besides Henry's, not even animal life. Panic tried to surface.

"I can't feel them."

"I can," Henry said. She didn't let the paradox distract her.

"Well?"

"You're glowing. Like a lot. More than ever."

"I know, just trust me on this. Let's go."

He nodded and he moved, fast. They ran an hour.

"Couldn't you have gotten us any closer?" she panted.

"I came back to where I landed the first time. It was the only place I really remembered." He didn't look at her, just forward. She was too eager up against his chill. He didn't even breathe hard.

On flat land, Henry let loose. She could keep up, but she regretted spending her energy. Henry only slowed to a jog when they came to the next tree line.

"It's going to get pretty thick," Henry pulled up to a walk. "Catch your breath. We will be there in ten minutes."

She followed him, silent. They crept through thick brush, but the leaves were fine and made no noise. She had three more minutes. Her breathing was back to normal.

No fatigue. Breathing stable, body working, head clear. Good.

"Henry." She took his arm and crouched a moment.

"You're still glowing." He joined her.

"I can't do anything about that, and besides, they know we are coming."

Henry nodded.

"You get Kekoa and Gambare. Let me handle everything else. Once you get them, take them straight back to the Tower."

Henry stiffened. Her marking strained against her will. He never looked at her like...*this*.

"We leave together."

"No, you take them back."

"No. We leave together."

"Shut up and do what you're told."

"No."

Idiot! They need evac first!

She wanted to smack him, but he continued.

"I can't leave, just like you can't leave Kekoa."

"They need to get home. That's what matters. Do not disobey me, Henry."

He didn't conceal his guilt. "I'm not leaving without my team. Not again."

"Just take them home!"

"I'm sorry." He snapped his head forward and moved on.

She wanted to scream at him. She wanted to kick him. She didn't. She couldn't further endanger Kekoa and Gambare. Henry was already being stupid enough.

I'll give him hell for this.

He already crossed from underbrush into open air—a big glade with three tall poles at the far side of the space. Bodies occupied two of them.

Ro could make them out. Gambare was strung up on her left. Kekoa was on the middle. Death hung Gambare at eerie angles. Kekoa was still dying. Slowly. She couldn't see anything else.

Focus! Focus! Focus!

She couldn't. So much dark red stained Kekoa's legs she choked. If he bled that much it meant he had tapped out all the specs in his suit.

She moved forward, and Henry caught her.

"Where is it?" Henry called. Kekoa shrugged.

"Scan for lifeforms," Henry said. She complied but found nothing, not even Kekoa.

"Where did it go?" Henry asked. Again, Kekoa shrugged.

"The target isn't here but I bet it isn't far. It looks like an animal, but it's intelligent. Looks half human half ape."

"Let's draw it out then." Ro pushed forward.

All three poles started oozing black, like ash seeping from the wood, swirling with air.

"Rolyn?"

CHAPTER SIXTY-FIVE

Ro froze. Her name. The way it really sounded. The way a Syll said it. Memories crystallized like ice in her skull. The disembodied voice was too familiar, too like her own. She stopped, rooted to the spot. Henry froze, too. Even Kekoa tried to pick his head up.

The ash hitched, as if a breath was taken. Between the second and third pole, a foot off the ground, the ash converged. Flying as if drawn by a hurricane, the ash took shape. A human form appeared.

"Dramatic, I know," Ro's voice said, but it wasn't her. It looked exactly like her: blue skin, blue eyes, black hair, same muscles, same weight, same height…same silvered blood.

"Ringer," Ro intoned. *How can it be?*

Ro recognized herself—her dream self—the one who burned and mauled. The one that shadowed her sleep.

"What?" Henry grit out.

"Ringer. That's me."

"You are you. What is that?"

"I am here. That over there is also me. That's a Ringer. My Ringer."

How can I save Kekoa? My Ringer will know my every attack, every defense. Can I distract it long enough to get Henry home?

"Ro, I don't know what the fuck is going on." Henry's hand gripped her arm. "How do I fight you?"

"Fight me?" she snapped. "You're getting them out of here, idiot!"

"No, no, this is wrong. Something's not right. We need to get out of here."

"I know. You should feel off. You can only make a Ringer of yourself, and I've never made one. There's no way this is a good thing, but unless you see something different than I am, I'm standing over there."

Henry's grip tightened.

"Rolyn, I have no need for the others. Come with me," her Ringer spoke. Henry pulled her behind him.

"We need to change targets."

"Absolutely not. You watched me fight with Pia. I wasn't full out. You can't take my Ringer on."

Henry stayed put, made immobile.

"Why does it always have to escalate, Rolyn?" her Ringer sounded forlorn.

Henry still didn't move.

"Get them out of here," Ro pleaded.

"Leave?" her Ringer called. "I'm afraid not." Her Ringer pointed a finger and sliced it through the air.

A ring of ashes shot outward from the empty pole. A grotesque, white creature paced inside. It looked female. It loped on all fours but had human hands and feet. Her face was disfigured, blue light pouring from round eye sockets.

"That's it," Henry murmured.

Ro's marking drew to that intensity, but Kekoa was bleeding out and she hadn't done anything about it. She walked forward, heedless of Henry.

"No, Rolyn." Her Ringer shook its finger. "You leave with me, not with the bait."

"Henry, nothing has changed. Kekoa needs us."

Henry didn't budge.

"Please, Henry…please."

Henry let go of her.

"Seriously Rolyn, last warning." Her Ringer beckoned with two fingers and one hand on its hip.

The monkey-girl stalked around Kekoa and Gambare's corpse. This wasn't combat; it was rescue. She used every brain cell she had to scrape together a survivable plan.

Her Ringer sighed. "I can't believe this is how it goes." It stood up straight, and its face lost its veneer. It flicked its hand. Its eyes never moved from Ro's face. A scream punched Ro's ear drums, a familiar voice lost in the moments before death.

She turned. A cut from navel to neck cracked through Kekoa's sternum. His blood didn't gush or spurt. It coated his body, like rain on a roof. His intestines, puffy, pink, and soft peeked from skin meant to hold them in. She tried to Possess him, but he was already Possessed, and the touch was familiar.

She looked into his eyes. They found hers. They quivered and dilated uncontrollably, but she didn't look away. She held his gaze all the way through, all the way until his eyes were dull, gelatinous orbs floating over blood stains.

The world faded. Her marking contracted before exploding in a flare of light. The Web pulsed through her, fueled by rage that transcended the human limitations imposed on her will. Her glow grew ten-fold, the light absorbing the blackness of her suit. She beamed like a small star.

Marked blood poured from her suit to cover her luminescent body. Her suit flexed, stiffened, adhered whenever she needed to. Every move was a choice of exhaustive possibilities, an arsenal for no other. Her marking-bound armor perfected her combat, her ultimate weapon.

Four hours.

The maximum time she'd held her blooded spec.

Her Ringer, easy in stillness, watched wearing a tormented expression. It made Ro's blood run thicker, pulse brighter.

Ro had no care for her own humanity. For the first time, she yearned to see a lifeless, broken body heaped at her feet.

It's my right to beat you.

Ro went all out from the beginning. She took the offensive. Her Ringer read the first feints, dodging. The fourth time, Ro connected. She concentrated her will, sharpening her blood across her knuckles. She slashed through skin. She pulled back and landed two more fast jabs, sinking crushing weight behind each blow.

On the second hit, her Ringer caught her by the forearm. Ro twisted and broke free.

They stood apart from each other, Ro panting, before they tangled again. Ro tried for speed and landed a blurring kick to the head. Ro snapped her leg back and used the momentum to launch her forward into a new combination.

It was the seventh strike. Her Ringer grabbed Ro's forearm, but this time slammed its knee into Ro's body. Ro sank back into her Ringer's hold. The onyx enveloping the Ringer's hand solidified. Its grip was unbreakable.

"I'm sorry."

Ro's suit under her Ringer's hands shrank back, revealing blue skin. Ro screamed as the Ringer squeezed harder and harder. Pressure unlike even the Web could exert exploded her molecules. Her Ringer let go when there was nothing left between its hands.

Ro backed away whimpering, sheltering the stump of her left arm.

"You are weak yet," the Ringer whispered.

Ro pushed the physical tragedy from her mind, focusing on survival. She could feel blooded seal over her stump.

Now limited, Ro avoided as much as she could. She dodged nine blows, blocked four, and took thirty-seven. Her shoulder and arm crunched as she tried to block one last hit. She sagged to the earth, beaten.

She struggled up anyway.

"I expected nothing less."

Her Ringer lunged, going for her hair. Ro evaded, allowing her Ringer to flow past.

She fought, hard. She could barely see, barely think, but she fought.

Her Ringer grabbed at her right hand. Ro pulled, but her Ringer's grip hardened into a vise again. Knowing what was coming, Ro used it as an advantage. She screamed and kicked out. She landed a few good blows as her fingers were crushed off. Her Ringer threw her body up. The roots of her fingers finally gave, letting her body fly into the sky with the force of the throw.

Ro had never known such savagery. Her right and left, both useless. Her upper body mostly broken. She vaguely saw the Ringer come after her, a vast black shape that flew toward her like death. A huge mass hit her in the ribs, forcing a scream she didn't think she had left. Fingers wrapped around her neck, squeezing her windpipe shut. Heat spread through her body as a new pain sliced across her consciousness.

"Die quickly, Rolyn."

She couldn't see…couldn't breathe…

The pain drowned in the sense of freedom, the sense of release. She had no more energy to stop her blood pouring from suit and body.

Her will gave.

She hit something hard. She couldn't move anymore. She had nothing left to give. She breathed what little she could as her life spilled from her body.

Grass filled her hazy vision. Every blade stood—tall, crooked, wide, broken. Some were dark green, and some were small and reaching. Some sprouted in two ways, and some had droopy tips.

Each blade moved. Some twitched with air. Some shivered with the earth. All of them grew and lived. Incomprehensibly, moving.

She fell into darkness, two strong arms pulling her under a shaded wing.

CHAPTER SIXTY-SIX

Kekoa screamed. Henry watched a shard of onyx rip his body in two, from sternum to stomach. The onyx faded to ash and settled on the ground like a memorial to the dead.

Henry's rage boiled as Kekoa died, but he didn't move. He could do nothing to save him.

He could still save Ro. His fear for her survival cleared the anger pushing through him.

Ro's control evaporated with Kekoa's life. She exploded. Her brilliance drowned the darkness of her suit. A nimbus of silver fire burned from her skin.

Henry never felt so small. He watched Ro evolve into something beyond brains or bodies—a being of light, spitting fire.

Ro shot toward the Ringer, and the beast charged. Henry tore his eyes from Ro. The beast's only advantage was speed. Henry trusted his eyes, waited, dodged. The beast blew past him and Henry put his foot in its back. The beast slammed into the pole under Kekoa's body. Its vertebrae crunched. It still quivered on its haunches, trying to stand. Henry materialized his knife. He pinned the beast's hand to the pole. It didn't screech or howl—its jowls snapped near his throat. Henry grabbed the beast's jaw.

Henry roared. Blood and bone squelched between his knuckles. Henry stood, kicked the knife to the hilt through the padded palm. A wail gurgled from the bloody hole in its head, but Henry never heard.

He had turned to Ro. He almost shut his eyes.

How long had he fought? Three minutes? Less?

Silver blood splashed the ground in puddles. The Ringer was airborne. Its onyx wings buzzed too fast for Henry to make out, but they were soundless in the air. In one hand, the Ringer gripped a shady spear. In the other, Ro's neck.

Ro hung limp. She didn't glow. She leaked—silver dripping from her boots.

He couldn't jump high enough if he tried.

The Ringer's spear flashed high and sunk into Ro like a dead fish, disintegrating to leave gaping flesh. The Ringer let go.

Henry sprinted toward her falling body, calling her. Desperation burned Henry's eyes, his vision blacking out the sight of her fall.

An indefinable crack rang through his ears, and ash fell from his body.

Like the tide, Henry's will surged through his marking without the splice. His marking bridged the seam and his intention, her name, his mantra.

Bright lines emerged between them, entwining her body, and clawing fear raked against Henry's conscious. His will enveloped her furious bid for survival that was the last string holding her together. Henry reached out for the brightest thread binding them and snapped his will. Possession drew her body toward him. Her weight, heavy and wet, hit him in the chest. He protected her as they fell.

When he rose, he could see. Ro was dying. Blood oozed through the battered skin from her chest up her face. Her body crumpled around broken ribs, stretching the spear wound above her hip. One hand was unidentifiable mush. The other, a stump at her forearm.

He pulled her unresponsive body close and pushed his will into her body, forcing the bleeding to stop, the lungs to breathe, the heart to pump.

The Ringer's face betrayed confusion. "H—Henry?"

Terror snapped his head toward the Ringer, missing its wide eyes for its outstretched fingers. Ash gathered, developing into an unmistakable shaft.

Henry wanted to fight.

He wanted to avenge.

He wanted to rip its hand off too.

He wanted Ro more. He wouldn't watch her die.

He kissed Ro's forehead and laid her down. He gripped her forearm tight and squeezed his Possession tighter.

He knelt on the ground, his other fist braced in front of his chest, mimicking every defensive Wing he'd seen.

The Ringer raised its eyebrows—familiar contempt on its unknowable face.

Henry didn't have the strength but he made his will maintain his Possession and reach out to the seam. The spear was faster than his lightning. It sunk into his shoulder, but his fingers closed around its shaft. It never came close to her.

His lightning jolted the Ringer, the seam forcing her into a dive that Henry pinned back to the crater with yellow spores. The spear disintegrated, leaving a deep puncture. Henry pressed a hand over the stinging fire swelling with the blood, grinning through exhaustion.

Henry flogged his will one more time, praying he could pull Ro through without inflicting more damage, and the seam swallowed them toward home.

The Web squeezed him through; the ecstasy nearly undid his overused will. Ro's weight tearing through his chest to his wounded shoulder grounded him.

Her arm slipped in his grip. He squeezed his fingers tighter, but her blood slicked skin sent his hand the wrong way.

He freed his bleeding shoulder and reached for her. The movement slipped till he only held her limp hand.

He couldn't stop his instinct.

His eyes opened.

Agony flared through his eyes, his sockets smoldering with electric destruction.

The Web sparked his marking.

The pain centered to suffering in his retinas, but something much stronger carried his sight.

Light seeped his mind, quenching a desert where Henry's ability lurked. His vision fractured into silver crystals, shading the world in prisms of light. Henry's ability emerged.

His worn will rose to its natural station, a cloak safeguarding him from the eternity of the Web he now saw. Vision was too small a word. Thread of all sizes connected Life of all measures across an infinite void—a silver net demanding space amidst a vacuum that would consume it. The entanglement of Life stretched as far as Henry could see, silver light carving a thread between him and the Commander that flashed his urgency.

He couldn't bear it all. He was so much smaller, lesser. His only place was awe.

A squelch on his palm taught him to never belittle Life again.

Blue streaked behind him, the Web lighting color as it caressed the blood draining from Ro's body. She was dying, and in this universe of knotted light, the corners of her lips turned up, a softness in her shut eyes that made Henry fear.

He focused his Possession around the faint pulse her Life beat, but his will wasn't strong enough for steady. Her Life fluttered before him, the Web dancing to her fading heartbeat, and she smiled into her death.

Henry cried.

He willed her body closer. His Possession obliged, her form sliding toward his. He held her tight, Possessed and close, wishing he could keep her.

The force landing on his feet tumbled him. He sheltered Ro's body, but other hands caught them both.

"Let go!" the Commander's voice cut through Henry's futility.

Henry obeyed, gasping as the pressure released him. He fought gravity. He didn't notice to the colorless world around him, rendered in monochrome shades. The blue draining from Ro's body consumed him before he collapsed.

CHAPTER SIXTY-EIGHT

Henry gasped. Consciousness opened his eyes to light bled of color. He lay on his back staring into the Tower's facsimile of the Web, a binding net only for the Commander's chosen. Millions of silver filaments crisscrossed the space around him, networking every living person in the Tower. Clusters of brightness stood out from the rest. A thousand times more light gathered around one body, silver armed, and a cocoon. If Henry peered, he could make out slivers of blue in between the layers of shielding her.

Metal clinked around his neck. Two heavy chains pinned him to a bed.

He saw Shai the moment he crossed into the Web. Henry watched the bundle of threads surrounding Shai reach toward him—a silver circle appeared next to him. Shai emerged, blotchy faced.

"Henry?"

The quiver in his tone, the glossy sheen on his eyes, the etching across his forehead.

"Hey, Shai."

Shai slumped by Henry's feet. He held his head in his hands, sniffed.

"I… I'm sorry. I should have been there. I—"

"Not your fault."

Shai's fist pressed into the mattress. "I miss Kekoa."

Henry's throat parched, and his cheeks grew hot. His eyes were too dry for tears.

"Ro?" he managed. All he remembered was silver blood, coating the floor, her hair, her skin…

"Touch and go," Shai sighed, wiping his cheeks. "They have her in this…tank, thing, filled with slime. She's chained up worse than you, but they put this breathing device on her. Some days they think she might wake up. Something to do with the slime changing colors, something about her brain activity. Kekoa could've explained it."

Henry turned wet eyes up, away from Shai, where the Web witnessed his fear without judgment. "Did you see her?"

"Yeah. She—fuck." Shai grit his teeth. "She didn't come back whole. I was there when—when she started to re-grow parts. It's still not done. I'm glad she's unconscious."

Henry couldn't agree. He wanted to see her—upright, walking and eating and laughing with the rest of them.

Henry tilted his head behind Shai. "Tissues."

Shai blanked. His head snapped up, hopeful eyes round.

"You can see?"

"Why wouldn't I?"

"You…you opened your eyes in the Web, man. You…you…"

Henry blinked. "Am I blind?"

"Burned your corneas out. Can't even see your pupils or your irises anymore. Your whole eyes are just…" Shai swiped his hand in front of his face. "Just silver."

Henry turned his sight to the beaming lines around them. "I can't see color anymore. But I can see through the Web. Can see you."

"That's incredible," Shai muttered, getting the tissues. "So, your marking?"

"It kind of makes sense. Wish I didn't go—"

Shai put his hand on Henry's ankle and squeezed. "You can see. Let's leave it at that today. Please."

Henry let his head fall back. "Sure, man." He paused. "How long have I been out?"

Shai scrubbed his hand through his hair. "You…you were fine. They just knocked you out to do some testing. I don't know what they did to you, though."

"What'd they do to you?" Better than asking the unspoken.

"What they'd do to any giant. Forced sedation. Three days. Never felt pain. That slime's incredible stuff."

Henry sighed. "How long was I out?"

"Eight days."

Henry closed his eyes, shutting off his marking. Darkness enveloped him; silence permeated his mind.

Eight days unconscious. Near two hundred hours lost.

"This part of why it took so long?" Henry shook the chains binding him.

"Yeah. They were deciding on what charges they were going to press."

"And?"

"Mutiny, accessory to assault, and kidnapping."

The bleak words settled on Henry like lies.

"Don't scoff," Shai chastised.

"We never even got one question answered before I fucked it up. Sorry I'm such a burnout." Henry grinned.

"Right when you got your marking too. That is some burnout shit, Henry." Shai lifted watering eyes from the floor.

"Shai. Don't worry. They won't send me home, or anywhere else, not now that I can use my marking."

Shai didn't answer.

"I'm serious. Bet this blows over. Special treatment, right?"

"Right." Shai squeezed the edge of the mattress a couple times. "I gotta—uh—"

"Trust me."

Shai's shoulders sagged. "I do. Don't fuck up anymore."

"I won't. Brother." He held out his fist.

"Brother." Shai bumped. "Get some sleep. Trial starts tomorrow."

Shai patted Henry's shoulder walking out.

Without Shai, doubt snuck between the light that blinded Henry.

Ro was alive. Barely.

He was going to trial. Soon.

They deserved punishment. He agreed with that. He didn't think anyone believed he had been inciting mutiny. He definitely didn't kidnap Ro.

Ro…shouldn't be alive. She did attack the Commander. No one in a secret section of the military would be healed like Shai described before being forced to confess and executed.

The thought made Henry's stomach roil, but he was still right.

None of it made sense.

None of it worked.

But he had made it to Wing.

He had broken Taizai's splice.

He had saved Ro.

His marking rippled across his vision, a wave of his power flooding through the Tower. A flash of pain hazed his senses, and he grinned.

I can take whatever comes next.

BIO

L.A. Magill lives in Rockville, Maryland with her husband and their cat. She met her husband in high school and knew, even then, he'd always make her laugh. She studied English, dance, and special education through college, earning a Master's degree in 2014. She taught for three years before turning to her passion, storytelling. She loves getting lost in distant worlds and uncovering their secrets. She is a lifelong nerd, animal lover, and outdoor enthusiast. She spends too much time playing video games to be so bad at them and endures chronic Tex-Mex cravings. *The Thread* is her first novel.

Stay tuned for more of L.A. Magill's work. You can find her, along with all JaCol's authors at www.jacolpublishing.com

www.ingramcontent.com/pod-product-compliance
Lightning Source LLC
Chambersburg PA
CBHW071725190726
48292CB00003B/618